W9-AGB-225

UNIDENTIFIED
WOMAN
#15

ALSO BY DAVID HOUSEWRIGHT

Featuring Rushmore McKenzie

The Devil May Care

The Last Kind Word

Curse of the Jade Lily

Highway 61

The Taking of Libby, SD

Jelly's Gold

Madman on a Drum

Dead Boyfriends

Pretty Girl Gone

Tin City

A Hard Ticket Home

Featuring Holland Taylor

Penance

Practice to Deceive

Dearly Departed

Other Novels

The Devil and the Diva
(with Renée Valois)

Finders Keepers

UNIDENTIFIED WOMAN
#15

David Housewright

MINOTAUR BOOKS

NEW YORK

UNIDENTIFIED WOMAN #15. Copyright © 2015 by David Housewright. All rights reserved. Printed in the United States of America. For information, address St. Martin's Press, 175 Fifth Avenue, New York, N.Y. 10010.

www.minotaurbooks.com

The Library of Congress Cataloging-in-Publication Data is available upon request.

ISBN 978-1-250-04965-0 (hardcover)
ISBN 978-1-4668-5063-7 (e-book)

Minotaur books may be purchased for educational, business, or promotional use. For information on bulk purchases, please contact the Macmillan Corporate and Premium Sales Department at 1-800-221-7945, extension 5442, or write to specialmarkets@macmillan.com.

First Edition: June 2015

10 9 8 7 6 5 4 3 2 1

FOR RENÉE AND RENÉE
AND RENÉE AGAIN

ACKNOWLEDGMENTS

The author wishes to acknowledge his debt to India Cooper, Pat Donnelly, Tammi Fredrickson, Randy Gustafson of the Ramsey County Sheriff's Department, Maggie Hood, Phyllis E. Jaeger, Keith Kahla, Ramsey County Commissioner Mary Jo McGuire, Sergeant Anita Muldoon of the St. Paul Police Department Homicide Unit (Ret.), David P. Peterson, Forensic Science Supervisor with the Minnesota Bureau of Criminal Apprehension, Alison J. Picard, Dr. James Schlaefer, and Renée Valois.

UNIDENTIFIED WOMAN
#15

ONE

It was snowing heavily when they rolled the girl off the back of the pickup truck onto the freeway.

What happened, I was heading east on that stretch of Interstate 94 where you cross from Minneapolis into St. Paul. Rush hour had expired long before, yet traffic was moving at a cautious pace out of respect for the inch of snow that had already fallen and the twenty-miles-per-hour winds that made it swirl, reducing visibility to about the length of a football field. A vehicle came up tight on my rear bumper. I knew it was either a pickup or an SUV because of the height of its headlights.

Nina was sitting next to me, her voice competing with the whump-whump of the windshield wipers and the hockey game being broadcast on the radio, my Minnesota Wild against the Tampa Bay Lightning—a regular occurrence that always made me shake my head, hockey in Florida. She was telling me that we needed to get something for the condominium we had recently purchased together, yet the sudden appearance of the vehicle distracted me.

"What do you think?" Nina asked.

"Hmm?"

"You haven't been listening to a word I've said."

Driving instructors everywhere warn that it's dangerous to hug the rear end of the vehicle in front of you, especially during a blizzard. I tapped my brake pedal politely to remind the driver. I figured the flash of my brake lights must have done the trick because the pickup pulled into the lane next to mine.

"Of course I've been listening," I said.

"Well, what do you think?"

"I think whatever you want to do is fine with me."

"Sure it is, until I actually do it, and then it's hey, I didn't agree to this."

The pickup accelerated until it was even with my car. The passenger looked down at me and said something to the driver. The pickup leapt forward and abruptly pulled into my lane.

Swoop and squat, I thought. I might even have said it aloud. A vehicle swoops in front of you and slams on its brakes, causing a rear-end collision that, according to state law, is always your fault. Usually the vehicle will contain several passengers—like the man wearing a heavy coat with a hood, squatting in the truck bed—who will testify that the extreme pain and suffering caused by the medically ambiguous injuries they sustained can only be alleviated by hefty insurance settlements. And if you happen to be driving a $65,000 Audi S5 . . .

I immediately applied the brake, causing the Audi to shimmy a bit on the snow-covered pavement as it slowed. The pickup accelerated at the same time, putting plenty of distance between us.

"What?" Nina said.

I took my foot off the brake.

"Nothing," I said.

Nina has often accused me of being cynical, of having an overly suspicious nature and a generally low opinion of my fellow man. So have many others, come to think of it. Watching the pickup speed away, I told myself they might be on to something.

And then the hooded man dropped the tailgate.

He scooted to the front of the truck bed and, with his back against the cab, used his legs to shove something out. I didn't realize it was a woman at first. She was lying horizontal across the bed, and I thought she could have been a thick carpet. Hell, she could have been a sack of potatoes. Until my headlights caught her blond hair twirling through the air as she fell.

It seemed to me a terrible way to end a relationship.

I stomped the brake so hard I thought my foot would go through the floor. My tires gripped the icy asphalt with a high-pitched shriek. The car fishtailed, yet I managed to keep it going in a straight line. The girl seemed to roll toward me as I moved toward her. I cranked the steering wheel hard to the right and the Audi skidded sideways. I lost sight of the girl. The car came to an abrupt halt, its nose hanging over the white line indicating the shoulder, its rear resting in the driving lane.

I thought of moving the car, but I didn't know where the girl was, so I worked the manual transmission into neutral, pressed the button that started my emergency flashers blinking, and released my seat belt. I pointed at the snow-covered bank that led from the valley that was the freeway up toward the residential streets.

"Get out, climb the bank, stay away from the car," I said.

Nina did not argue, did not question, did not hesitate. Instead, she did exactly what I asked, and in the brief moment while I was still thinking about her, my inner voice reminded me that I was lucky to have a woman who trusted me that much.

I opened my own door; the sound of the wipers and a Wild power play followed me as I escaped the Audi. The girl was lying on her back next to the rear tires. Her wrists were tied together with twine. I didn't know if I had hit her or not. There was no blood that I could see, but I knew that meant nothing. Her eyes were open and staring at me as I bent over her.

"Are you okay?" I asked—a stupid question that she made no effort to answer. She had just been thrown from a pickup truck traveling at least fifty miles per hour. Of course she wasn't okay. This wasn't the goddamn movies. How badly hurt, though? I couldn't wait to find out. I gripped the back of her shirt under her shoulders—she wasn't wearing a jacket despite the January cold. I lifted and pulled, cradling her head between my arms the way they taught me back at the police academy.

Yes, it was risky to move her. I knew what was about to happen, though, and there was nothing I could do to stop it.

I dragged her body in a straight line across the asphalt and down into the ditch that ran along the freeway. If she was in pain, she did nothing to show it.

The ditch was filled with two months' worth of snow, and I sank several inches with every step, yet the lack of friction made it easier to slide the woman along. When I reached the bottom of the ditch, I maneuvered so that I was pulling the girl away from the Audi. I managed maybe fifteen yards when the inevitable happened. A driver, following the long curve of the interstate, saw my car too late, hit his brakes, slid sideways, corrected course, and plowed his vehicle into the passenger side of the Audi. Both vehicles lurched forward about ten feet. A few seconds earlier, the girl and I would have been buried under the wreckage.

I settled the girl against the snow. Her eyes were closed now. The flakes melting on her face and the distant yellow freeway light gave her a ghostly appearance. I knelt and placed two fingers across her carotid artery. She was warm to my touch, and I could detect an uncertain pulse. I couldn't work the knot, so I cut the twine that bound her wrists with a tiny pocketknife I always carried. Afterward, I draped my coat over her, tucking it in around her throat.

Nina trudged toward me. I held up a hand to hold her back. At the same time, a skidding sound caused my head to snap around. I was just in time to see a second car crash into the car that crashed into my Audi, although with considerably less force. A third car managed to stop in time, only the driver behind him wasn't as capable. His car hit the third car with enough force to push it into the second car.

"Oh my God, this is going to be a bloodbath," I announced to no one in particular.

I left the girl, climbed out of the ditch, and moved to the cars. The radio in my Audi continued to broadcast the hockey game, although the windshield wipers had ceased working. I yanked open the passenger door of the second vehicle. The air bag had deployed, and the driver was sitting there with an expression that suggested he had no idea what had just happened. The woman next to him seemed more cognizant. There had been no air bag on her side of the car, and she was holding her shoulder under the seat belt strap with one hand and her forehead with the other. Blood seeped between her fingers.

I took the handkerchief from my back pocket and folded it over. I pulled her hand away from the wound, covered it with the white cloth, and returned her hand. She didn't seem to mind at all.

"I told you you were driving too fast," she said. "I told you. Didn't I tell you?"

I'm not sure the driver even heard her.

"Try not to move," I said.

She turned her head, looked me directly in the eye, and said, "Huh?"

"Try not to move."

"Move what?"

Another car piled into another car, which was hit by yet another car.

The snow grew thicker and heavier.

The wind blew harder.

Nina appeared at my side. She held up her smartphone for me to see.

"I called 911," she said. "They're sending help."

I could only nod. I watched the freeway behind us. Some

vehicles, unscathed, were caught in what was fast becoming an enormous traffic jam stretching all the way back to the Mississippi River bridge. Others were skidding and sliding and bouncing around like bumper cars. The magnitude of it all was beginning to overwhelm me. It was Nina asking, "How's the girl? Did you hit her?" that brought the world sharply back into focus.

"I don't know," I said, one answer for both questions. "Is the operator still on the phone?"

"Yes."

I took the smartphone from Nina's hand and spoke into it.

"There are car accidents piling up all around us," I said. "We need paramedics. Ambulances. Police. Send everybody. Also, and this is important—are you listening?"

"I'm listening, sir."

"This isn't just an accident scene. It's a crime scene. A young woman was purposely thrown out of a moving pickup truck. That's what started it all. She's alive, but I don't know for how long."

"What is your name, sir?"

"Rushmore McKenzie. I used to be a cop with the St. Paul Police Department."

I added that last bit in case the operator thought I was some kind of nut job—she wouldn't have been the first.

"You will remain at the scene, Mr. McKenzie," she said. It wasn't a question.

I returned Nina's phone just as a Wild player deflected the puck past the Tampa Bay goalie. The radio announcer gleefully shouted, "He scoooooooooooores."

And another car hit another car.

"We should shut that thing off," Nina said.

In the end, 37 assorted vehicles were damaged in what the *Minneapolis Star Tribune* labeled the most massive highway pileup in state history, easily exceeding a recent 25-car melee in Des Moines, Iowa. In case anyone was feeling smug about it, though, the newspaper also reported that the accident paled in comparison to a 140-car, fog-induced pileup in Texas, a 100-car accident near Fargo, North Dakota, and an 86-car pileup in Ohio. This was Minnesota, after all, and we liked to keep score.

Footage of the accident, including aerial shots, appeared the next morning on all of the Twin Cities TV stations that pretended to deliver the news, as well as ABC, NBC, CNN, and The Weather Channel. Most Minnesotans who saw it felt an inexplicable sense of pride, what comes from living in a place where not much happens that's of national interest. In each case, it was reported that the accident was caused when a car struck an unidentified woman that was trying to cross the freeway on foot at night.

I saw Bobby Dunston's hand in that last bit—he was always one to keep his cards pressed firmly against the buttons of his shirt.

Dunston was a commander in the St. Paul Police Department's Major Crimes and Investigations Division. They had roused him from his warm and happy home—which was coincidentally less than a mile from the scene—when the cops concluded that I was right, there was fuckery afoot. He saw me talking to one of his detectives and a lieutenant wearing the maroon hat and overcoat of the Minnesota State Patrol. The sight made him abruptly turn away, stand with hands on hips, and look up at the snow-filled sky.

It's a pleasure to see you, too, my inner voice said.

He turned around.

"Hey, boss," the detective said. "This is McKenzie. He used to be one of us."

"I know who he is," Bobby said.

He glanced over my shoulder and his face brightened considerably. Nina was resting against the bumper of an MSP cruiser. The paramedics had draped a blanket over her shoulders, and she held it closed over her leather coat with a gloved hand. Despite that, she was shivering. I don't know if it was because of the cold, the wind, the snow, or the chaos around her. Probably all four.

Bobby gave her a hug.

"Are you okay?" he asked.

"Don't worry about me," Nina said. "I'm fine. How are Shelby and the girls? It must be awful getting pulled away from them on a night like this."

He brushed the snow off her bangs and kissed her cheek. I knew what he was thinking because I had thought it myself on numerous occasions. There she was, looking and feeling miserable under miserable conditions in a miserable situation, yet she was more concerned about someone else. For the second time that evening, my inner voice reminded me how lucky I was.

"You should sit in a car, get warm," Bobby said.

"What, and miss the show?"

Eastbound I-94 had been closed on the Minneapolis side of the Mississippi River, and angry, put-upon drivers were being detoured to the side streets around us. Westbound vehicles were moving at a crawl because drivers had slowed to get a good look at what was going on as they drove past, which in turned caused several fender benders that snarled traffic even more.

The portion of I-94 where we were standing was no longer a freeway. It was a parking lot, and a surprisingly bright one, too, given the freeway lights, vehicle headlights, the blinking red and blue light bars on top of emergency vehicles and tow trucks, and the helicopters overhead with their searchlights— all of it reflecting against the slanting snow. Paramedics moved between the cars checking occupants for injuries. The man and woman in the vehicle that crushed my Audi had both been transported to Regions Hospital. Others had followed, yet I was impressed by how few of them there were. Experience told me, though, that come morning many people who insisted they were perfectly fine now would realize that they weren't. Chiropractors and auto repair shops were going to make a killing off of this.

Drivers gathered in small groups to exchange insurance information. Skirmishes broke out between some of them that were quickly broken up by St. Paul cops, Ramsey County deputies, and state troopers, most of whom didn't seem to be getting along any better than the accident victims. Undamaged vehicles were being carefully guided around and through the accident scene, their drivers thrilled to escape intact with a story to tell. It wasn't easy. Snow was piling up at an alarming rate, and the plows weren't able to get to it. Cars with smashed bumpers and other damage—including mine—were being towed off one at a time. Yet their owners described their experiences in typically Minnesota fashion to the TV reporters who had somehow managed to get their camera equipment through the melee.

"It could be worse," they said.

Yeah, it could be snowing, my inner voice added. *Oh, wait . . .*

Nearly two inches had fallen since the girl was pushed out of the pickup truck, and I found myself stamping my feet to keep them from being buried.

Bobby gave Nina's shoulder a big-brother pat and returned to where we were standing.

Hey, that's my girl you're manhandling, pal, my inner voice complained.

"Okay," Bobby said.

The three of us all began speaking at once. He waved us silent and gestured at his detective. The detective told Bobby everything I had told him, adding that Ms. Truhler had corroborated my story.

"We also found the twine McKenzie claimed he cut, and there were deep abrasions on the girl's wrists, so . . ."

Bobby turned to the officer from the state patrol, who pointed upward at a traffic camera fixed to a light pole.

"Already checked it out," he said. "Footage confirms McKenzie's story, too, only because of the blowing snow, hell, we can't even identify the truck, much less the license plate number. What we know for sure is that the pickup left the freeway at the Cretin-Vandalia exit."

"What about the girl?"

"Paramedics took her to Regions," the detective said. "She was unconscious. I don't know her exact condition. The medics said . . . I guess it's not looking good. There was no ID on her. We searched the scene as best we could in the snow. No coat, no bag."

While he spoke, I found myself tugging at the zipper of my own coat. The paramedics had returned it to me before they transported the girl. It was a dress-up coat, though, made for hopping from warm cars to restaurants and clubs, not for standing around in a Minnesota blizzard.

"Anything, McKenzie?" Bobby said. "Anything at all you can tell me?"

I pretty much repeated everything his detective and the trooper had already told him.

"In other words, you got nuthin'," Bobby said.

"Sorry."

"Bobby," Nina called.

"Nina?"

"It was dark."

"I know it's dark."

"No, no, I mean the color of the truck. It was dark. Black or dark blue. It was a Ram truck, too. I recognized the emblem on the tailgate."

"Are you sure?"

"Yes. Sorry, I didn't get a license plate number."

Bobby looked at her with the expression of a man who was trying not to smile.

"Thank you," he said. "Okay. Lieutenant, would you be kind enough to send the camera footage to my office?"

"Happy to."

"Thank you. Detective"—he rested a hand on the elbow of his fellow officer—"get down to Regions. Let me know about the girl's condition. Let me know when they think we can talk to her."

"Sir."

Bobby returned to Nina's side.

"I bet you could use a ride home," he told her.

Nina nodded.

"How 'bout me?" I asked.

"You can come, too. Sit in the back. Try not to make any noise."

Money can't buy happiness, or so I've been told. On the other hand, it was because I had plenty of dough that I wasn't particularly upset that my Audi was now a pile of rubble in the SPPD's impound lot. Unlike most of the other drivers caught in the accident, I didn't need to worry about replacing it. I didn't have to wonder how I was going to get around until I did. I was concerned only with the inconvenience.

The next morning, I kissed Nina good-bye, hopped into my backup car—a battered Jeep Cherokee—and drove to the lot located just south of Holman Field, the airport along the Mississippi that served downtown St. Paul. I had to produce two forms of ID just to inspect the vehicle, never mind removing contents or ransoming its freedom. I took several photographs of it from all sides with my smartphone and sent them to my insurance agent. Afterward, I called his office. A woman I knew as Theresa answered on the fifth ring, recited the name of the insurance agency, asked if I would hold, and then put me on hold before I could reply. She came back three minutes later and apologized.

"It's been crazy," she said. "We get a lot of calls the first couple times it snows, people relearning how to drive in winter, you know? Today, though, the number of accidents—we only got four and a half inches, for goodness sake. You'd expect better from Minnesota drivers in January."

"About that. This is McKenzie, and my Audi . . ."

"Hi, McKenzie."

"Hi, Theresa. Like I was saying . . ."

"I was telling Pat the other day that we haven't heard from you since, what is it, now? Four months? I said you were due."

"Yeah, yeah . . ."

"What happened this time? Machine-gun fire?"

"Considering the amount of business I've given you guys over the years . . ."

"I'm not complaining. I just want to know. My kids have been asking for new McKenzie stories."

"This time it wasn't my fault. I got caught in that pileup on I-94 last night."

"Please tell me that you didn't cause it."

"Not exactly. Look, can I talk to Pat? I sent him some photos."

"He's on another line, but you know what, I bet he'll take your call."

Theresa put me on hold again. Thirty seconds later, Pat answered. His voice sounded tired.

"Did you know that I have over a thousand clients?" he asked.

"No, I didn't know that."

"So why do I spend most of my time talking to you?"

"Because we went to school together and you like me?"

"No, that's not it."

"I e-mailed some photos."

"Uh-huh . . . Hang on . . . I'm pulling them up . . . Oh, c'mon."

"Do you think it can be fixed?"

"Your car? No, I don't think it can be fixed. We'll send an adjuster out to take a closer look, but geez, McKenzie, what did you do?"

I explained. Pat sighed heavily.

"This might become complicated if other drivers involved in the accident decide to blame you," he said.

"It's not my fault. The cops said so."

"Uh-huh. Well, you know where to download the forms. Be sure to get the case number from the police."

"Been there, done that."

"Way too often, if you ask me. You know, McKenzie, I have only about a dozen drivers who pay higher insurance premiums than you do."

"Gives me something to shoot for—the top ten."

"You might make it with this one. Two words, McKenzie, something to think about—mass transit."

"Always a pleasure talking to you, Pat."

"We'll be in touch."

I ended the call, just in time to receive a second one. I answered the way I always do. "McKenzie."

"Where are you?" Bobby Dunston asked.

"St. Paul impound lot, why?"

"Meet me at Regions. SICU."

"When?"

He hung up without answering. I took that to mean "Right frickin' now."

The Surgical Intensive Care Unit was located on the third floor and was damn near impossible to reach by a visitor using Regions Hospital's overly complicated elevator and corridor system. On the other hand—and I'm speaking from experience when I tell you this—if you come in through the emergency room, they can whisk you right up there.

I talked my way past a nurse-receptionist and found Bobby leaning against a wall and looking down as if his shoes were the most interesting things he had seen in a long time. He was standing across from a recovery room. Beyond the sliding glass walls of the room I could see the figure of a woman lying on a bed, her head wrapped in white bandages, a cast extending from the elbow of one arm down far enough to enclose a couple of fingers. Cables attached her to a monitor; wavy red, green, and blue lines and ever-changing numbers kept track of her vital signs.

"How is she?" I asked.

Bobby pulled out a notebook. For most things he used his smartphone or one of those tablets. For others it was still paper and pen. He began reading.

"Three broken ribs, two broken fingers, broken wrist, broken clavicle, broken scapula, one punctured lung, one bruised lung, blood in the chest cavity, they call that a hemothorax. Cracked spleen, fractured liver, dislocated kneecap, major road rash—abrasions over half her body; there's gravel and bits of pavement imbedded in her skin. The big thing, though, she has a fractured skull. Some blood vessels ruptured. The bleeding put pressure on the brain. They had to drill holes to drain the blood and alleviate the pressure."

"Epidural hematoma," I said.

"The same thing happened to you a couple of years ago."

"I remember."

"Traumatic brain injury," Bobby said. "The docs are concerned because they don't know how extensive it is. Could be . . ."

"Traumatic?"

"Yeah."

"Jesus."

Bobby showed me the woman's photo on his phone. Her face was puffy and pale, setting off the ghastly scrapes on her chin and forehead. Her blue eyes were open and staring at the camera, yet they seemed to be out of focus, as if she had no idea what she was looking at. My impression was that she had been very pretty once. I hoped she would be again.

"Recognize her?" Bobby asked.

"No. Should I?"

"I don't know. Should you?"

"What are you thinking? That they dumped her in front of my car on purpose so I would be the one to run her over? Some kind of revenge thing?"

"Yeah, I thought about it. Have you?"

"All night long. Listen, Bobby. I don't know her, and I'm not involved in anything right now that would piss someone off."

"Take a good look."

I took Bobby's phone, stared at the image for a few moments more. She bore an uncomfortable resemblance to Bobby's younger daughter, Katie. I didn't tell him that, though.

"I don't know her." I returned the cell. "Who is she?"

"Unidentified Woman Number Fifteen."

I that took to mean the police had been unable to put a name to her face despite running her fingerprints through the FBI's Integrated Automated Fingerprint Identification System, a database with over 100 million files including prints from people who served in the military or bought a gun in some states or worked a sensitive civilian job. A search through the National Crime Information Center's missing persons files and the Minnesota Missing and Unidentified Persons Clearinghouse must have proved inconclusive as well.

"Look at the bright side," I said. "If she was in the morgue, instead of Unidentified Woman Number Fifteen, the toe tag would read 'Jane Doe.'"

"There is that."

"Someone must know her. Someone must miss her."

"Besides the three men who tossed her onto the freeway?"

"I can only identify two of them as being men."

"Yeah, yeah, yeah . . ."

"Are you going to ask the media for help? Run her photo on the nightly news?"

"I haven't decided yet. McKenzie, why would they push her out of a speeding truck?"

The obvious answer was to kill her, so that's what I said.

"Why not just shoot her in the back of the head, bury her in the snow? We wouldn't find her body until spring if ever."

"They wanted to make it look like an accident."

"Better ways to do that. Besides, did they think no one would see them?"

"They were pulling away from me at the time, so, yeah, maybe they did think that, the way the snow was falling. The guy just dropped the tailgate too soon. If the pickup hadn't come up so close to my bumper in the first place, I doubt I would have paid any attention to it."

"Did they think the highway cameras wouldn't see them?"

"There are cameras everywhere—on the freeways, at street corners, in shopping malls, in front of stores and apartment buildings, gas stations. How often do you think about them?"

"Not often."

"Bobby, are you asking these questions because you want me to answer them or are you just thinking out loud the way you do?"

He didn't say.

"Anyway, when the girl comes to, you can ask her," I said.

"She regained consciousness before they wheeled her into surgery—the second surgery. She doesn't remember a thing."

"People who suffer a head injury often don't remember details of the accident that caused it. They call it traumatic amnesia."

"Just because you dated a psychiatrist back in the day doesn't make you one. Besides, she didn't just forget the accident, she forgot everything, and I mean everything, including her name."

"That sounds more serious."

Bobby gave me one of those looks.

"Or not," I added. "Listen, whatever it is, it's probably just temporary. What do the doctors say?"

"They say it's probably just temporary—if she's telling the truth."

"Why wouldn't she be?"

"All I know is, she didn't do what I would have done if I came to all busted up in a hospital emergency room, if I couldn't remember who I was or how I got there. She didn't panic. She didn't scream for her mother or a doctor or a policeman or a superhero from the Marvel universe. She didn't demand assistance or rail at her attackers or promise retribution. Instead, she accepted it all as if it was the natural order of things. As if she believed the world was a place where sooner or later they threw you off the back of a speeding pickup truck."

"Bobby, why am I here? Why are you telling me all this? You haven't discussed an open case with me in years, not since I quit the cops."

"I might need a favor."

TWO

Nina and I never argued when we were just sleeping together. There was the occasional spirited discussion concerning subjects like music and restaurant food and the use of the shootout to settle regular-season hockey games. For the most part, though, we got along extremely well—to the point where we would watch other couples bickering and shake our heads in bafflement. *What is wrong with these people?* we'd ask ourselves. Then we decided to live together and everything changed. Behavior that was inconsequential before suddenly became monumentally important. We started pointing fingers at each other, declaring this is right, this is wrong, this is good, this is bad, our declarations based solely on personal preference. I quietly told friends that maybe we didn't belong together after all, only to learn that she had told them the same thing.

Bobby Dunston said to relax, said we were just going through a period of adjustment. We had both lived more or less alone for most of the past two decades, answering to no one, he reminded us, and we were set in our ways. Bobby's wife, Shelby, on the other hand, decided to intervene—mostly on Nina's behalf, which was aggravating. I had known her since college and was convinced that if I had been the one to spill a drink on her dress instead of Bobby, it'd be the two of us bickering.

Our disagreements became acute when we started looking for a home. Nina lived in the out-of-the-way northeast St. Paul suburb of Mahtomedi, and we certainly weren't going to move there. I had a house in much more convenient Falcon Heights, complete with a backyard pond that attracted all kinds of wildlife—ducks, wild turkey, the occasional deer. Yet that didn't work for Nina, don't ask me why. It soon became apparent that, given our conflicting demands, there wasn't a suitable house, town house, condominium, apartment, or loft anywhere in all of the greater St. Paul area.

Finally Nina told me she'd found a place, loaded me into her Lexus, and drove west. I told her this was unacceptable when we crossed the Mississippi River.

"I will not live in Minneapolis," I announced.

Nina kept driving until she pulled up to an eight-floor glass and brick structure built to resemble a 1930s warehouse nestled between the northeast corner of downtown Minneapolis and the river. There was a convenience store, liquor store, pizza joint, and coffeehouse on the ground floor. Plus, it was within easy walking distance to several jazz clubs, restaurants, Orchestra Hall, a bunch of theaters including the Guthrie, the train, the Nicollet Mall, and the stadiums where the Vikings, Twins, and Timberwolves played ball—facts that Nina happily shared with me.

"Sweetie, we're just wasting time," I said.

"It won't hurt to look," she said.

She must have arranged our visit ahead of time, because she guided me past the security desk without a word to the guards, over to a bank of elevators, and eventually to a seventh-floor condominium that she unlocked with a card key attached to a plastic tag that bore the name of the building.

"This isn't going to work," I told her.

I walked through the doorway. The entire north wall of the condo was made of tinted floor-to-ceiling glass with a dramatic view of the Mississippi River. If that wasn't enough, there was a sliding glass door built into the wall that led to a balcony. I might have said, "Wow," but I really don't remember.

The south wall featured floor-to-ceiling bookcases that turned at the east wall and followed it to a large brick fireplace. To the left of the fireplace was a door that led to a small guest bedroom with its own full bath. Against the west wall and elevated three steps above the living area was the most spectacular and elaborate kitchen I had ever seen, including a gas stove—it's always better to cook with fire.

Nina led me past the kitchen to a master bedroom that also featured floor-to-ceiling windows. Adjacent to the bedroom was a huge walk-in closet complete with shelves and drawers. The closet led to a bathroom with double sinks and a glass-enclosed shower big enough for two people to play tag in. Beyond that there was a storage area with enough room to park a car.

"Yeah, but sweetie, it's Minneapolis," I said.

I followed Nina back to the living area, and she began pointing.

"There's a half bath and closet for guests on the other side of the kitchen. We can put a desk and computer over there and a dining room set over here and a sofa and chairs for a nice conversation pit near the glass and in the center of the room sofas and chairs facing the fireplace. A big-screen TV goes above the fireplace. Oh, we can put a grill on the balcony. I already measured; there's plenty of room."

"Nina . . ."

"There's twenty-four-hour security; I know that's important to you. There's an underground garage, a full gymnasium on the second floor, a party room, and a garden on the roof."

"Nina, stop . . ."

"I know you'll like this. If we pool the money we'll realize from selling our houses, we will not only be able to pay for the condo, but what's left over we can put into an account that will pay our building fees for the next fifteen years."

"It's beautiful, Nina. It really is. But, sweetie, I can't live in Minneapolis."

"Why not?"

"Because I'm a St. Paul boy."

"Then why do you live in Falcon Heights?"

"I told you, it was an accident. I thought I was buying a place in St. Paul. It wasn't until I made an offer that I discovered the house was on the wrong side of the street, that I was actually moving to the suburbs."

"Why didn't you withdraw the offer, then? Besides, that was almost seven years ago. You could have sold it after your father passed. You could have moved back to St. Paul. You didn't."

"There's no sense talking about it. I will not live in Minneapolis."

Nina smiled like she knew something that I didn't and crossed the large living area until she was leaning against the bookcase. She folded her arms across her chest and smiled some more. I got the feeling that I had already lost the argument, yet I didn't know why.

"Yes, the bookcases are beautiful and the view is beautiful, but Nina . . ."

Nina moved her elbow. I heard a click. The bookcase swung open to reveal a secret room.

"Whoa," I said.

I moved quickly to her side. Nina stepped back and swung the bookcase open farther. The room behind it was about eight feet by ten and carpeted. I tripped a sensor, and a light went on when I stepped inside.

"You can keep your guns in here," Nina said. "And the safe with all the cash and fake IDs that no one is supposed to know about. Look."

Nina pointed to a corner where there were a half-dozen cable outlets.

"The place is wired. You can set up cameras and alarms and whatever else you want. The images can be sent to the security desk downstairs if you prefer, or you can monitor everything from here, use it as a panic room. The sales guy said that once the door is locked from the inside, the room is damn near impregnable. I know you like your gadgets and gizmos, Mc-Kenzie. This might be the coolest gadget you'll ever own."

"Except that it's Minneapolis," I said.

"You'll get over it."

To my great embarrassment, I did—and haven't my St. Paul friends been giving me a hard time about it ever since?

After we bought the condominium, I thought our problems were over. I had made a huge sacrifice moving to Minneapolis and deserved a little slack, right? Things just seemed to get worse, though, because now we were skirmishing over furnishings and deciding which drawer would hold the silverware and whether we should shelve our books by author or subject matter and what towels to buy for which bathrooms because our old ones simply were no longer good enough.

I did something then that I had promised Nina I would do months earlier. I bought her a piano—a baby grand piano with ebony polish, to be precise—and had the delivery guys set it up near the glass door leading to the balcony. I had a moment of panic when the woman I hired to tune it arrived late, yet it was sitting there, ready to be played, when Nina returned home.

"Hi," she said as she walked through the door.

"Hi," I replied from the sofa, where I was pretending to watch ESPN.

She stopped. Said, "Oh. My. God." Dropped her bag and rushed over to the instrument. "You bought this for me?"

"I said I would," I reminded her.

"You have always kept your promises. You have never broken a promise to me in all the years I've known you."

"Well . . ."

Nina tossed her coat on the floor, sat on the bench, and began to play. She started with some boogie-woogie.

"It's tuned," she said.

"Of course it's tuned. What kind of guy would give his girl an untuned piano?"

She segued into some Dave Brubeck and Bill Evans, followed by Chopin's Prelude in E minor before playing the adagio from Rachmaninov's Second Symphony, one of my favorite pieces of music. While she played I gathered up a huge throw pillow with the logo of the Minnesota Twins—which Nina preferred I get rid of—and laid beneath the piano to listen. A good half hour passed before she stopped playing and crawled beneath the Steinway to be with me. As we embraced, I was reminded of the final line in the Charles Dickens novel *Great Expectations*—"I saw no shadow of another parting from her."

We haven't had a serious argument since.

And then they rolled the girl off the back of the pickup truck.

I was lying beneath the piano when our landline rang, a rare occurrence since most people we know call our cell phones. I was propped up against the Twins throw pillow, which no longer seemed to annoy Nina, with a clear view of the HDTV above the fireplace. Fox Sports North was broadcasting a rare Minnesota Twins evening spring training game from Fort Myers, and I was watching it with the sound off. Meanwhile, Nina was having a difficult time teaching herself a Gershwin piano prelude, Number Two, I think, which was a hoot because whenever she made a mistake she would shout things like "fudge nuggets" and "geez willigers." Should she ever cut loose with an honest-to-God high-octane expletive—that's like tornado sirens going off. It is wise to pay attention.

"Dang," she said when the phone rang.

"I got it," I said.

I crawled out from under the Steinway and crossed to the desk we had located by the bookcases.

"McKenzie," I said.

"Mr. McKenzie, this is security. We have a woman who would like to come up to your condominium."

"What's her name?"

"She doesn't seem to have one. She says, just a moment . . ." I heard a muffled sound over the telephone receiver, and then the guard spoke clearly. "She says her name is Fifteen."

"I'll be right down."

I hung up the phone. Nina quit practicing and called from the piano.

"The woman they pushed out of the pickup truck six weeks ago is in the lobby," I told her.

I moved toward the door. Nina said, "I'm coming with."

The young woman was surrounded by security guards, yet they didn't mean her any harm. It was as if they wanted to be near in case she should swoon; she looked so fragile that it seemed it could happen at any moment.

She was wearing black boots, jeans, and a purple ski jacket zipped all the way to her throat—all of it new. Her hands were in her pockets. She had the expression of a junior high school student summoned to the principal's office without knowing why.

I approached from the elevator and extended my hand. "I'm McKenzie," I said. That was as far as I got. Nina swooped past me.

"Look at you," she said and wrapped a protective arm around the young woman's shoulder. "Are you okay?"

"It's hard to say."

"My name's Nina Truhler."

"I'm . . . They call me Fifteen."

"One of my favorite numbers. Let's get you upstairs."

"I don't want to impose. The man said . . ."

"What man?"

"The policeman."

"Bobby Dunston?"

"Commander Dunston. I didn't know his first name. He said McKenzie—are you McKenzie?"

"I am," I said.

"You saved my life."

How do you respond to something like that?

"Think nothing of it," I said.

"He said you might help me."

"And we will," Nina said. "Come along."

Nina led Fifteen toward the elevators. As they passed, she gave me a look I've been seeing more and more as our relationship developed. It said, "What the heck?"

I waited until they were on the elevator and going up before turning to the security guards.

"How did she get here?" I asked. "Did you see someone dropping her off?"

The guard behind the desk pointed at one of the many monitors that allowed the guards to scrutinize all the corridors and public areas inside the building as well as the sidewalks and streets that marked its perimeter. The name on the tag pinned above his jacket pocket read SMITH.

"She came on foot from the direction of the train station," he said.

"I want you to monitor her every movement as long as she's in the building," I said. "Anyone she meets, speaks to, waves at; any vehicles and their drivers that seem to show interest in her when she's outside—I want to know about it. Okay?"

One of the guards behind me chuckled and said, "All right."

I turned to him—his name tag read JONES—and back toward the desk. Smith smiled.

"Of course we checked you out, Mr. McKenzie, before you moved in," he said. "SOP—we do it for all the tenants. Orders from the company that manages the building. We know your reputation. We're delighted that you're staying here. The job gets boring sometimes, you know?"

The security guards looked if they expected me to start performing magic tricks.

Oh, for God's sake, my inner voice said.

Nina and Fifteen—I guessed that's what we were calling her now—were sitting knee-to-knee in the chairs we had arranged near the piano. Nina took the young woman's hand in hers as they spoke quietly, earnestly. I didn't announce my presence. Instead, I scooped my cell off the desk and made my way to the secret room. I found the hidden switch, swung open the bookcase door, and stepped inside, shutting the door behind me. A minute later, I had Commander Robert Dunston on the phone.

"What the hell?" I said.

"I told you six weeks ago that I might need a favor," Bobby said. "This is it."

"What favor, exactly?"

"Take care of Fifteen for a few days."

"I don't know what that means."

"McKenzie, I've already kept her in the hospital weeks longer than I had any right to. I don't have grounds to hold her as a material witness. But I can't just cut her loose either. The people who tried to kill her are still out there; the reason they tried to kill her still exists."

"Whatever that is."

"I interviewed Fifteen many times, showed her the footage of them heaving her off the back of the pickup. She still insists she doesn't remember a thing."

"Maybe she doesn't. It's extremely unusual, but that kind of amnesia does happen, right?"

"That's what the doctors say. If you were one of her attackers, though, would you bet your life on it, bet that she doesn't remember and won't remember? My biggest fear is that they've been waiting for her to leave the hospital so they'd have another chance at her."

"So you sent her to me?"

"If you were still living in Falcon Heights, I wouldn't have done it. Your old house, that place was about as secure as a bag of Old Dutch potato chips. Your condo, though? It's like a fortress."

"Hardly. A seasoned professional—"

"These people—three of them, at least two males—they're not pros. What they did before, that was sloppy. There was no guarantee that the girl would have been killed even if you had run her over. They are determined, though. Something else. Fifteen's skull fracture was caused when she hit the freeway, not by a blunt object. They wanted her to know what was happening when they rolled her out of the truck; they wanted her to suffer. Which raises the question—why? What reason did Fifteen give them to try to kill her like that?"

"You're assuming that she's not an innocent victim? That it wasn't the husband and a couple of guys trying to get rid of the wife?"

"There's no indentation on her third finger left hand that indicates a wedding ring. Besides, if she had been married, the husband would have come forward by now. He would have had to."

"A mistress who was about to put the kibosh on someone's marriage?"

"You're just guessing now."

"Aren't you?"

"The thing is, I don't believe she lost her memory. I believe she decided not to give up the guys who tried to kill her—or even reveal her own name—because she's afraid we would learn things that would put her in big trouble."

"Bigger trouble than this?"

"I'm going to make another assumption. She and her pals are

dirty as dirt can be. She turned on them and got caught. Or maybe they turned on her. Either way, the lady is in danger."

"Give her to the ten o'clock news, then. Make her a celebrity. Unidentified Woman Number Fifteen—the media loves that crap."

"What if I'm wrong? What if Fifteen really is telling the truth about not knowing who she is?"

"Then Mommy and Daddy will come forward to claim their lost little girl."

"Except Mommy and Daddy aren't looking for her. There's been no missing persons report that resembles her filed anywhere in the country. Or Canada, for that matter."

"After six weeks? Someone must be looking for her."

"You mean besides the men who already tried to kill her?"

"Bobby, you are going way above and beyond with this. You are not following department procedures."

"Yeah, like you always obeyed the rules when you were in harness."

"Whether I did or not, you always did. Always. You're the best cop I know, and this is very uncoplike behavior."

"I don't want to cut her loose, then come into the office tomorrow morning and read a bulletin that says she's been killed."

"Why do you care so much?"

"It's my job to care. Besides, McKenzie, don't you think she looks a lot like Katie?"

"No."

"Liar."

"What do you want me to do?"

"Hang on to her for a few days. Lying or telling the truth— if you spend time with her, talk to her, she might drop some hints that could help us learn who she is. She might do something foolish, try to make contact with people she knows. Hell, she might even contact her pals, remind them she's still alive; go the extortion route. Once we get a handle on her, we can figure out who's trying to kill her. And why."

"What if she does none of those things? If she really did lose her memory?"

"I don't know. Give her to the media, I guess. Hope for the best."

"All right, I'll do it. I owe you one."

"You owe me a helluva lot more than one."

"True, but this is going to cover all debts."

"Fair enough."

"One more thing. The clothes she's wearing—they're new. The money for her train fare. Where did all that come from?"

"I took it out of petty cash."

"I didn't know the Major Crimes Division had petty cash."

"A lot of things have changed since you were a cop."

I turned off the phone and stood in the center of my man cave. There was hockey equipment, golf clubs, bats and balls and a Paul Molitor–autographed baseball glove that I haven't used in years, gun cabinets—some locked, some unlocked—shelves loaded with knickknacks and memorabilia, and a small desk with a laptop. Inside desk drawers were a stack of bills—twenties and fifties, $25,000 worth—and a couple of passports, credit cards, and driver's licenses with my picture and someone else's name. A few years ago I had to "disappear," and it was difficult because I hadn't been prepared. Now I was. I had kept all of this in a safe when I lived in Falcon Heights. Unfortunately, the safe was imbedded in my basement floor, and I had to leave it behind. I'd been meaning to get a new one installed in the secret room, only I hadn't gotten around to it.

I wasn't thinking about that, though. I was thinking about amnesia.

I found a number in my cell phone's contact list and called it up. A few moments later, I was speaking to Dr. Jillian De-Marais. She was a psychiatrist. For a brief period of time, back when I was with the cops, she had been my psychiatrist.

Afterward, we started sleeping together. That didn't work out, and we became enemies. Time passed, though, and now we were friends again. The circle of life.

"I need help," I told her.

"I've been telling you that for years."

"Seriously."

"Okay, what?"

"Tell me about amnesia."

"Traumatic, hysterical, anterograde, retrograde, transient global . . . ?"

"Work with me, Jill."

"Traumatic amnesia is usually caused by a hard blow to the head."

"I know that one."

"Hysterical amnesia is almost always triggered by an event that the patient's mind can't cope with."

Like being thrown from a pickup truck, my inner voice said.

"Patients forget not only their past but their very identities. They wake up without any sense at all of who they are. Driver's license, credit cards, pictures in their wallets are meaningless to them. The person in the mirror is a complete stranger."

"That sounds promising."

"You think so? In most cases the memory returns either slowly or in a rush, usually within forty-eight hours. The patient might forget the cause of the memory loss. Beyond that, though, recovery is usually complete."

"Okay, that's not it."

"McKenzie . . ."

"Jill, please."

"Patients with anterograde amnesia can't learn anything new; they've lost the ability to make new memories. Retrograde amnesia means they can't remember anything that happened before the event that caused the memory loss. Transient global amnesia is a mild form of memory loss usually associated with vascular disease in older patients."

"Retrograde, then."

"What about it?"

"Can you fake it?"

"We call it malingering."

"Jill . . ."

"Of course you can. According to one study, nearly thirty percent of all criminals sentenced to life imprisonment claimed amnesia at their trials."

"How can you spot a faker?"

"Malingerer."

"How can you—"

"There are ways, tests."

"Like what?"

"McKenzie, do you know someone with retrograde amnesia? Because this is so rare, I'd like to meet him."

"Her."

"Of course. A damsel in distress, no doubt."

"I think that might be a good idea, if you talked to her."

"I have a patient waiting, the last of the day, so what I want you to do—call my service and we'll set up an appointment, probably the day after tomorrow. I'll give you the ex-boyfriend rate."

"Is that higher or lower than your usual fee?"

"Oh, much, much higher."

I left the man cave and carefully pushed the bookcase back in place until I heard the click that meant it was locked. By then, Nina and Fifteen had left the chairs and were now sitting on stools across from each other at the island in the kitchen area. We didn't have a kitchen and dining room, just "areas." Fifteen was devouring a plate of leftovers as if she had never tasted food before—a chicken and cashew stir-fry that I made with my own orange marmalade barbecue sauce.

"This is amazing," she told me.

"Do you like Chinese food?" I asked.

"I don't know. I like this, though, so . . . It's way better than hospital food, that's for sure."

I watched her face as she ate—a pretty face with eyes just a shade darker than cornflower blue. I was pleased that the scrapes on her chin and forehead had healed, leaving not a blemish on her smooth skin. She caught me staring and lifted her short golden hair a few inches above her ear.

"Want to see the scars where they drilled the holes in my head?" she asked.

"I'm sorry. I was staring."

That's why it's short now, my inner voice told me. *They cut her hair when she was in surgery.*

"You were looking at me the way the policeman looked at me, like he wanted to see what was inside," Fifteen said. "Problem is, I don't know what's inside. I would tell you if I did."

"I apologize for being rude."

"No, I—I apologize. I never thanked you for what you did. They showed me, the policeman showed me the film from the highway camera. He thought it might . . . I saw what you did. Thank you. I'm so sorry about your car."

"The policeman is an old friend of mine. He's very concerned for your welfare. He asked me to help, and I said I would."

"People have been very kind to me since I woke up."

"I have another friend, a psychiatrist—Dr. Jillian DeMarais."

"That tramp?" Nina said.

Fifteen covered her mouth with her hand in a failed bid to hide her smile.

"One of McKenzie's ex-girlfriends," Nina told her.

Fifteen smiled some more.

"She'd be happy to see you if you're willing to see her," I said. "Maybe the day after tomorrow?"

"I don't know," Fifteen said. "I've spoken to so many doctors in the past month. Can I think about it?"

"Of course."

"It's just that . . . it's so scary. Not knowing who I am, not knowing where I came from, I mean. I get images in my mind, but they're cloudy, you know? I can't quite make them out. It's like looking at something through a telescope that's out of focus. If you could just turn the knob—only I can't."

Is that true? my inner voice asked. *Or is she playing a part? Jennifer Jones in* Love Letters *or Geena Davis in* The Long Kiss Goodnight *if you prefer shoot-'em-ups.*

"It must be terrible," Nina said.

"I want to know, yet at the same time I don't," Fifteen said. "What if I find out that the people who tried to kill me, that I deserved it?"

"No one deserves that," I said.

"You've been so good to me already."

"We're happy that you're here," Nina said. "You're going to stay in our guest room. My daughter is away at college, and she's left plenty of clothes that you can borrow."

"Wait. You have a daughter in college?"

"Erica. She's a sophomore at Tulane University."

"No way. Grade school, maybe junior high. But college? I would never have guessed."

Nina took Fifteen by the elbow and started leading her toward the guest room.

"We're going to get along just fine," she said.

I busied myself by policing the kitchen. Nina returned alone twenty minutes later.

"Fifteen's trying on clothes," she told me.

"Okay."

"I like her."

"You don't know anything about her."

"She's sweet."

"A pretty girl and pleasant, giving off a please-help-me vibe . . ."

"I've heard that voice before. You're overly suspicious."

"Nina, the young lady could be everything she appears to be. She could also be the most conniving, black-hearted bitch, a woman with carefully honed skills of persuasion, who knows when to smile and laugh and cry and pretend to be vulnerable to get what she wants, who knows just which buttons to push and exactly when to push them."

Nina thought about it for a moment and announced, "I like her," again.

"So do I. That's the problem."

I poured Nina half a glass of Riesling and treated myself to a Summit Ale. We sat on the big sofa in front of the fireplace. I had a nice conflagration going when Fifteen emerged from the guest room. She wore Erica's pajamas and fluffy pink slippers and had wrapped herself in a thick pink robe. She looked like she was eleven years old.

I noticed that Fifteen was limping slightly and asked her about it.

"My knee still hurts a little," she said. "Kinda funny when you think about it, I had so many broken bones." She flexed the fingers of her hand. "They all healed real nice, but my knee . . . and sometimes—sometimes, I get an ache deep inside—just an ache. And headaches, too. The doctor said that I might not get completely back to normal for like two years."

Just saying it seemed to dredge all the pain to the surface at once. Fifteen closed her eyes and remained still for a moment. When she opened them they were wet, and she brushed at them with her knuckle.

"I'm okay, though," she said.

Nina patted the cushion next to her, and Fifteen sat facing the fire.

"Thank you," she said. "Thank you for taking care of me."

"Would you like a drink?" I asked.

"I don't know if I'm old enough to drink."

"Coffee?" Nina asked. Before Fifteen could answer, Nina

went to the coffeemaker in the kitchen area. She poured a generous amount into a mug. "Cream? Sugar?"

"I don't know," Fifteen said.

"I like mixing in some Hershey's syrup with a dollop of whipped cream."

"That sounds wonderful."

Nina made the beverage, returned to the sofa, and served it. She stood watching while Fifteen took a sip.

"This is really good," the young woman said.

"A poor man's café mocha," Nina said.

"I know that."

"Do you?" I asked.

"I know a lot of things. I just don't know how I know them. I remember movies—we had cable at the hospital—but I don't remember seeing them. I know music, too, songs. When I hear them on the radio, I can sing along, only I don't know where I learned them. Ever since you brought me here, I've been staring at your piano. I think I know how to play, but I don't remember taking lessons."

"Go 'head," Nina said.

"Is it okay?"

"Certainly."

Fifteen went to the piano and made herself comfortable on the bench as if she had done it a thousand times before. She lifted her fingers over the keyboard—and froze. Her face scrunched up with effort and her muscles strained as if she were trying to open a stubborn jar, yet her fingers did not move.

"It's okay," I said.

"No it's not. It's not."

Fifteen slammed her fists down on the piano keys. Nina went quickly to her side, sat on the bench next to her.

"What am I doing?" Fifteen said. "I don't know if I can play the piano. I don't know if I like music. Or Chinese food. Or coffee. I don't know my family, if I have a family. Or friends. Where I went to school. I don't even know if I like me. I mean, if I'm a good person or . . . I don't know how old I am. I don't know anything."

"Try this," Nina said. With her right hand, she picked out the opening notes to Beethoven's "Ode to Joy." Fifteen gathered herself and listened. Nina played the notes again.

"I've heard that before," Fifteen said.

Nina played the notes a third time. Fifteen flexed her fingers as if she wanted to be sure they still worked. She rested them gently on the piano keys and closed her eyes. A moment later, Fifteen played the same notes Nina had. She didn't stop where Nina had, though. She opened her eyes and continued playing. She played the entire song all the way through.

"How did you guess?" Fifteen asked.

"It was one of the first songs I learned when I was taking lessons," Nina said. "I think every piano instructor in the world teaches that piece. Try this one."

Nina played the opening to *Eine kleine Nachtmusik* by Mozart. Fifteen did the same. She stopped abruptly and wrapped her arms around Nina. She wept into her shoulder.

I finished my beer and opened another.

THREE

I was making Spanish omelets when Nina came into the kitchen area, opened the refrigerator, and removed a jug of orange juice. I was dressed in sweats and Nikes. She was wearing black knee-high boots and a clingy burgundy knit dress, reminding me that smart, tough, funny, and kind weren't her only attributes. She filled a tumbler with juice and drank half of it.

"Where's Fifteen?" she asked.

I gestured toward the balcony. Fifteen was outside, leaning on the rail, wearing one of Erica's down vests.

"What are we going to do with her?" Nina said.

"I don't know, but eventually your daughter is going to return home, and I'll bet she'll want her room and clothes back."

"Do you think Jillian can help her?"

"That tramp?"

"I admit I liked her better when you two were still calling each other names."

"I dialed her service earlier. I have an appointment scheduled for eleven tomorrow."

The mention of time caused Nina to glance at her watch.

"I gotta go," she said.

"What about breakfast?"

"I'll grab something at the club."

Nina took up her coat and bag and headed for the door.

"I'll be home early," she said.

That was unusual for her. Usually Nina stayed at Rickie's until well after one in the morning, although she was getting better lately at delegating responsibilities to her assistants and taking more time for herself.

"Who's playing tonight?" I asked.

"Your girlfriend, Connie Evingson."

"Girlfriend? I barely know the lady well enough to say, 'Hi, how are you?'"

"How many times have you seen her in concert in the past two years?"

"I haven't kept track."

"Uh-huh."

"Maybe we'll come down later for dinner and, you know, catch the show."

"Uh-huh."

Nina stopped and regarded the young woman standing on the other side of the glass wall for a moment. She draped her bag over her shoulder, went to the balcony door, slid it open, and poked her head out. She said something I didn't hear. Fifteen smiled at her and waved. Nina closed the door.

"I'm off," she said. "Call if you're coming down."

Usually I get a kiss good-bye. This time I didn't.

I finished making the meal and went to the balcony. I slid open the door and stepped outside, closing the door behind me. It was barely twenty degrees, but there was no wind on our side of the building, and that made the temperature more bearable. Fifteen kept leaning on the railing, showing no sign of being cold. I stood with my back to the glass and shivered.

"It's so beautiful," Fifteen said.

From where we stood, you could see the curve of the Mississippi River as it approached St. Anthony Falls and the lock and dam, the ice and snow that covered much of it, and the patches of water that remained unfrozen where steam rose up. On the east side of the river, Nicollet Island, where they launched the Minneapolis Aquatennial fireworks, and Father Hennepin Bluffs Park, where Nina and I used to watch them while sitting in canvas chairs. On the west side, parts of downtown Minneapolis, including the Guthrie Theater, Mill City Museum, and Gold Medal Park. Plus the Hennepin Avenue, Third Avenue, and Stone Arch Bridges that connected the two banks. And far to the right if you leaned over the railing, the I-35W freeway bridge that had been built to replace the one that collapsed a few years ago, taking with it thirteen lives and much of our peace of mind.

"It seems much higher than it really is because of the way it looks down into the river," Fifteen said.

"I suppose."

"This view . . . There's isn't a single building in Deer River that is more than two stories. I was in high school before I even saw an elevator. Tell me, McKenzie, living so high up, does it make you feel big or small?"

"Actually, it makes me feel a little nauseous. I have a touch of acrophobia."

"You're afraid of heights?"

"Just a bit."

"Why do you live in a building like this, then, with a balcony and glass walls and a view?"

"Well, you see, there's this girl . . ."

"You moved here for Nina? Wow. That is so cool. No one has ever done anything like that for me. At least . . . I don't remember, but it doesn't feel like it."

"You're still very young," I said. "Give it time."

"You think?"

"You're very pretty. Once you get past all this, you won't have any trouble finding somebody."

"Yes, but finding some*one,* that's the trick, isn't it? McKenzie, do you mind if I take a walk down there? Along the river?"

"Do you mind if I go with?"

"Are you asking because you think I'm in danger? Your cop friend, Commander Dunston, he thinks I am. That's why he sent me here."

"Breakfast is getting cold."

Fifteen dug into her omelet the same way she had consumed the Chinese dish the evening before—as if food were something she had just discovered.

In between bites, she said, "You are a marvelous cook."

"Yes. Yes, I am."

"Modest, too. Tell me, how does this work?"

"What do you mean?"

"You and Nina? I know she has a job. She said she was going to her office. Are you like, a househusband?"

"I hadn't thought about it. I suppose I am."

"She supports you?"

"No, not at all. We—Nina owns a restaurant and jazz joint in St. Paul called Rickie's, that she named after her daughter. It's her pride and joy. Both the club and Erica."

"Erica's not your daughter, too?"

"Nina and I aren't married."

"Ahh," she said around a mouthful of the egg dish. I wasn't surprised. We get that a lot.

"What about you?" Fifteen asked.

"What about me?"

"What do you do?"

"I'm what the screenwriters call independently wealthy."

"Really? How did that happen?"

"I used to be a police officer in St. Paul. One day, working on my own time, I tracked down a rather enterprising embezzler with a substantial price on his head. Actually, it took longer than a day. Anyway, I retired from the cops to collect the reward. The idea was to give my father a comfortable retirement, only he passed six months later."

"I'm sorry."

"Thank you."

"So, what do you do now?"

"Whatever I feel like."

"Must be nice."

"It has its moments."

"So, you basically took the reward money and started living a new life."

"Pretty much."

"God, I wish I could do that."

"You are, aren't you?"

"It's not the same thing. I mean, how can you start a new life if you don't know what the old one was like? It could have been the worst life ever. Or it could have been the best. I might have been in love. Someone might have loved me. I like to think I was a good person, McKenzie, except . . . except if I was, why did they try to kill me—kill me that way?"

"I have an appointment scheduled for you to meet my friend at eleven tomorrow morning."

"Tomorrow and tomorrow and tomorrow creeps in this petty pace from day to day, to the last syllable of recorded time, and all our yesterdays have lighted fools the way to dusty death."

"Shakespeare. *Macbeth.* I'm impressed."

"Who's Shakespeare? Who's Macbeth?"

Food was consumed. Dishes were cleared. Heavy winter clothes were donned. Fifteen was smaller than Erica, yet not by so much that she was uncomfortable in her clothes.

We took the elevator to the lobby. I threw a wave at Smith and Jones, but their attention was focused on the girl and they didn't notice. Outside the door, we hung a right and made our way along icy sidewalks and ramps to a path near the bluff above the river that had been cleared by a miniplow. We followed it west. It was like walking through a trench. The snow on each side was piled nearly to our shoulders. The Cities hadn't received more snow than usual; it was just that it had been so damn cold that very little of it had melted. There was more snow on the ground at that time in March than in the past thirty-plus years. Which made sightseeing problematic.

Nina was a talker. She noticed everything and loved everything, and she enjoyed pointing out the things that she noticed and loved from the dynamic lighting displays on the top floors of Target Plaza South to the authentic cobblestones beneath her feet. Fifteen, though, was quiet. I didn't know if that meant she was uncomfortable with my presence—or with herself—or if it was just her natural state. As for me, I tended to be more watchful than talkative. I didn't study the skyline or the river. I studied the people. Probably that was my cynical, suspicious nature again. It was also the reason why I spotted him.

Tall, with a blue jacket and a gray knit cap; I first picked him up when we hit the sidewalk at Gold Medal Park, and he was there when we reached the Stone Arch Bridge, a former railroad bridge now reserved for bicycles and pedestrians. (Nina would have told you it was the only arched bridge of stone on the entire river and that it was built in 1883 by James J. Hill for his Great Northern Railway.) When we strolled across the bridge, he trailed behind.

Normally, I wouldn't have cared. The area was filled with people who were doing exactly what Fifteen and I were doing, some of whom could be accused of following us as well. It was his unwavering pace that made me anxious. He always remained thirty yards behind us—never gaining, never losing ground. His presence reminded me whoever tossed the girl off a speeding truck might be keen to do it again.

We took our time crossing the bridge, reaching Father Hennepin Bluffs Park on the far side. From there we walked the plowed and shoveled sidewalks until we reached St. Anthony Main, a shopping, restaurant, office, and condominium complex. I guided Fifteen to the Aster Cafe. She stepped inside as if this had been our destination all along.

The Aster was considered by one local magazine to be "the best place to go on a first date" because of its spectacular view of the Minneapolis skyline, the tree-lined cobblestone street outside its front door, its perfect-for-cool-summer-nights courtyard, and the live jazz and bluegrass music it staged—mostly kids just starting out but also veterans like Bill Giese and Gary Rue. I picked it simply to see if our tail would follow us inside. He did. I pretended to ignore him.

I ordered black coffee; Fifteen had a mocha plus something called a Minnesota Malted Waffle, served with berries and whipped cream, despite eating breakfast less than ninety minutes earlier.

Our friend also had coffee.

"Do you think I lost weight?" Fifteen asked.

"Excuse me?"

"You saw me before I went into the hospital. Do you think I lost weight?"

"I couldn't say. A pound or two? Everyone loses weight in the hospital; all the meals are so nutritiously prepared."

"The portions are small, too. I was hungry all the time."

That explains why she attacked every meal as if it were her first, my inner voice said.

"I don't think losing weight is going to be a problem for you," I said.

Fifteen lifted a fork filled with waffle and whipped cream to her mouth, paused, and said, "You're cute." Which I took as her diplomatic way of saying, "What a jerk."

"There's a man sitting at a table off your left shoulder near the window," I said. "I want you to take two more bites of food and then look at him."

Fifteen did exactly as I asked. I thought her body stiffened at the sight, yet I couldn't be sure.

"Have you seen him before?" I asked.

"I don't remember. Why?"

"He's been following us."

To her credit, Fifteen finished her waffle without missing a beat.

"Are you sure?" she asked.

"Let's find out."

I paid the bill and escorted Fifteen back into the street. We retraced our steps, walking casually. At least I was casual. At one point, Fifteen took my hand in hers and did not let go until we reached the bridge. That's when I glanced behind me. He was there, exactly thirty yards back.

"What are we going to do?" Fifteen asked.

I gave her hand a squeeze.

"Patience," I said.

When we were halfway across the bridge, I guided Fifteen to the railing. She leaned against it as if enjoying the view of St. Anthony Falls, the Third Avenue Bridge, and Nicollet Island in the distance. At the same time, I turned my back to the railing, removed the glove from my right hand, and unzipped my coat. I made sure our companion saw me.

He kept walking while looking straight ahead as if I weren't there.

I pivoted slowly, watching intently as he passed.

I gave him a good thirty-yard head start before I nudged Fifteen.

Together, we drifted to the middle of the bridge again and walked toward downtown, this time following our follower. He picked up his pace, increasing the distance between us to about a football field by the time he reached the end of the bridge. He turned right and soon disappeared. We turned left and headed back to the condominium. I did not see him again, and I looked hard.

I rezipped my coat and replaced my glove.

"McKenzie?"

"Yes, sweetie?"

"Are you carrying a gun?"

"Nope."

She took my hand again.

When we returned to the condo, I announced that I was going down to the gym.

"You're going to work out?" Fifteen said.

"I try to get in an hour a day."

"Doesn't walking all that way count?"

Well, sure, I told myself, if all I was concerned with was maintaining my girlish figure. Unfortunately, I have on occasion been asked to perform, shall we say, vigorous activities, and a walk in the park just wasn't going to cut it. Especially at my advanced years. I didn't tell Fifteen that, though. She seemed jumpy enough. Instead, I said, "It's good for the heart."

Instead of her heart, Fifteen patted her flat stomach.

"I suppose a little exercise couldn't hurt. May I come with?"

"Of course."

Fifteen dashed into the guest bedroom and returned a few minutes later dressed in Erica's workout clothes. The shorts were loose around her waist and backside, yet the top was snug. I tried not to notice.

The second-floor gym had most of the machines you'd find in a pay-by-the-month workout facility, but no trainers. Still, I had spent enough time—and money—in fitness clubs over the years that I knew how everything worked. Fifteen, it turned out, seemed to know as well. There were plenty of grunts and groans along the way, yet forty minutes later her body glistened with perspiration and the warm glow of good health. As for me, I was pushing harder than usual, trying to impress the girl.

What's wrong with you? my inner voice asked. *She's a child.*

I have no idea what you're talking about, I told myself. I'm just working out.

You know exactly what I'm talking about. Stop it.

No harm, no foul, I reminded myself.

Really, McKenzie? Really?

"I'm sweating like a pig," Fifteen said.

The remark ended my internal debate.

"You look great," I said.

"Do you think so?"

"You've done this before."

Fifteen used her wrist to wipe the sweat off her forehead.

"If I have, it hasn't been recently," she said.

"At least six weeks, anyway."

She became very quiet after that, and I apologized.

"You don't need me to remind you of your problems," I said.

"I'm reminded nearly every minute of every day. McKenzie, do you think we have a soul? A biblical soul? One of the doctors I talked to when I was in the hospital, he said when we lose our identity we lose our entire sense of self—that's what he called it. He said we lose our understanding of who we are. I was eating ice cream at the time and I said I liked it and he said it's not enough that we like ice cream, it's knowing that we like ice cream that makes us the people we are. Where we went to school, who our friends are, all the things we've done or were done to us, the sum total of our experiences, all that defines us as a person. He was kind of a douche, but I know what he meant.

"Only, do you think we could forget all that and still be a good person? Maybe forgetting it all can help us become a good person. We're not born jerks. We become jerks over time. If we forget our crimes and whatever else turned us into jerks, we would stop being jerks, wouldn't we? We could become the people we were always meant to be and not worry about all that other stuff. I mean, out of sight, out of mind. Forget it like it never happened, and what's left over—that's our soul and it can be whatever we make of it. Don't you think?"

"Possibly," I said. "We'll ask my friend tomorrow."

"I don't think I want to see your friend."

"She might help you remember who you are."

"I don't know if I want to remember who I am—who I was. Not if I can start over."

If they'll let you, my inner voice said. I was thinking about the men who tried to kill her in such a terrifying manner. *They still remember who you are. And the crimes you committed.*

Fifteen held my hand and leaned against my shoulder on the elevator ride back to the seventh floor, and continued to hold my hand as we walked to the condo. She released it when I unlocked the door and held it open for her. Once inside, I announced that I was going to take a shower. She said she was going to do the same. I went to the master bedroom, closing the door behind me. I took off my shirt and kicked off my Nikes and passed through the walk-in closet to the bathroom. I heard a gentle knock on the door and returned to the bedroom. Fifteen had opened the door and was standing just inside.

"What is it?" I asked.

"I was thinking. You've been so kind to me. I was thinking . . . if you want to . . ."

"If I want to, what?"

"If you want—you're not married."

"Pretend that I am."

Fifteen's face colored a deep crimson. She turned abruptly and hurried from my bedroom.

"I'm sorry," she said over her shoulder and then, "Oh God, oh God. El, what were you thinking?"

Are you happy now? my inner voice said.

Thirty minutes passed, and I was sitting behind the desk next to the bookcase and surfing Web sites on the PC, looking for information about amnesia. An hour later, Fifteen emerged from the guest bedroom. She was dressed in the same clothes she had been wearing when she arrived the day before. She looked like she had been crying, and for a moment I felt I should gather her in my arms and tell her, "It's going to be all right"—which, all things considered, was probably the worst thing I could do.

She spoke to me from across the room. Her voice was soft, though, and I couldn't hear what she said.

"Hmm?" I asked.

"I should get out of here."

"That's a good idea. Why don't we run down to Rickie's later and get something to eat, listen to some jazz. You should change, though. Wear something nice."

"But . . ."

"No buts. Nina runs a high-class saloon."

Fifteen hesitated.

"Go on," I said.

"McKenzie, you have a generous soul."

"Sweetie, I could tell you stories that would bring tears to your eyes."

I maneuvered the Jeep Cherokee out of the underground garage, across Washington Avenue, to the Sixth Street entrance of I-94. Since Fifteen was sitting next to me, I took the carpool lane, something I seldom get a chance to do. A white Toyota Corolla followed close behind. There was only the driver in the car, though, and it annoyed me. I violated most motorized vehicle laws on a regular basis; this one I took seriously. Go figure.

It was only a minute or so before we reached the stretch of freeway where Fifteen had been thrown from the pickup truck, where my Audi was destroyed. She seemed to know it, too, the way her body stiffened and her jaw clenched.

"Are you okay?" I asked.

She nodded, yet did not relax until we approached the Dale Street exit, a couple of miles down the road.

I took the exit and hung a right. The Toyota stayed with us. It continued to follow when I went east on Selby Avenue. I pulled into the lot next to Rickie's, parking the Cherokee so that the nose was pointed toward the street. The Toyota drove past and kept on driving. I stayed in the Cherokee.

"What?" Fifteen asked.

NPR was on the radio.

"Just waiting for the news report to finish," I said.

"You care what's happening in Somalia?"

"It's a small world, after all."

The Toyota didn't return.

Nina must have told the staff about our houseguest, because they positively fawned over her. Fifteen enjoyed the attention, although I began to suspect if she heard the words "poor thing" one more time, violence might follow.

It was decided that Fifteen was indeed old enough to drink— certainly the strawberry lace dress that she had pilfered from Erica's closet supported that impression—and they started pouring her elaborate concoctions containing vanilla ice cream and rum that she drank with a straw. When she started on her third, I suggested that she might want to modulate her intake, but she assured me that she could handle her milk shakes.

Dinner was pan-seared scallops with a bean and pancetta ragù that Nina's head chef served herself.

"If you don't care for it, I'll make something else," she said.

That caused a double take. I had never heard Monica Meyer utter a word before that was even remotely solicitous, especially about her food.

Fifteen made sounds that seemed almost sexual in nature and announced, "This is amazing."

I said, "If you're looking for suggestions, Chef . . ."

"No one cares what you think," Monica said.

That's my girl, my inner voice said.

"McKenzie is a great cook," Fifteen said.

Monica patted her shoulder. "I'm sure you'll be better soon," she said.

Monica left the table, and Fifteen said, "She's not a nice person."

"Actually, she is," I said. "We just like to tease each other."

Fifteen shook her head as if she didn't believe me.

After dinner, Fifteen and I found a table in Rickie's upstairs performance hall. Connie Evingson had a terrific jazz repertoire. I've heard her channel everything from Lerner and Loewe to Django Reinhardt, from Peggy Lee to the Beatles, and she was drawing on all of it, with a four-piece orchestra backing her up. Halfway through her first set, she threw me a wave from the stage and I gave her one back, and then quickly glanced around to see if Nina had noticed. Fortunately, she was downstairs. The exchange gave Fifteen a smile that a moment later became a frown.

"Did you tell Nina that I tried . . . that I hit on you?" she asked.

"No. Why would I do that?"

She gave it a few moments' thought before answering, "Then I will. I have to."

"No, you don't."

"She's been so kind to me, it's only fair."

"Fifteen, wait—"

She was out of her chair and heading for the steps that led to the bar downstairs before I got the words out.

Evingson did a nice mash-up of Paul McCartney's "Yesterday" and the more up-tempo "Yesterdays" by Otto Harbach and Jerome Kern, and I thought, I'm the one who's going to get mashed up when Nina gets her hands on me.

Fifteen returned ten minutes later. Her eyes were bright and shiny.

"I told her," she said. "I told Nina what happened. I told her everything; that I went into your bedroom."

"What did she do?"

"She hugged me and kissed my cheek and said, 'Don't ever do it again.'" Fifteen spoke as if she couldn't believe her own words. "Someone that kind—McKenzie, Nina's even nicer than you."

"Everyone says that."

We settled in and listened. Evingson sang "Wouldn't It Be Loverly" from her first CD. Out of the corner of my eye I could see Fifteen's lips move with the lyrics—*All I want is a room somewhere, far away from the cold night air* . . .

She sighed deeply when the song finished, and I wondered if like Eliza Doolittle, she had come to a decision.

The three of us left Rickie's together. I arranged it so that Nina and Fifteen rode in Nina's Lexus. I sat in the Jeep Cherokee and waited while Nina started her car, let it warm for a minute, and drove off. I followed cautiously behind. Traffic was light at that time of the morning. If there was a white Toyota Corolla lurking about, I didn't see it.

Nina and Fifteen reached the condo ahead of me. When I entered, Judi Donaghy, another one of my favorites, was on the stereo system and threatening to *drink muddy water and sleep in a hollow log* at a volume that invited ill will from our neighbors. Fifteen was in the middle of the room dancing and twirling about with reckless glee, completely unconcerned that Nina and I were watching. Or that I took several photographs of her with my cell phone.

"How many ice cream drinks did she have?" Nina asked.

"Let's just say that if we learn nothing else about the girl, we know she's not lactose intolerant."

Nina managed to attract the young woman's attention.

"Coffee?" she asked.

"Can I have another one of those mochas?"

"Sure."

Nina poured a mug from a coffee and espresso maker I had purchased a couple years ago. Fifteen waved at it as she danced.

"Jura-Capresso," she said. "Retails for about thirteen hundred dollars."

"That's exactly right," I said. "Although I got a deal on it."

Fifteen pointed.

"The Baccarat vase on the dining room table?" she said. "Full-lead crystal handmade in France, worth about four hundred and fifty."

Nina leaned in, giving Fifteen a good look at her diamond pedant necklace—a large diamond cradled by a circle of smaller diamonds that I bought at Nordstrom's. Fifteen lifted the pendant off Nina's chest, glanced at it, and let it fall.

"Eighteen hundred," she said as she danced away.

Nina looked at me, and I nodded. She seemed impressed but I don't know if it was from Fifteen's expertise or the fact that I paid so much.

"You're starting to make me nervous," I said. I showed her my watch. "What about this?"

She stopped moving for a moment and looked close.

"McKenzie, you're filthy, stinking rich and yet you wear a thirty-dollar Casio? Where did you get this? Sears?"

"How did you do that?" Nina asked.

Fifteen paused before answering. Most of her cheerfulness seemed to dissipate.

"I have no idea," she said. "Maybe I worked for a department store or something. Or I was a personal shopper—there are people you can hire who will shop for you. Make sure you're always in fashion. Maybe I did that."

"I used to date a woman who had a personal shopper," I said.

"The psychiatrist?" Fifteen asked.

"No, a corporate attorney."

"You'd be amazed at the riffraff McKenzie spent time with before I came along," Nina said.

Fifteen repeated the word "riffraff" and laughed more heartily than the joke deserved.

"Let's get you to bed, young lady," Nina said. She sounded just like she did when she spoke to her daughter.

Nina returned from the guest room ten minutes later.

"She's going to feel it in the morning," she said.

"That's what happens when you have too much ice cream."

"Were you ever going to tell me that Fifteen hit on you?"

"She didn't actually hit on me. It was more like she was testing the waters. You can't blame her—I'm such a fine figure of a man. Besides, if I told you about every attractive woman that tried to pick me up . . . actually, now that I think about it, it would be a pretty short conversation."

"Let's keep it that way."

Nina prepared for bed and I watched because, well, it was one of my favorite things to do. It reminded me of a poem by Page Hill Starzinger, the one where she wrote: *I want to squander you.*

"I've had this feeling all day," Nina said. "A feeling that something bad is going to happen. Only I don't know where it'll come from, this bad thing. I don't know which door to lock."

"Don't worry about it. It's an easy thing to say, harder to do, I know. Worrying, though, isn't going to help."

"You speak from experience."

"Trouble is like rain. It's gonna fall eventually. How we deal with it depends on where we are at the time."

"Inside a toasty warm condominium above the city lights or on the street under an umbrella."

"Sometimes without an umbrella."

"We've been together long enough, McKenzie, that I understand this. It's just . . . I want to help Fifteen."

"So do I."

"We can't actually adopt her, can we?"

"You're talking about a woman you've known for barely more than a day."

"She's a good person."

"How can you tell?"

Nina tapped the center of her chest.

"The heart never lies," she said.

"Of course it does. That's what's wrong with it."

FOUR

Nina was gone a good hour before I decided it was time to rouse our guest. I knocked on the bedroom door. Fifteen grumbled something unintelligible. I carefully balanced a tray with one hand while I opened the door and stepped inside. I set the tray on the table next to the bed.

"I feel terrible," Fifteen said.

"You should see yourself from my side."

"Oh, God."

I motioned toward the tray.

"First, the water," I said. "Rehydrate the body. Second, the fruit smoothie. There're bananas in it to replace your lost potassium and electrolytes. The egg sandwich. Protein and carbs are a good source of nutrients, plus the eggs contain an amino acid that'll help break down the toxins in your body and reduce the nausea."

"You're kidding me, right?"

"Fifteen, I've had enough hangovers over the years that I have it down to a science. Exercise is also good, so after you've eaten, get dressed. We'll go for a walk along the river before your appointment."

"McKenzie, I don't want to see your friend. I'm grateful,

but—I know exactly what she's going to say. The same thing the other doctors said. There's no Hollywood ending for me. Getting hit on the head again isn't going to restore my memory like it does in the movies. Seeing something or someone familiar, that won't trigger it either. What she'll tell me, if it's physical, the result of damage to the brain, I'll probably never get it back. If the memory loss was caused by stress, by the trauma of falling off the truck, the memories might still be there inside my head, only I'm subconsciously suppressing them, and getting them back, it's possible, but it's going to take a lot of work."

"It's up to you, but sitting around here all day isn't going to do you any good."

"The way I feel right now, sitting around here all day sounds like exactly what I should do. Can we make it some other time, McKenzie—meeting your friend? Would that be all right?"

"Eat your breakfast."

Dr. Jillian DeMarais had a suite of offices in One Financial Plaza, about a mile from my place. It seemed like a shame to waste the appointment, which I knew Jill would charge me for anyway, so I strolled over there. It was cold; what else was new? The Cities were hammered by an arctic cold front a couple of days after Thanksgiving and hadn't experienced a moment above freezing since. The holidays, Valentine's Day, St. Patrick's Day, the St. Paul Winter Carnival, and Hockey Day in Minnesota had helped ease the pain, except now it was mid-March and winter was starting to get very, very old indeed. Even knowing that the Twins were working out in Florida wasn't enough to cheer me up.

I waited for Jill in her outer office. There were four paintings, one to each wall—a Degas, Matisse, Chagall, and Van Gogh—and not for the first time I wondered if she had ever used them as a kind of Rorschach test. *Tell me which painting you like best. Tell me why.* In the course of our relationship, I found myself attracted to each one in turn, until I had both accepted and rejected them all. I had no idea what that said about me, and I was afraid to ask.

At ten fifty-five on the button, the door to her inner office opened, and Jill escorted a sour-looking woman in her early thirties out of the suite with a string of encouraging adverbs. It wasn't until the woman was gone that Jillian acknowledged my presence.

"Where's the patient?" she asked.

"Decided not to come."

She nodded as if it happened all the time.

Jill motioned for me to enter the inner office. She sat behind her desk, and I took a chair on the opposite side. There was a sofa and a couple more chairs against the far wall, and I wondered briefly about the stories she must hear every day.

"Tell me about this damsel in distress," Jill said. There was no "Hello," no "How are you," no "You're looking good." Jill had always been a no-nonsense kind of woman. It was one of the things I liked about her that eventually helped break us up.

I told her everything, including what Fifteen had told me just before I left the condo.

"She's right," Jill said. "If she damaged certain areas of the brain, the hippocampus, for example, then no, she probably won't regain her memories. If the memory loss was caused by psychological disorders, therapy, psychotherapy, becomes a viable option."

"Is it possible that she's faking—"

"Malingering."

"Could she still remember music, for example?"

"Oh, yes. The community has been trying to figure that one out, but yes, amnesiacs can lose all memory of their past lives—and yet remember music. We think it's because music memories are stored in a special part of the brain. The superior temporal gyrus or the frontal lobes. There's a famous conductor in England—"

"Jill. I'll take your word for it."

"Just trying to give you your money's worth, McKenzie."

"Could she remember the price of things, like, say, a diamond pendant?"

That caused Jillian to lean back in her chair.

"I don't know," she said. "Not everyone is the same. Usually the memory loss is complete. Occasionally . . . Memory isn't unitary. There's more than one kind of memory. Something else that we're just starting to understand, amnesia doesn't destroy personal habits."

"So if Fifteen was in the habit of pricing objects, she would still be able to do that?"

"I would really like to meet this woman, McKenzie."

"Would she be able to remember something specific, like the first time she rode on an elevator?"

"I wouldn't think so, but . . ."

"But everyone is different. How can I find out if she really is malingering?"

Jillian smiled at my use of the word.

"There is a wide variety of tests available that can help detect patients who fake anterograde amnesia," she said. "It's more problematic to assert whether or not a patient is feigning retrograde amnesia. The variables in question tend to be largely out of the examiner's control. We have an Autobiographical Memory Interview, which uses samples of personal semantic memories across the patient's life span, such as information about school days, but that requires cooperation of friends and family members with intimate knowledge about the patient's life. There is also the Public Events Test, which involves recall and recognition of news events. Unfortunately, none of this is foolproof. Even if strong suspicions occur, it's difficult to make accurate conclusions without a patient confession, which is rare."

"Then there's nothing I can do?"

"You can try the Dead or Alive Test."

"How does that work?"

"Get a list, say one hundred names, and ask the patient if that person is alive or dead. If the patient had no memory of these people, then it'll be like tossing a coin. The results should be near fifty-fifty. However, if the patient scores below chance, below the baseline of genuine amnesiacs, it might be because the malingerer is attempting to sabotage her own performance. In her attempt to *prove* that she has amnesia, she will score worse than patients with genuine amnesia. It's not conclusive; you need to remember that, McKenzie. One cannot say with absolute certainty that the patient is simulating without a confession."

"How do I get a confession?"

"You can always ask. From what I remember, McKenzie, you could charm a girl into almost anything."

The return trip took me past the Depot on Washington Avenue, which was once the Chicago, Milwaukee, St. Paul, and Pacific Depot Freight House and Train Shed before it was converted into a couple of hotels, indoor water park, and ice-skating rink. I liked to look through the huge windows at the skaters gliding across the ice inside. I've skated most of my life; still played hockey thirty weeks out of the year with Bobby Dunston and a bunch of friends from our misspent youth. The thought occurred to me—skating is like riding a bicycle. You never forget. If I convinced Fifteen to lace them up, would she remember? Would muscle memory kick in? Assuming she actually did know how to skate. You'd be surprised at the number of people living in Minnesota who can't. Probably the same percentage as those who are unable to swim despite our 11,842 lakes.

That's when I saw it, a white Toyota Corolla parked across the street.

I might have blown it off as a coincidence except there was a serious-looking young man sitting behind the steering wheel. I might have blown him off, too. I couldn't identify him as the driver of the Toyota that followed me the day before—if I had been followed. He most definitely was not the man who tailed us across the Stone Arch Bridge. However, the engine was running even though it was clear that he wasn't going anywhere; clouds of exhaust were being snatched by the wind and pushed across the street. He was just trying to stay warm as he watched—what? I stopped and tried to work out the angles. From where I stood, yeah, he could be conducting surveillance on the front doors of my building as well as the entrance to the underground garage.

I went back down the avenue, crossed at the light, and came up behind him, debating my options as I walked. The one I settled on was getting his license plate number and running it past Bobby. I slipped the cell phone out of my pocket, took a couple of shots as unobtrusively as I could, and kept walking. The young man continued to stare at my building. He didn't turn his head to look at me—or anyone else, for that matter.

I crossed again at the light a block ahead and moved directly to the building, fighting the impulse to glance over my shoulder to see if he was still there. Once I was inside, the security guards swarmed toward me. Smith was the first to speak.

"We've monitored a car driving around the building," he said. "It circled us four times."

"We don't believe he was looking for a parking space," Jones said. "There were plenty available."

"A white Toyota Corolla?" I asked. I recited the license plate number. "It's parked a couple blocks down with a clear view of the doors."

Smith and Jones glanced at each other. Disappointment etched their faces.

"I told you we should have walked the perimeter," Jones said.

"Do you want us to run the plate?" Smith asked.

"I got it."

"Are you sure?"

I hesitated. They both seemed so earnest, so wanting to be involved. Well, it probably is boring being a security guard watching locked doors all day.

"Do you have resources?" I asked.

"Yes," Smith assured me. "Oh, yes. We do."

"Run the plate, then. Don't do anything foolish, though, okay?"

I was concerned because not too long ago a woman sued the state for invasion of privacy after she discovered that nearly every law enforcement officer that she had ever encountered— over a hundred guys!—had pulled her record at one time or another for no better reason than to learn her name and marital status. Yes, she was that attractive. She was awarded a million-dollar settlement, and the Department of Public Safety had been clamping down ever since.

"We're on it," Smith said.

"Just a name and address for now, guys. If we need more, I'll let you know."

Smith and Jones were both smiling when I caught the elevator.

Spreading joy wherever you go, McKenzie, my inner voice said. *What a guy.*

The TV was on when I entered the condo; TCM was broadcasting a John Garfield film. I loved old movies and stopped to watch a few scenes. Fifteen was lying on the sofa facing the screen, sound asleep, the remote in her hand. Somehow she had managed to work it, amnesia or no. I slipped the remote from her hand, turned off the TV, and covered her with an afghan that I took from the back of a chair. I went to the PC and started compiling a list of names, one hundred in all, half alive, half dead—it was actually a lot harder than it sounds. While I typed them into a Word document, the landline rang. The sound of it woke Fifteen, who looked around as if unsure where she was or how she got there. Her head snapped toward me when I picked up the receiver and said, "McKenzie."

"Mr. McKenzie," Smith said. "We ran the plate."

"Go 'head," I said. I deliberately ignored his name for fear that Fifteen would know who I was talking to.

"The owner is Doug Howard, age twenty-four. His permanent address is on Portland Avenue in Richfield, Minnesota. His driving record is clean. Not so much as a parking ticket. Is that helpful?"

"Very much."

"Should we try to get a look at his criminal record?"

"Not now," I said. "Maybe later."

"Okay."

"Thanks for calling."

"Anytime."

I hung up the phone. Fifteen cocked her head as though she expected an explanation.

"My insurance guy," I said. "We're still working out the details on my car."

Fifteen nodded as if she knew it all along.

How did you become such a good liar? my inner voice asked.

Practice, practice, practice, I told it.

"So, how do you feel?" I asked.

"Much better. Almost normal."

"Ahh, to be young again with all recuperative powers still intact."

"You're not that old."

"It's like a used car. It's not the years, it's the mileage that counts."

Fifteen didn't say if she agreed or not.

"Did you see your friend?" she asked.

"I did."

"What did she say?"

"She said pretty much what you told me she'd say. She'd still like to see you, though."

"Maybe later, okay?"

"Okay. In the meantime, one thing Jillian told me is that your memory loss might not be complete. You remember the price of things." I gestured at the HDTV above the fireplace. "You remember how to use a TV remote."

"Actually, it took me a while to figure that out."

"She gave me a simple test that might give us an idea of the extent of your memory loss if you're up to taking it."

Fifteen lifted her hands and let them fall to her sides. "Sure," she said. I had the impression that she was trying to humor me. I explained the test without mentioning that it was designed to detect malingerers and started in.

"Abraham Lincoln."

"Dead."

"George Washington."

"Alive."

"Rod Carew."

"Alive."

"Brett Favre."

"Dead."

"Woodrow Wilson."

"Dead."

"Otis Redding."

"Alive."

It went on like that for the first fifty names and I noticed she was batting nearly .500—half right, half wrong. That's when I decided to be a smart guy and threw her the splitter down and away.

"Doug Howard"—the only nonfamous name on the list.

She stumbled, started to say "Alive," corrected herself and said "Dead."

I kept going as though nothing had happened. She knew

I was onto her, though. In the next fifty names, she got thirty-two wrong and only eighteen correct.

"Okay," I said.

"Okay what?"

"Okay, I'll give the results to Jillian later and hear what she has to say."

I stood up and stretched, trying to appear unconcerned.

"The names," Fifteen said. "Were they all famous people?"

I knew exactly what she was fishing for and gave it to her.

"Not all," I said. "Doug Howard—the security guys caught him circling the building earlier and asked if I knew who he was. I didn't. Do you?"

"I don't think so. At least I don't remember. You say he was watching the building?"

"That's what the security guys think. They're keeping an eye out for him."

"Do you think he's watching because of me?"

I could have lied, but I wanted to see how she would react.

"Yes, I do," I said.

"How would he know I was here?"

I shook my head.

"I thought I was safe," Fifteen said. "I'm not."

"Yes, you are."

It was her turn for some head shaking.

"No," she said. "They're not going to let me alone; they're not going to let me go. Sooner or later, they're going to take me and it'll be the same damn thing all over again."

"Who are they?"

"The men who tried to kill me the first time."

"Who are they?" I repeated.

"I don't remember."

"Fifteen, what you need to know, Nina and I are on your side. Especially Nina, so don't worry about me being friends with Bobby Dunston, okay? If there's a choice to be made, I'll go along with her every time. Besides, I'm not a cop anymore. I'm not in the business of arresting people for their past crimes." I emphasized the word *past*. "If there's anything you want to tell me, it won't go further than this room. I promise."

Fifteen nodded, yet I don't think she believed me.

"Who are these men?" I asked. "Why are they trying to kill you?"

"I don't remember."

"According to the twelve-step programs, there are two days you should never worry about. One of them is yesterday. Yesterday is gone."

"What's the other day? Tomorrow?"

"That's what they say, except I worry about tomorrow all the time."

"Tomorrow and tomorrow and tomorrow . . ."

"Exactly right. If you want to take care of tomorrow, fix today. I will help you if you let me."

"Why? Why would you help me?"

"I believe in the promise of spring."

Fifteen drifted to the huge windows and looked out at the frozen world beyond.

"I guess we all do," she said. "We wouldn't live here if we didn't."

We both stopped talking after that until the silence became too loud.

"Feel like going down to the gym and working out?" I asked.

"My knee is aching again." Fifteen grabbed her knee and massaged it to emphasize her point. "You go, though. I'll be all right. I need to think."

"Are you sure?"

She nodded.

I went into the master bedroom and changed my clothes. Fifteen was still staring out the window when I returned.

"Be back in about forty minutes," I said.

"Take your time."

"Fifteen? If it helps, what you said the other day, about the soul? I think you're on to something."

Thirty minutes later, Smith ran into the gymnasium. He was woefully out of shape for a security guard and spoke between labored breaths.

"The girl," he said. "She left the building. Went out the door. Carrying a backpack. We tried to call. You didn't have a phone. Saw you on camera . . ."

My first thought was to chase after Fifteen, but in shorts and a T-shirt, I wouldn't last ten minutes on the streets of Minneapolis in March.

"Where did she go?" I asked.

Smith shook his head.

"Jones is following her," he said.

"Good man."

I had just gotten the words out when Jones spoke to Smith over the radio that was attached to the lapel of his jacket.

"I lost her," Jones said.

"What do you mean you lost her?" I said.

Smith repeated my question into his mic.

"Target was headed to the train station. I thought she was going to get on the Green Line to St. Paul. She didn't. She—she disappeared. Just now. I looked. She's gone."

"Dammit," I said.

I guess she didn't believe you after all, my inner voice said.

Smith asked a question then that impressed me for the simple reason that I hadn't thought of it myself.

"The man in the white Toyota—Howard. Did he see her leave?"

"I don't know," Jones said. "The car is gone."

"Is that a good sign or bad?" Smith asked me.

"Hell if I know."

I searched the condo when I returned to determine what Fifteen might have taken with her in the backpack. Afterward, I made three phone calls. The Minneapolis Police Department was the first to respond.

I was filling out a theft report with an officer when Nina burst into the room, leaving our door open behind her.

"What did you do?" she wanted to know.

"Sit. I'll explain in a minute."

Only Nina didn't sit. She stood there glowering while I finished with the officer. The officer told me where and when I could get a copy of the report online and left the condo. He had to step around Bobby Dunston to get out.

"What did you do?" Bobby wanted to know.

"I screwed up. Twice. The first time was when Fifteen arrived. I let her see me going into the man cave."

The bookcase door was still open, and I led Bobby and Nina inside.

"What good is a secret room if you don't keep it secret?" Bobby asked.

"None at all."

"What did she take?"

"Four guns—a .25 Colt semiautomatic, .38 Smith & Wesson wheel gun, nine-millimeter Beretta, and my Walther PPK. They're all registered. I gave the numbers to the Minneapolis cops."

"Why did you do that?" Nina wanted to know. "They'll arrest her. Is that what you want?"

"It's the only excuse we have to search for her," Bobby said. "Except for the guns, Fifteen has committed no crimes that we're aware of."

"I don't want her arrested."

"I'll withdraw the complaint after we find her," I said. "If that doesn't work, I'll hire my own lawyer to defend her; G. K. can discredit me on the witness stand."

Nina's expression suggested that she'd pay real money to see that. Yet having an excuse to search for Fifteen was only part of the reason I called the police, and Bobby knew it. The other part—I needed to protect myself in case the guns started showing up at crime scenes.

"Why did she leave?" Nina asked. "McKenzie? She was safe with us. I told her that. Didn't you tell her that?"

"She didn't believe us. When she heard me use Doug Howard's name, she didn't believe us at all."

"Who's Doug Howard?"

"Is that what made her run?" Bobby asked.

I told them about my morning.

"Ahh, McKenzie," Bobby said.

"You thought she was lying about having amnesia. Now we know for sure."

"How did Howard know Fifteen was here?" Nina asked.

"Probably followed her when she left the hospital."

"What are we going to do?"

Bobby ignored the question and asked, "What else did she take?"

"Five thousand dollars in cash," I said. "I didn't tell the MPD about the money, though."

Bobby nodded his head as if he understood perfectly.

"What are we going to do?" Nina repeated. "Fifteen is all alone. She's all alone and she's scared. She's probably trying to hide."

"What do you know about Howard?" Bobby asked.

"Only what I told you."

"I don't even have a legitimate reason to pull his jacket."

"Maybe not, but you're going to do it anyway."

"We need to find her," Nina said. "Should we offer a reward?"

"What would the notice say?" Bobby asked. "Wanted—a pretty, young, blue-eyed blonde with pale skin? In Minnesota, that shouldn't generate more than ten thousand phone calls. I'm sorry, Nina. I don't mean to be rude, only it would be like looking for a needle in a stack of needles. We don't even have a name."

"That's not entirely true," I said.

Nina looked at me with high expectations. Bobby's expression suggested annoyance.

"Have you been holding out on us, McKenzie?" he asked.

"She let it slip the other day. Her name is El."

"Elle? As in Elle Macpherson, the model? Or short for Ellen, Eloise, Eleanor?"

"Or just the letter L," Nina said. "Linda, Laurel, Loraine . . ."

"Something else," I said. "Yesterday morning on the balcony, she said that there wasn't a single building over two stories in Deer River."

Bobby tried to contain himself and nearly succeeded. Yet for the briefest of moments an expression flicked across his face that I had seen before, albeit not very often. It was the one that said, "You're smarter than you look."

FIVE

I started at the Holiday Stationstore off U.S. Highway 2 just inside the city limits.

"Yeah," I said. "I have a place, a cabin, about fifty miles north of here. I must have driven through Deer River a thousand times to get there, and this is the only place I've ever stopped. I ran into a couple of kids in the Cities, though, especially this pretty young thing called herself El, and they said I should give DR a try. Do you know El?"

I spoke the name loud enough for everyone to hear. The woman working the cash register didn't know it. Neither did anyone else by the way the other customers acted.

I tried the same gag over a mug of tap beer at the joint next door and received a head shake from the bartender for my trouble. The folks at the Outpost Bar and Grill, Otte Drug Store, and the U-Save Food Store also claimed they had never heard of a blue-eyed blonde named El. I found it very discouraging. Small towns don't have much of a transient population. Everyone who was there was usually there to stay, and I figured the thousand or so people who lived in Deer River would know everyone else. I was starting to think I had figured wrong.

Next, I pulled into the parking lot of the Deer River High School, home of the Warriors. The school was housed in an aging flat brown building, and if it had any athletic fields, they were buried under three and a half feet of snow. It must have been doing something right, though, because the plaque just inside the front entrance proclaimed that *U.S. News & World Report* had awarded Deer River a bronze medal, designating it as one of the best high schools in the country.

The secretary was old enough that she could have turned over the first shovel of dirt when the school was built. She looked up expectantly when I approached. I asked if there were copies of the yearbook dating back the past five years that I could look at. She asked why. I told her that I wanted to look up a young lady I met in the Cities—a girl called El. She asked why. I asked if she knew El. She responded by picking up a phone and making a call. I told her that wasn't necessary. She told me to wait. I did.

Less than a minute later, another woman approached. She extended her hand and told me her name. "Ms. Bosland." She was surprisingly young and pretty and I thought, as I shook her hand, that if I were still in school I might have tried to date her. I told her what I wanted.

"Mr. McKenzie." She spoke my name slowly like she was trying to memorize it. "We are not in the habit of revealing personal information about our students to strangers."

"Let me speak to the principal."

"I am the principal."

Wow, school has changed, my inner voice told me.

"Finally, someone I can talk to," I said aloud. I shook her hand a second time and repeated my request, this time making it sound like I wanted dinner and a movie with drinks at my place afterward. She still refused.

"What about prospective employers who only want to know if she graduated?" I asked.

"You can't even tell me her full name, so I doubt she sent you a résumé or filled out a job application. But I'll bite—are you a prospective employer? What company?"

"I just want to look up El's picture in the yearbook." Even as I said it, I knew I sounded creepy.

Both women folded their arms in unison, their movements so similar that I wondered if they were family, if the principal was the secretary's great-granddaughter. It was apparent that neither of them was going to budge unless I told them a story, and the only one that came to mind was the truth. I couldn't tell them that, so I excused myself. Their cold stares followed me out the door and across the parking lot to my Jeep Cherokee.

I thought about calling Bobby Dunston. Perhaps he could contact the principal from his office and ask her to cooperate with me. It sounded a lot like admitting defeat, though, and I wasn't ready for that.

I had purchased the Cherokee when cars were cars and not floating personal computers. It had none of the gadgets— including a seat warmer—of my late, lamented Audi, which I had every intention of replacing in June or when the snow melted, whichever came first. So I dug the smartphone out of my pocket, pleased that I had bars. Experience had taught me that coverage Up North was iffy at best. I piggybacked the high school's Wi-Fi connection and googled the Deer River, Minnesota, public library, figuring that it would probably have yearbooks. There wasn't one.

"Well, dammit."

Night had fallen, along with the temperature. The snow under my boots crunched like gravel as I walked across the parking lot toward the entrance of the small roadhouse just off Minnesota Highway 6, north of town.

O'Malley's was an oasis of light in a world of sorrowful blackness. Except for the distant stars shimmering above, there was nothing else to comfort a traveler as far as the eye could see. Along with light, there was warmth. I felt it radiate from the building as I approached; heard it in laughter and Golden Oldies as I opened the door.

The mornin' sun is shinin' like a red rubber ball, the Cyrkle sang from the jukebox.

Hang a left and there was the restaurant, filled to capacity, a trio of smiling waitresses scurrying from kitchen to tables and booths, taking and filling orders. To the right was a bar, also full of customers, a regulation-size pool table making it more crammed than it needed to be, a young man circling the table and twirling his cue like a samurai sword and someone shouting "just shoot the frickin' ball" in a way that made others laugh.

It was only 6:00 P.M. on a Thursday by my watch, yet the place was rocking like Saturday night in downtown Minneapolis. I thought that was probably because Deer River was two hundred miles from downtown Minneapolis and there was nowhere else to go and nothing else to do on a cold winter's night. It was a condescending attitude to take, I admit, but you should hear sometimes what small-town folk have to say about us city slickers.

The only empty stool was at the far end of the stick beneath the head of a twelve-point buck that had seen better days. I managed to get there without inconveniencing the pool player. There were amusing signs on the wall about credit, as well as jokes involving Ole, Sven, and Lena. Conversations seemed to include everyone within earshot. The bartender could have been the girl who grew up down the street. She looked to be about twenty with sandy hair, hazel eyes, and a figure the old man would have labeled "pleasingly plump." The thing was, though, it seemed as if all the light in the place came from her smile.

She set two menus in front of me before I was comfortably seated, one listing the daily specials. She left, served a few patrons, and returned. The Everly Brothers were on the juke-box now, telling Little Susie to wake the hell up.

"Whad'llya have?" she asked.

I requested a Summit EPA, a craft-beer brewed in St. Paul, my hometown, that she didn't serve, then switched my order to Schell's Pilsner, which she didn't have either. She stared at me, an expression of infinite patience on her face.

"Grain Belt?" she suggested.

"On tap?" I said.

"Comin' right up."

The bartender returned a moment later with a twelve-ounce mug. She pointed at the menus and asked, "Do you want to order something to eat?"

"In a minute."

She started to move down the stick and I said, "I must have driven past here a thousand times on the way to my lake cabin, yet I've never stopped."

"What makes us so lucky this time?"

"A young lady I met in the Cities told me to give it a try. Girl named El."

"El? You know Ella Elbers?"

He shoots, he scores, my inner voice announced.

I pulled out my smartphone and tried to keep my hands from trembling as I called up Fifteen's pic, the one of her dancing in a dress made of strawberry lace. I zoomed in and showed the photo to the bartender, who took the phone from my hand.

"Oh my God, she cut her hair. So cute."

"You're friends?"

"Of course we are. We grew up together. Went to school together. Didn't she say?"

"No. She just said to stop in O'Malley's the next time I was up here."

"The bitch. Didn't even tell you to say hi? That's cold."

I spread my hands wide as if to announce, "That's El."

The bartender returned my smartphone.

"I haven't heard from El in God, three months," she said. "Oh, hey, in case she didn't tell you." The bartender extended her hand and I shook it. "I'm Cynthia Desler. Cyndy. With two Y's. Some people call me M."

"What does M stand for?"

"Nothing. It used to stand for Marie. When I got divorced, I switched from my ex's name back to mine, but the court clerk screwed up. He left the Marie part out. Now it's just M. You believe that? I lost my middle name. My friends call me M now whenever they want to tease me. What a world. How do you know El? Oh, wait . . ."

Cyndy moved down the bar and began assisting patrons with drink and food orders. How she knew they wanted help I couldn't say. It wasn't like they were waving—at least I didn't see them wave. Yet a competent bartender has a sense for such things, and she was clearly good at her job. A few minutes later, she returned with a fresh Grain Belt.

"This one's on the house. Any friend of El's is a friend of mine."

"El and M."

"Yep. BFFs going all the way back to kindergarten."

That's how long you've known Bobby Dunston, my inner voice reminded me.

I lifted the beer mug in a toast.

"You're very kind," I told the girl.

The smile, which never seemed to leave her face, cranked a few watts brighter as if it was a compliment she heard before yet never tired of.

"How long have you been tending bar?" I asked. "You don't look nearly old enough."

"Better than that, I'm the manager. Didn't El—no, of course, she didn't say. I'm going to kill that girl."

"Still, you're pretty young for the job."

"What can I tell you? Ingvar hired me part-time to wait tables when I was in high school, made it a full-time job when

I graduated. I proved I was smarter than everyone else, so when I turned twenty-one he put me in charge. That was last year."

"Ingvar?"

"Ingvar Ragnvaldsson."

"Lord almighty."

"Yeah, well, that's why he called the place O'Malley's. Smartest business decision he ever made, besides hiring me, that is. If he had used his own name—I can pronounce it because I've had a lot of practice. Everyone else trying to get it out, they'd tell themselves, 'You know what? I've already had too much to drink.' Oh, oh . . ."

She cocked her head to listen. I heard it, too. The opening *ba—ba, ba—ba* to an old Partridge Family song. She moved away until her backside was resting against the mirrored shelf behind her, the most serene smile on her face. And David Cassidy sang "I Think I Love You" from the jukebox. Nearly everyone in the bar joined in, all of them directing the lyrics toward Cyndy M. Inexplicably, I found myself singing along—*Though it worries me to say, I never felt this way*—which made her laugh out loud.

The song ended, people applauded, Cyndy shouted, "Enough now, enough," and took care of her customers. It was a good fifteen minutes before she returned. She pointed at the beer mug.

"Freshen that up?"

"Sure," I said.

I also asked for a Philly cheese sandwich. She took care of both orders.

"You get that a lot?" I asked. "Your customers serenading you?"

"Couple times a week. Same song. Do I look like Susan Dey, the actress who played Laurie Partridge in the TV show?"

"Not really."

"Yeah, well, when I was younger and thinner . . ."

"Younger? Thinner?"

"I have a child, a daughter. That'll age you. And believe me when I tell you childbirth goes right to your hips. That's why I didn't move to Minneapolis with El. A bunch of us planned to go after we graduated. Seven of us. Three girls and four guys. There was nothing sexual about it, though. No one was partnering up. We were like brothers and sisters. Growing up in DR, we took every single class together from preschool through senior year, you know? Anyway, the seven of us were going to try our luck in the Cities, rent a house together, get jobs, maybe go to community college and then try to get into the U. It was going to be fun. Then I got pregnant with Lizzie. Then I did what they say you're supposed to do. I married her father, who I loved at the time, but who turned out to be a jerk who stole my middle name. And here I am."

Cyndy spoke the words with the melancholy tone of what might have been. Yet she did not linger long, choosing instead to change the topic of conversation. I liked her for that.

"How do you know El, anyway?" she asked.

"We were involved in a car accident."

"You wrecked her Ram truck? And she let you live?"

The pickup was hers, my inner voice said. *They tried to kill her using her own truck. Assholes.*

"No, no, no," I said aloud. The mechanism in my brain that controlled lies was in overdrive. "It wasn't as bad as all that. I dinged her in the parking lot. The damage was less than my deductible, so we took care of it without bothering our insurance companies. While we were working it out, I invited her to a party that I threw a week ago. That's where the photo was taken. She said the next time I came through Deer River I should check out O'Malley's. And here I am."

Cyndy nodded like it all made perfect sense to her, and then she asked a question that tripped every one of my internal alarm systems.

"Do you know where she is?"

Wait, wait, wait, my inner voice screamed. *Kids today stay in constant touch with Facebook; they tweet and text every moment of their lives as it happens. It's possible Cyndy hadn't heard from El in over three months, like she said. But what about the friends who went to the Cities with El? Had she not heard from them as well? It's possible Cyndy didn't know El had been in the hospital for six weeks, but she must have known that her BFF was missing. Maybe that's the point. Maybe she's worried about her friend. So what are you going to tell her?*

"I don't remember her address off the top of my head," I said. "I think I have it written down somewhere at home, but I've never been to her place, so . . . Don't you know?"

"Not since she moved. Just a sec."

Moved? What does that mean?

Cyndy disappeared for a moment. When she returned, she was carrying three plates loaded with food. She set two of them down in front of patrons sitting at a small table on the other side of the pool table. The third she gave to me.

"Don't go anywhere," she said and busied herself with her many customers. I took that to mean she wanted to talk some more.

I ate the Philly cheese sandwich, which tasted like it had been microwaved after spending several months in a freezer. While I ate, I felt movement at the door. I turned to see Ms. Bosland enter. She was accompanied by a woman who appeared to be several years older than she was.

A fellow teacher? my inner voice asked.

Ms. Bosland glanced around as if she wanted to see if there was anyone in O'Malley's she recognized. Her eyes fell on me and her expression changed from curiosity to surprise and back to curiosity again. A waitress ushered her and her companion to a table for two in the restaurant area that I could see through the door. I watched her. She watched me. Back in my dating days I would have taken that as an invitation, yet something in her eyes told me to keep my distance.

I looked for Cyndy M and found her chatting with a couple of guys barely older than she was at a table near the jukebox. I wouldn't have thought much about it except one turned his head to look at me. A moment later, the second did the same.

By then I had consumed my third beer and excused myself to the facilities. It took me a few moments to work out the location, down a short corridor just off the kitchen. When I exited, I found Ms. Bosland standing outside the women's room. She did not speak. Instead, she extended her hand. My first thought was that she wanted to shake hands again. There was a balled-up napkin in her palm, though, and when I took it from her she stepped inside the woman's restroom without speaking.

I returned to my stool and managed to unfold the napkin without drawing attention to myself. Ms. Bosland had written a phone number there. I glanced through the door. She had not returned to her table. I pulled out my cell phone, inputted the number, and stuffed the napkin in my pocket. Ms. Bosland answered on the first ring.

"Did you get what you wanted, the information that you wanted?" She was speaking from the restroom, and the confined quarters gave her voice an echo.

"Some of it," I said. "Not all."

"I couldn't speak to you at the school; people would know. It would be different if you were a policeman, but you're not, are you?"

"No."

"If you want to talk, it needs to be in private."

"I understand."

"I doubt it."

"Tell me."

"Do you know where the Northern Lights Inn is?"

As a matter of fact, I did, and told her so—it was located on the outskirts of the town of Marcel, about twenty-five miles north, near where I turn off Highway 6 to head to my cabin. Yes, I really did have a place Up North.

"Meet me there in ninety minutes," she said. "Don't let them follow you."

"Who is them?"

Ms. Bosland hung up her phone without answering. I glanced at my watch. It was closing in on 8:00 P.M. Cyndy M was back behind the bar, and I waved her over.

"I need the check, sweetie," I said.

"Leaving so soon?"

"I need to get to my place. Crank up the heat. Make sure the water pipes haven't exploded while I was gone."

"Where is your cabin?"

"On Lake Peterson near Spring Lake," I said—one of the few things I told the woman that wasn't a lie.

She nodded as if she knew exactly where it was, went to the register, and returned with my bill. I paid in cash, leaving a tip slightly over twenty percent.

"How long are you going to be up here?" Cyndy asked.

"Just a day or two to check the place out, take care of a few things."

"Be sure to stop on your way back home."

"I'll do that."

By then I was dressed for winter. I headed for the door. At the same time, Cyndy drifted to the table near the jukebox where the two young men were sitting. She said something and they started donning their coats. They seemed to be in a hurry, although one of them did stop long enough to drain his beer.

I stepped outside wondering what I was going to do about them.

I kept it casual, moving to my Jeep Cherokee as if I had nowhere in particular to go and all the time in the world to get there. I started up the SUV and put the heat on high, angling the vents so that the air blew on me. When the air changed from cold to warm, I pointed the Cherokee toward Highway 6. Meanwhile, the two young men left O'Malley's and jogged to their own vehicle; I watched them in my rearview mirror. They were starting their car when I pulled onto the highway and headed north.

I did the calculations in my head and decided that they weren't *after* me in the sense that if I wasn't careful, I could end up in a ditch somewhere. And they didn't want me to lead them to Ms. Bosland—how could they have known about our conversation? More likely, Cyndy M sent them to learn if I was for real, if the story I told her about just passing through on my way to my lake home was legit. So I decided to prove that it was and lead the boys right to the front door. 'Course, I was never very good at math. Also, there was the X factor that I had left out of the equation—why would she care?

The boys kept their distance, which I found encouraging. They didn't want me to know they were back there. At one point, I think they tried to follow with their headlights off, not a good idea even if the highway wasn't slick with ice and packed snow. I did not slow down or speed up or drive evasively for twenty miles; I barely touched my brake until I approached the intersection. Go right on Highway 286 and I'd be in Marcel in ten minutes. Go left on County Road 4 and I was headed to Spring Lake.

I went left.

The boys sped up to close the distance between us, took the turn, and drifted back again, giving me plenty of space. I drove west toward Spring Lake at about ten miles below the posted speed limit, slowing into the corners and accelerating out of them—I mentioned the ice and packed snow on the pavement, right? The boys became confused by my defensive driving. They'd speed up, slow down, speed up, and slow down again, no doubt wondering who in hell gave that crazy old man a driver's license anyway. Just outside Spring Lake I took a right, driving north toward Big Fork on County Road 29. This led me to the turnoff for my lake home.

It was plowed to accommodate the folks who lived on Lake

Peterson year-round, including the old man who kept an eye on my cabin in exchange for a couple bottles of eighteen-year-old Macallan. I followed it slowly. The road was more or less private. The only people who used it were those of us with property on the lake. Tailing me right up to my front door would have looked suspicious, so I expected the boys to break off pursuit. Unless—I felt a sudden chill that had nothing to do with the icy temperatures outside the cab of the Cherokee—unless they didn't care. I recalled a quote from Sherlock Holmes.

The lowest and vilest alleys in London do not present a more dreadful record of sin than does the smiling and beautiful countryside . . . Look at these lonely houses, each in its own fields, filled for the most part with poor ignorant folk who know little of the law. Think of the deeds of hellish cruelty, the hidden wickedness which may go on, year in, year out, in such places, and none the wiser.

I didn't know about poor ignorant folk who know little of the law, but a single gunshot in the city would attract a lot of attention, not to mention an army of cops. Up North, though? If you emptied an AK-47 in the forest, would anyone hear?

I watched the boys through my rearview mirror as I drove. They stopped at the mouth of the road and watched me watching them until a slow curve took us out of sight of each other.

I exhaled deeply.

Get a grip, McKenzie, I told myself.

No, my inner voice insisted. *You've been too damn nonchalant as it is. You came up here to get a line on El, to find out where she might be hiding. Only you haven't thought it through—the men who heaved her out of the pickup truck, they're looking for her, too.*

I stayed on the road until I met another. This one took me away from my cabin, which was just as well. I had closed up my place in October, draining the water pipes and shutting off the power. Push comes to shove, I'd probably be better off sleeping in my Cherokee.

I stayed with the second road, following the lake shore past several driveways, until it circled back toward the county blacktop. I stopped at the entrance to 29 about a mile up from where I had entered, my lights off, and stared down the pavement. It is never entirely dark in Minnesota in winter. The snow and ice nearly always find one source of illumination or another to magnify and reflect, like the quarter moon and half a billion stars that glistened in the clear night sky. I gave it a full five minutes. There were no other vehicles that I could see, so I made my way back toward Marcel, thinking at the time, Easy peasy puddin' 'n' pie.

SIX

Northern Lights Inn wasn't nearly as boisterous as O'Malley's, and I wondered if the polished furniture, spotless glassware, carefully directed lights, uniform shirts on the help, and list of top-shelf alcohol without prices had something to do with it. Or it could have been the half-dozen flat-screen TVs. Most of them were tuned to the NHL, a couple were following the first quarter of a West Coast NBA game, and one TV was showing a tape-delay woman's volleyball game from Penn State, all with the sound off. None of the games involved a Minnesota team, though, and most people were ignoring them.

I found a stool at the bar. I was both surprised and relieved when the bartender set a bottle of Summit Extra Pale Ale in front of me—it meant I wasn't that far from home after all.

It was a rounded bar. From where I sat, I couldn't help but notice a young man sitting on a stool, watching me while pretending not to. His coat was unzipped, and I could see the butt of a handgun beneath it. We were supposed to see it, the other customers and I. Ever since Minnesota changed its permit-to-carry laws, you find them. The chronically insecure who believe that three to four hours in the classroom and ten minutes on the firing range make them a Hollywood action hero, and the bullyboys who need the sense of power that carrying a gun gives them. They want you to see the gun hanging under their arms or clipped to their belts; want you to know they're packing; want to see the look in your eye when you realize that against them you don't stand a chance. Having gone armed many times in the past, I tended to remain unimpressed. As far as I was concerned, anyone who carried a concealed weapon who wasn't involved in some manner of law enforcement or security was an asshole. There were no exceptions—myself included.

I nursed the ale until 9:30 P.M., when Ms. Bosland arrived.

Of course she's punctual, my inner voice said. *She's a high school principal.*

She had her older friend in tow, and neither of them acknowledged my presence. Instead, they found a booth against the wall and sat across from each other, chatting amicably. Drinks were ordered and served while I watched. I half expected Ms. Bosland to leave for the restroom. When she didn't, I figured what the hell, gathered the remains of my ale, and moved to the booth.

The bullyboy's head turned to watch me.

"Mr. McKenzie, it's good to see you again," Ms. Bosland said. "Have you met my friend Camila Susko?"

"I haven't."

I extended my hand. Susko shook it.

"Join us, please," Ms. Bosland said.

Susko scooted until her back was hard against the wall, giving me more space on the bench than I needed. I sat. Ms. Bosland smiled at me, yet there was no mirth in it. She spoke softly.

"I apologize for the chicanery," she said. "I . . . we . . . need to be careful."

Now there's a word you don't often hear in polite conversation, my inner voice said. *Chicanery.*

"Why?" I asked aloud.

Ms. Bosland cocked her head as if she were surprised by the question. I turned to Susko.

"Why?" I repeated.

It was Ms. Bosland who answered.

"We're young, single, what many men might consider pretty—and we work for a small-town high school," she said. "We're held to a higher standard."

"At the same time, being young, single, and what men call pretty in a small town—it's like wearing a target on our foreheads," Susko said. "I've had men try to pick me up at parent-teacher conferences."

"Me, too," Ms. Bosland said. "Many times."

"Several years ago, I allowed myself to become involved with the divorced father of one of my students. I've been wearing the scarlet letter ever since." Susko drew an imaginary letter *A* across her chest to emphasize the point. "Do you know what I mean by scarlet letter?"

"Yes."

I nearly told her that I was one of the few people I knew who had actually read *Moby-Dick* all the way through without being forced to, but I was afraid she'd think I was showing off.

"She means we need to be careful who we're seen with," Ms. Bosland said.

"I know what she means," I said.

Do you believe this? my inner voice asked. *I'm not sure I believe this.* On the other hand, the bullyboy at the bar had spun on his stool so that he was now facing us. There was a grin on his puss that I didn't like. *Maybe there's something to it.*

I waited. When the silence became uncomfortable enough, Ms. Bosland leaned in and spoke even more softly than before.

"El was one of my favorite students," she said.

"Ella Elbers?" I asked.

She nodded, not at all surprised that I knew the young lady's name.

"She was utterly fearless," Ms. Bosland said. "My first year in Deer River, it was decided that the school would put on a play—an abridged version of *Macbeth*. This was not my idea, I assure you. Deer River did not have the resources for such a production. Despite my opposition, however, I was chosen to direct. Low girl on the totem pole, I was told. In retrospect, I believe the principal did not entirely approve of me or my"— she quoted the air—"graduate school notions of education and was hoping for failure. Any excuse to be rid of me. It's ironic, when you think about it. I'm from Rochester, Minnesota, and wanted very much to teach there. Jobs are scarce, however. It took me two years to secure this position. Now he's teaching in Rochester and I'm the principal."

"You're doing a very good job," Susko said.

"Thank you."

"Tomorrow and tomorrow and tomorrow," I said.

"Yes, yes, *Macbeth*," Ms. Bosland said. "El was supposed to play Lady Macbeth. However, at the last possible moment, the boy who was cast to play the lead dropped out. I don't know if it was stage fright or hepatitis C or what."

"He might have decided, his friends and family might have convinced him, that it wasn't manly to be an actor," Susko said. "Although, given the number of people Macbeth slaughtered . . ."

"We were going to cancel the production until El stood on a chair and started reciting Macbeth's speech just before he murders Duncan—*Is this a dagger that I see before me, the handle toward my hand?* She had memorized both parts. I found that astonishing. So the show went on with El playing Macbeth. It was the fiasco our dearly departed principal had hoped for. Lights blew out; actors forgot their lines; El's understudy, the girl who played Lady Macbeth, she was like a deer in the headlights. Cyndy Desler, the young woman who now runs O'Malley's—I believe you spoke to her earlier this evening. She was Great Birnam Wood. Her sole responsibility was to push a couple of cardboard trees across the stage. They fell over. One of them landed in the lap of a grandmother in the first row.

Everyone laughed—except when El was on. She held the stage, as they say. When it all mercifully ended, the audience gave her a standing ovation."

"Why are you telling me this?"

"At the beginning of the school year—I was made principal in August—El gave me a hand-carved ivory cameo trimmed with fourteen-karat yellow gold and said I was the best teacher she ever had. I had the cameo appraised. It was worth six hundred dollars. I wasn't the only one, either. She has given expensive gifts to a great many of her acquaintances. Now, you tell me, Mr. McKenzie. A twenty-two-year-old girl living with friends in Minneapolis—how could she afford such generosity?"

"I don't know. You tell me."

The two women exchanged glances; whatever message was passed was too subtle for me to read. I filled the silence that followed with a question.

"You told me before to make sure I wasn't followed. Why would anyone follow me?"

"Everyone knows you're here to learn about El," Ms. Bosland said.

"Who's everyone?"

"It's Deer River. People look out for each other."

See, you were right about small towns, my inner voice said.

"Okay," I said aloud. "Then tell me what is it that they're afraid I'll learn."

The women gave each other another glance; another private message was exchanged.

"It would be better if people didn't know we were helping you," Susko said.

"You mean besides the kid at the bar?"

Susko glanced at the bullyboy, yet Ms. Bosland did not, which made me think she already knew he was there.

"His name is Tim Foley," Susko said. "A former student."

"They're all former students," Ms. Bosland added.

"He's probably wondering why we let you sit here."

"Why did you let me sit here?" I asked.

"We want to help El if we can, Mr. McKenzie," Ms. Bosland said. "If you could tell us where she is . . ."

Once again my internal alarm systems went off; once again I was reminded that I wasn't the only one looking for El. I tried not to show it.

"I don't know where she is," I said.

The women leaned away from the table simultaneously and passed yet another clandestine message.

"Stop that," I said.

"McKenzie," Ms. Bosland said, "why are you looking for El?"

"I think she's in trouble. I want to help."

"What kind of trouble is she in?"

"I don't know."

"What kind of help will you give her?"

"That depends on why she's in trouble and with whom."

"What if it's none of your business?"

Four guns and five thousand in cash makes it your business, my inner voice said.

"She can tell me so when I find her," I said aloud. "Your turn."

"My turn?"

"Why are you trying to help her?"

Ms. Bosland spoke solemnly, as if all the answers to all the questions in the universe could be found in her words.

"I'm a teacher," she said.

While I let that settle over me, Susko said, "We believe El is involved with some dangerous people."

Ms. Bosland said, "The last time we saw her she seemed so frightened."

"What people?" I asked.

"People from the Cities."

"Not her Deer River friends, the ones who went to the Cities with her?"

"No, of course not."

"Can you tell me who they are, these dangerous people?"

Both women shook their heads.

"Can you tell me what made her afraid?"

They shook their heads again.

"Have you any idea what El's involved in?"

And still more head shaking.

"We were hoping you could tell us," Susko said.

"What about her family?"

"There's only her mother and her little sister, Ellen," Susko said. "El-2, they call her. She's a sophomore at DR. She and her older sister are very close, yet she hasn't heard from El in over six weeks and she's very concerned."

"How do you know?"

"She's in my homeroom."

"That doesn't tell me very much."

"We need to be careful."

"You keep saying that. I'm beginning to think that's why the kid is sitting at the bar watching every move I make. What's his name? Tim? He's your bodyguard, isn't he?"

"All we know about you is that you're from the Cities," Susko said.

"I could be one of the people El is afraid of. Fair enough."

"That's not the only reason he's there," Ms. Bosland said.

My inner voice said, *Oh puhleez.* Aloud I said only, "Oh?"

"We want answers, McKenzie. No more beating about the proverbial bush. Who are you? Why did you come to Deer River? Don't you dare tell me you just want to help."

"Don't you tell me you're just looking out for a former student."

Ms. Bosland turned her head toward the bar and gestured with her pretty chin. The bullyboy rose from the stool and shuffled toward us.

"Seriously?" I said.

The women watched as the bullyboy moved closer to the booth. He swept the ends of his coat back to reveal the wheel gun clipped to his belt, looking every bit like a Wild West gunfighter about to throw down on a hapless sodbuster in the Long Branch Saloon. Probably I should have been conciliatory, should have found a way to defuse the situation. I might have, too. Except he said, "Is this dumb fuck from Minneapolis giving you trouble?" and I lost all interest in diplomacy.

I came out of the booth, my right fist leading the way, and caught him just below the eye. He flew backward and bounced off an empty table, a chair, and finally the floor. I was quick to his side. I pulled his gun from the holster and held it by the butt with two fingers as if it were something you didn't want to handle without washing your hands afterward.

"You pulled a gun on me." I spoke loudly enough for the entire room to hear. "Talking quietly with an old friend from Rochester and you pull a gun on me because you're jealous. Did you see that?"

Nearly all the customers of the Northern Lights Inn were now watching me. Most of them hadn't seen what happened. The spectacle of the bullyboy on his back cursing as he massaged his face coupled with my words, though, would convince them that they had. Enough of them would support my story that I didn't need to worry should the county deputies be summoned.

The way the help responded, however, I doubted a call would be made. One employee took the gun from my hand and asked if I was all right. Another apologized profusely and said drinks were on the house. A third helped lift the bullyboy off the floor, telling him, "This is the last straw, Foley. I don't want to see you in here ever again."

I turned toward the ladies, glancing first at Ms. Bosland, who seemed genuinely unstrung, then at Susko, who was busy gathering up her belongings.

"I don't know what you ladies offered this young man to stand up for you, but he's going to want more."

"This was a mistake," Susko said. "We should never have arranged this."

Honestly, I didn't know if she was talking to Ms. Bosland or me.

"Why did you—"

"Don't talk to me," she said.

She hustled out of the inn, leaving her friend sitting alone in the booth.

That was silly, my inner voice told me. *Punching that poor kid.*

He had a gun.

Since when are you afraid of guns?

It's the principle of the thing.

Principle my ass. You hit him because he called you a dumb fuck from Minneapolis.

I'm from St. Paul.

No one cares.

Ms. Bosland was still in the booth. She was staring at me with a peculiar expression on her face, as if she couldn't decide whether she was horrified or impressed.

Why don't you get the hell outta here before you make it worse?

And then it got worse.

I realized it the moment I stepped out of the Northern Lights Inn and found the two young men who had been following me earlier—the men I thought I had evaded—flanking my Jeep Cherokee. Their heavy winter coats were zipped to the throat and their gloved hands were empty, so I walked toward them. They separated, one moving to my right, the other to the left, as if they knew exactly what they were doing. We stopped, forming a triangle, each just out of striking distance from the other, our breath floating like a cloud above our heads in the frigid night air.

"I admire your persistence," I said.

"There are just so many places you can go up here if you're not going home," said the taller of the two.

Ms. Bosland emerged from the bar, followed closely by the bullyboy. He said something and Ms. Bosland spun around and gave him a hug. She spoke quickly, buzzed his cheek, and hurried to a car not far from the entrance. The engine was already running, and the vehicle drove off the moment Ms. Bosland settled into the passenger seat.

"Did you see that?" the taller young man asked.

"Yeah, Tim Foley and Ms. Bosland," the smaller one said. "Wonder what that's all about."

"Man, what do you think it's all about?"

"I had her, you know, Ms. Bosland, before she became principal. I had her for geometry. Never missed a day, never a minute late to class, yet I didn't learn a damn thing."

"That's cuz you confused it with biology."

Both young men laughed like it was a joke they had shared before.

"Guys," I said. "Remember me?"

"Yeah, yeah, yeah, McKenzie," the smaller said.

"We don't like when strangers come around asking about our friends," the taller said.

It wasn't fear that caused my body to shiver, only the simple act of moving from the toasty warmth of the inn into the subzero parking lot. Still, it's hard to fight outside in Minnesota in the winter, especially when the temperature dips down to negative digits. The spirit might be willing, but the flesh is layered with bulky coats and sweaters, not to mention thermal underwear, and covered with thick gloves, cumbersome boots, and stocking hats. Which isn't to say that you can't hurt a guy through all that padding. It just takes a lot more effort.

"We think you should go home," said the smaller.

"Okay," I said.

"Okay what?"

"Okay, I'll stop asking questions and go home."

The two young men glanced at each other, an expression of skepticism on their faces.

"I know you don't believe this, but Ella is my friend, too," I said. "I'm trying to help her."

"You're right," the taller said. "We don't believe you."

"You didn't even know her name until M told you," said the smaller.

They both took a step closer.

"Guys," I said. "Please. Don't do this. It's really cold."

"You came to the wrong town, old man," the smaller said.

Old man?

"You might be twenty years younger, but I'm twenty years smarter," I said.

The way they kept coming, I didn't think they believed me.

Legs, legs, my inner voice reminded me. Without karate's emphasis on the use of legs, it would be virtually impossible to defend against two or more attackers. I stepped backward and brought my hands up, keeping my eyes on both young men at the same time. If I could disable one fast enough, the other might back off. I decided to go after the taller one first, thinking a front kick to the groin might do the trick, if I could get my heavy boot up fast enough.

That's when I heard the voice screaming behind me.

"You sonuvabitch."

The two young men stopped advancing and turned their heads to look, so I did the same. The bullyboy called Tim Foley was sprinting across the parking lot and closing fast. He was waving a tire iron above his head with his right hand. Apparently the staff of the Northern Lights Inn had refused to return his gun.

Well, good for them.

When he came close enough, the bullyboy swept the tire iron in a downward arch, aiming for my head. I stepped inside the blow, which seemed to surprise him. The tire iron hit nothing but air. At the same time, I grabbed his right arm and shoulder, then squatted and turned, heaving him up over my hip, which was more judo than karate, but what the hell. He landed on the ice-packed pavement with a solid thud and slid forward, dropping his weapon. The bullyboy's momentum carried him into the legs of the taller young man, knocking him down like a bowling pin, which wasn't my intention yet pleased me just the same. The smaller man went to his friend's side. There was some moaning and groaning that I didn't pay much attention to. Instead, I picked up the tire iron and turned toward the trio.

"What the hell, Foley?" the smaller man said.

Tim rolled to his knees and fought to keep from vomiting.

"He's asking questions about El," he said.

"Are you sure it's not because he made you look bad in front of Ms. Bosland?" the smaller man said.

"Fuck you."

"Whatever."

The smaller man was trying to help the taller man up. He saw me standing there with the tire iron in my hands and let him fall back down again. He brought his hands up like he was saying no to a second helping of ice cream.

"Now, mister . . ."

"Seriously," I said. "I'm going home. You got a problem with that?"

"Me? No. Hell no. You drive carefully now, you hear?"

I flung the tire iron into the darkness beyond the lights of the parking lot. That didn't seem to make any difference to him. I went to the Jeep Cherokee while he helped his buddy to his feet. We all ignored the bullyboy.

I started the Cherokee and drove off. I kept checking my rearview mirror. If the young men were following again, they did it with their headlights off.

The parking lot was virtually deserted by the time I reached O'Malley's—midnight on a cold weekday in Deer River, I decided. I stepped inside. Two older men maneuvered around me and out the door, leaving the bar empty.

"Good night, M," one shouted.

I didn't see her, but I heard Cyndy's voice in reply.

"'Night."

I glanced inside the restaurant. It was also empty except for a middle-aged couple sitting at a table for two and having the kind of fierce whispered discussion that rarely ends well. I unzipped my coat, stuffed my hat and gloves in my pockets, drifted to the jukebox, pumped in a couple of quarters, and selected a song.

Please allow me to introduce myself, I'm a man of wealth and taste . . .

Cyndy appeared from wherever she was hiding.

"Sorry, we're closing early . . . Oh, crap."

"It's good to see you, too," I said.

"What are you doing here?"

"You said to stop by on my way home."

"You're leaving?"

"Just taking the advice of the two young men you sent after me."

Her eyes grew wide and an expression of concern crossed her face.

"Are they all right?" she asked.

"Why wouldn't they be?"

She didn't answer. Instead, she gestured with her chin at the jukebox.

"I've never liked that song," Cyndy said. "Why should the devil get any sympathy?"

"Because he's so misunderstood?"

Cyndy retreated behind the bar. She took two glasses and a bottle of Jim Beam and set them in front of her.

"Join me," she said.

I removed my coat and laid it across the pool table. Just as I was settling on a stool, the middle-aged couple left the restaurant. They were holding hands as they exited the door.

Guess things worked out after all, my inner voice said. *Good for them.*

Cyndy poured an inch of bourbon into a glass and pushed it in front of me. "Friend or foe?"

"I could ask you the same question."

"You're not here to help Ella."

"Yes, I am."

"You didn't even know her name."

"That's true."

"No one's seen or heard from her in over six weeks, but you said that you saw her at a party last week."

"The bit about the party was a lie. I did see her, though. Yesterday, in fact."

"Well?"

"It's kind of a long story. I'm trying to decide if I trust you enough to tell it."

"And you expect me to talk about her?"

"El is missing. She really is this time."

"Missing or hiding? See, that's the problem, McKenzie. If you're looking for El because she's missing, I'm inclined to help. If you're looking for her because she's hiding . . ."

"Ms. Bosland said the last time she saw her, El seemed frightened. She said that El was frightened by dangerous people from the Cities."

Cyndy picked up her glass and swished the alcohol around, yet did not drink.

"Bosland isn't from around here," she said.

"Do you know who these people are, why they're dangerous?"

"No."

"Ms. Bosland said—"

"Why should Bosland care about El? What's it to her?"

"You tell me."

"McKenzie, listen, I don't know what Ms. Bosland said or why. El never told me she was frightened, never said anything in her posts or texts. Last time we actually spoke—it was at Christmas—she said she was having a wonderful time, that the Cities were great and I should come down and visit, find a baby-sitter for Lizzie so we could party with her boyfriend."

"What boyfriend?"

Cyndy backed away from the bar; her expression suggested she had revealed something that she meant to keep secret.

Let it go, my inner voice told me. *Come back to it later.*

"Why do you think El is hiding?" I asked aloud.

Cyndy didn't answer.

"I know about the expensive gifts," I said. "What was she into? Tell me."

"Who are you, McKenzie? Why are you here?"

There was something akin to menace in Ms. Bosland's voice when she had asked those questions earlier. Cyndy M's voice, though, was filled with concern. So I told her. I told her all of it, starting with the blizzard six weeks earlier and ending with El fleeing my condominium. Somewhere during the story, Cyndy's smile disappeared. I never saw it again.

"She's okay?" Cyndy's voice demanded that the question and answer be the same. "She's okay now?"

"She gets headaches. Her knee still bothers her."

"But she's okay?"

"She seems to be."

"Her memory, though."

"She might have been . . . faking." I nearly said "malingering."

"Why?"

"Do you know who Doug Howard is?"

"No."

"He's not one of the Deer River tribe?"

"No, and the others—they're like brothers and sisters. The men who tried to kill El, they have to be someone else."

"Even the best families can have a falling-out."

"I don't believe it."

"That brings us back to the original question. Why do you think El might be hiding?"

"I knew she was into something. When she came home, not just during the holidays, but whenever she came home, she always had expensive gifts, like you said. Clothes and jewelry. I asked how she got the money for it all. She laughed it off. She said if a girl is smart, there's plenty of easy money to be had. I might be a small-town girl, McKenzie, but I know the streets in the Cities aren't paved with gold. Anything where you get a lot of money for not much work isn't going to be honest."

"When was the last time you heard from El?"

"I saw her at Christmas, like I said. We traded texts and Facebook postings until after New Year's. A couple weeks before . . . before the accident."

"And then?"

"And then, nothing."

"What about the rest of your friends?"

"We weren't as close, so not hearing from them—I wasn't surprised not hearing from them except . . . except when I sent texts asking about El, no one replied. I asked Tim about it—"

"Tim?"

"Tim Foley. He was one of the original seven that moved to the Cities. Well, six after I dropped out. He came home last, what was it, November?"

"Why?"

"Not everyone is cut out to live in the city. I think it's much harder to go from here to there than it is to go from there to here. Anyway, I asked him about El and the others, what they were doing. He wouldn't tell me anything. Which is like—why wouldn't you tell? Why keep secrets? That's when I realized something was wrong, and then not hearing from El . . . You showing up like you did, I thought you might be the reason something was wrong."

"What is her boyfriend's name?"

"Oliver Braun. Although . . ."

"What?"

"One of El's posts, one of her last posts, she wrote how the U's food service department sells ice cream made by the students that's just as good as Ben and Jerry's and how she's been going through it one flavor at a time since Oliver suddenly can't go a single evening without visiting his mother."

His mother? my inner voice asked. *What does that mean?*

"El's texts and posts, what other names did she mention?" I asked aloud. "Did she upload photos of people she met in the Cities?"

"She wrote about the Deer River crowd and their landlord, someone named Leon—Leon Janke, something like that. I guess he's a real sweetheart. She also mentioned . . . besides Oliver she mentioned some of his friends, and a couple of guys she met in the Cities, Mitch and Craig, but she didn't post many pics. I can go back and look. Postings on Facebook last forever. Mc-Kenzie, Mitch and Craig—do you think they're the ones who tried to kill her?"

"We'll have to ask them, won't we? I'm going to give you my cell number. If you find out anything about Oliver, about Doug Howard and the others, anything that might tell me where to look for El, you call."

"I will."

"In the meantime, your other friends, the ones who went to the Cities with El, I want their names, addresses, cell numbers, whatever you can give me."

"They wouldn't have hurt El."

"They might know who did."

"Maybe they're in danger, too."

"Maybe."

Cyndy wrote out the information on a napkin. She told me the address was for a duplex the Deer River tribe was sharing near the University of Minnesota campus.

"They live on the top floor," she said.

"Earlier you told me that El had moved," I reminded her.

"She house-sits sometimes."

"Is that a job, babysitting people's homes while they're on vacation?"

"I think so."

I held up the napkin.

"Don't tell your friends you gave this to me," I said.

"I'm trusting you with a lot, McKenzie."

More than Fifteen did, my inner voice said.

It took me three and a half hours to drive home on an icy highway. Probably I should have spent the night in a motel, except the thought of my own warm bed kept me on the road even though I was fast approaching an entire day without sleep. Along the way, I stopped to top off my gas tank and buy black coffee and strawberry Twizzlers. I was tempted to call Bobby Dunston's office and recite into his voice mail Ella Elber's real name as well as the other names and numbers Cyndy had given me. I knew he wouldn't get the message until morning, though, and decided to wait. As for calling him at home—I had learned long ago that's not something you do, call a policeman's home late at night if it isn't a dire emergency.

I tried not to wake Nina when I returned to the condominium. As I slipped silently beneath the sheets, though, she rolled over and rested an arm across my chest.

"Bobby wants you to call him," she said.

"First thing in the morning."

"How was your trip?"

"No one died."

"Hmm," she purred in reply.

SEVEN

When I said first thing in the morning, what I meant was sometime after ten o'clock. Imagine my annoyance when my cell phone started singing at a quarter past eight. I would have ignored it despite Nina's NHL-quality elbow to my ribs, except I thought it might be Cyndy M with more information.

"McKenzie," I said.

"Dunston," Bobby said. "Meet me at the Highland Park arena. Meet me now."

"Why?" I asked, but he had hung up before I could get the word out.

"I hate it when he does that."

"Hmm," Nina said and rolled over.

The ice arena in Highland Park, usually considered a "Jewish neighborhood" because most of St. Paul's synagogues were located there, was actually called the Charles M. Schulz— Highland Arena, named for the creator of Charlie Brown, Snoopy, and the other Peanuts characters. It's where Bobby and I and our ne'er-do-well friends have been playing pickup hockey for the past decade and a half—the scene of many happy moments, and I thought of it fondly.

I knew that was about to change, though, when I pulled into the parking lot and found a half-dozen police cars surrounding a steel-blue Ford Taurus, its doors wide open. The arena was about to be added to a long list of locations in the Twin Cities that tightened my stomach, that caused me to look away.

That's the park where they shot Chopper in the back.

That's the house where they raped and murdered Jamie Carlson.

That's the fast-food joint where I killed Cleve Benjamn.

That's where they snatched Victoria Dunston off the street.

That's where we found her.

Someone had posted the customary three-inch wide yellow tape—POLICE LINE DO NOT CROSS—but the way the cars were arranged, no one was going to get close anyway. I parked on the south side of the lot and walked over, afraid of what I would find. The temperature had climbed to thirty degrees; there was even some giddy talk on the radio that it might reach above freezing, yet I did not feel it. Officers and techs turned to look at me as I approached. I felt embarrassed by my appearance. I had been quick to leave my apartment after Bobby had called, and my teeth were unbrushed, my face unshaved, my bed-hair matted beneath a stocking hat, and I was wearing yesterday's jeans.

Bobby juked between two squad cars and intercepted me. He rested a hand on my shoulder.

"It's not her," he said.

I hadn't realized until that moment that I had been holding my breath. I stopped caring what I looked like.

Bobby led me under the tape and past several officers until we were close to the truck. He wanted me to get a good look at the young man slumped across the passenger side of the front seat. I had no idea who he was and said so.

"Take a good look."

I did.

"According to his ID, his name is Oliver Braun," Bobby said.

Oh, God, no.

"Student at the University of Minnesota, majoring in political science. Lived with his parents in Little Canada."

No, no, no . . .

"The Taurus is in their name. Preliminary findings indicate he was killed between eight and twelve last night. I'm guessing closer to midnight because the arena was closed by then, no one around to see. That's all we have so far."

Tell him, my inner voice said.

Wait, I told it.

Why?

Just wait.

"You didn't bring me here just to confirm the kid's identity," I said aloud. I nearly added "That's not like you," but didn't.

"Jeannie," Bobby said.

Jean Shipman stepped forward. She was young, beautiful, and smart as hell—at least that's how Bobby once described her to me, although I didn't see it. She had been Bobby's partner before they made him a commander and remained his cohort of choice on those occasions when he stepped away from his role as a practicing bureaucrat and actually did some investigating.

"Hey, Jeannie," I said.

"That's Detective Shipman to you."

Did I tell you—she didn't care for me one bit.

Shipman was holding a clear-plastic evidence bag. She held it up for me to see. The bag contained a .38 Smith & Wesson wheel gun.

"Look familiar?" she asked.

"No," I said.

I wasn't answering her question, though. I was answering the one that formed in the back of my head the moment I learned the kid's identity. *Is El responsible for this?*

"It's yours, all right," Shipman said. "Serial number matches the S&W you told the Minneapolis cops was stolen from your house—assuming it was stolen."

Dammit, El.

"Only it's not the murder weapon," Bobby said.

Wait. What?

"You seem surprised," Shipman said.

"We found it on the floor of the car," Bobby said. "It hasn't been fired. The kid—he was killed with a knife."

I had no idea what to say, so I said nothing.

"Again, you seem surprised," Shipman said.

"Let's chat, shall we," Bobby said.

He led me back under the yellow tape and away from the crime scene. Shipman followed along. As we walked I heard someone say "Fucking McKenzie," but I didn't look to see who it was. I still had plenty of friends with the St. Paul Police Department, men and women I had worked with who didn't seem to mind at all that I quit to take the reward on Teachwell. I also had plenty of enemies, cops who very much minded, who were upset that I had sold my badge for exactly $3,128,584.50. Then there were those who were convinced I had hit the lottery and wished they could do the same.

"Well?" Shipman asked.

"Well, what?"

"How did the gun get here?"

"Obviously, either Fifteen gave it to him or Braun took it from her."

"So obvious we won't even consider the possibility she held it on him while someone else gutted the kid with a knife."

"Why leave the gun behind?"

"What's your theory?"

I was surprised how much it distressed me to say it. "Fifteen's lying in a ditch somewhere and a second party now has my guns."

"We're getting a little ahead of ourselves," Bobby said.

"Where were you last night?" Shipman asked.

"Seriously, Detective, you're asking me that question?"

"Where?"

"Deer River, Minnesota."

"Witnesses?"

"Several." I recited a few. "Plus, I used my credit card. You can check the times."

"You know I will."

"Stop it," Bobby said.

"She started it," I said.

"You think you're so damn smart, McKenzie," Shipman said.

"What can I say? They gave me tests. Rushmore, they said, you have a superior mind. It's a burden I've been carrying ever since."

"You two make me so sad," Bobby said.

Because he actually sounded sad, Shipman and I stopped talking and just stood there glaring at each other.

"McKenzie, tell me something I don't already know," Bobby said.

"Fifteen's real name is Ella Elbers, sometimes called El. She's twenty-one or twenty-two, from Deer River. She moved down here a couple years ago with a few high school friends."

I pulled out the napkin and recited the names and address Cyndy M had written there. Shipman read along over my shoulder, transcribing the names into a notebook.

"What else?" Bobby asked.

Time to come clean, my inner voice said.

Instead, I told him El had a habit of bestowing expensive gifts on her BFFs, but that none of them knew where the money came from.

"She's well loved up there," I added. "Her friends are worried. They haven't heard from her for over six weeks. Look, what about Doug Howard? What do you have on him?"

"Nothing," Shipman said.

"What does that mean?"

"Nothing means nothing. Checking him out was a waste of valuable police resources. The reason he was parked on Washington Avenue near your overpriced condominium was because he was waiting for his wife, who works for the Spaghetti Factory, also located on Washington Avenue."

"How do you know?"

"Straight-up solid police work, McKenzie. I asked him. And his wife."

"My children behave better than you two," Bobby said.

"He was wasting my time," Shipman said.

"I didn't know that," I said. "I thought—wait. If El didn't know who Howard was, why would she have been afraid of him? Why would she have run?"

"She caught your paranoia. It's contagious."

"You think she's hiding, then."

"If Elbers had wanted to go into hiding, she would have taken one gun for protection and all of the money, all twenty-five grand. Instead, she took four guns and five thousand dollars. She took only what she thought she needed."

"Needed for what?"

"Baby's gone a-hunting."

"I don't believe it."

"There's something you should know," Bobby said. "A call was made from the landline in your apartment. It was placed about fifteen, twenty minutes before Fifteen—Ella Elbers—took off. To Oliver Braun."

At the sound of his name, we all turned to gaze on the crime scene.

"Do you want to explain that, McKenzie?" Shipman asked.

Tell them!

"Oliver Braun was El's boyfriend," I said aloud.

"McKenzie," Bobby said, "you're just telling us this now?"

"They might have broken up around Christmas. I was looking into it."

"Dammit, McKenzie," Shipman said. "That's obstruction."

"How do you know about the call anyway?" I asked. "Did you subpoena my phone records?"

"You're a suspect in a homicide, you bastard."

"Since when?"

Bobby sighed heavily and glared at Shipman.

"We checked the kid's cell phone," he said. "His call log captured your number and the time when the call was made. The call lasted three minutes."

"You didn't check my phone records?"

"Of course not."

I glared at Shipman, too.

"Detective," I said, "and I use the term loosely—you're the reason there are so many bad cops on TV."

"Says the bastard who's withholding evidence," Shipman said.

I lowered my voice and spoke to Bobby, not caring if Shipman heard of not.

"I think El meant it when she told me she wanted to change her life," I said. "I think that's precisely what she's attempting to do. Fix today and tomorrow will take care of itself. One of the dumber things I've said."

"Now you agree with us?" Shipman said.

"I don't think El is responsible for this, if that's what you mean."

"You don't get to make that call."

No, you don't, my inner voice said.

On the other hand—"I don't believe that she killed Oliver," I said aloud. "If you want to change my mind, you had better come up with better evidence than you have now."

"What a bastard you are, pretending you're still a cop," Shipman said.

"Stop calling me that."

"You two know that I love you both," Bobby said. "Right?"

Bobby returned to the crime scene, Shipman and I watching his back as he walked away.

Yeah, but he loves you more, my inner voice said.

Let me explain how things work. The cops in St. Paul and Minneapolis might labor in separate jurisdictions, yet they are more than willing to help each other out; happy to search for a suspect or a car, check out an address, gather intel and report back to the other agency. But that didn't mean a detective was welcome to cross the river and flash her badge anytime she damn well pleased. If Shipman—I assumed it would be Shipman—wanted to interview the kids living at the address I had supplied, protocol dictated that she first notify the Minneapolis Police Department and, if the case was hot enough, arrange for one of its officers to accompany her. This wouldn't be a problem. It would take time, however. Which gave me a head start.

The duplex was smartly located on Thirteenth Street between Hennepin and Como, two bustling avenues with active bus lines. It was about a twenty-minute walk from Dinkytown, a retail community bordering the University of Minnesota that catered mostly to students; five minutes by bike if you rode with reckless abandon, which almost no one ever did in winter. There were two mailboxes flanking the front door. The one with the "1/2" added to the address featured six names including Ella Elbers and Tim Foley, the latter name crossed out.

The door was unlocked. I stepped past it into a foyer. There was a door to my right that led to the downstairs apartment. Someone had attached a wicker vase to the jamb and filled it with artificial flowers so lifelike that they gave off a pleasant, almost sweet aroma. In front of me was a narrow staircase that spiraled upward. While climbing it, I thought it must be a bitch getting furniture up and down.

I knocked on the door at the top of the staircase, waited for a response that did not come, and knocked some more. When that also went unanswered, I tried the doorknob. It turned easily.

Who leaves their door unlocked these days? my inner voice asked.

Small-town kids who don't know any better.

I don't believe it.

Neither do I.

I opened the door and called out. Silence followed. I touched my right hip where my gun would have been if I had thought to bring it. Asshole or not, sometimes it pays to carry a concealed weapon.

I stepped inside the living room. A place gives off a kind of empty vibe when there's no one home; I moved cautiously just the same. I found furniture—sofas and tables, plus shades on the windows, paintings on the walls and rugs on the floor. Yet there were no TVs, laptops, CD players, books; no clothes strewn across the floor, no discarded pizza boxes. Five kids couldn't possibly be this neat, I told myself.

I called out again.

There were four doorways leading out of the living room. I checked each one in turn. The first three led to bedrooms. Each contained mattresses without sheets, and closets and bureaus without apparel of any kind. The fourth door led to the kitchen. There were no glasses, plates or bowls in the cupboards and no silverware in the drawers. I checked the refrigerator. It had been cleaned out but not turned off—there was ice in the trays in the freezer.

A door in the kitchen led to a bathroom that also was empty. I examined the medicine cabinet and linen closet. Nothing. I returned to the kitchen.

Clearly the kids had moved, I told myself. But where? When?

I went back through all the rooms, this time checking waste-baskets. They were empty as well, except for the larger basket in the kitchen. There I found discarded bags, wrappers, and paper cups from several fast-food meals that couldn't have been more than a couple of days old. Under the debris I discovered a sheaf of flyers. There were ten colored copies advertising a winter garage sale in Arden Hills on Saturday and an equal number of flyers promoting a garage sale in Woodbury on Sunday. I took one copy of each and stuffed them into my inside coat pocket. I left the rest for Detective Shipman.

I stood in the kitchen, hands on hips, searching for something that I might have missed. That's when I heard the creak of a floorboard behind me. I tried to spin around. Hard metal hit me above the right ear. An explosion that sounded like fireworks from a long way off filled my head; red and white lights blinded me. I went to my knees thinking, You didn't lock the door behind you, you dumb sonuvabitch. A wave of nausea filled my stomach and tried to force its way out of my throat. I was able to push it back down.

My vision cleared slowly. I looked up. I saw the handgun first. A heavy black automatic. I saw him a second later. Bigger than I was by a couple of inches, heavier by a couple of pounds. He stood at a professional distance, his eyes hidden by sunglasses. I knew he was tough because the top button on his winter coat was undone.

"Who are you?" he asked. He could have been asking for directions to the nearest shopping mall for all the emotion in his voice. Meanwhile, my inner voice was screaming.

He doesn't recognize you!

I tried to keep calm.

"Who are you?" I said aloud.

I didn't know the name, yet I knew the face. He was the man who had followed Ella and me across the Stone Arch Bridge to the Aster Cafe. I kept it to myself, though. Why give him more incentive to shoot me than he already had?

"Right now I'm the guy pointing a gun at your head," he said. "You gonna fuck with me, what?"

Play it innocent, my inner voice said.

"Hey, I'm just looking for a friend," I said aloud. "I wasn't trying to burgle the place. The door was open . . ."

"What friend?"

Since her name was already listed on the mailbox, I answered. "Ella Elbers."

"Yeah, yeah, yeah, now I remember. You're the guy in Minneapolis. So she got away from you, too, huh?"

Dammit!

"So what do you want her for?" he asked.

"To get her recipe for coq au vin."

"Cute. What's your name?"

He doesn't know who you are, my inner voice said. *You were just a guy walking with the girl, as far as he's concerned.*

"Call me Ishmael," I said. "What's yours?"

He took a step closer, raised the gun like he was going to hit me again, stopped, and backed away, leveling the gun back at my face.

"Nice try," he said. "Goad me into making a mistake. Draw me close enough for you to fuck with me. Know what? I don't need to know who you are or what you're doing here. Get up. Real slow."

I did.

"Turn. All the way round."

I turned.

"Real good. Now. Hands flat against the table. Keep 'em there. Move your feet back toward me. A little more. More."

I was positioned as if I were doing push-ups against the kitchen table. Even then he was careful, using quick taps of his fingertips to search the areas where I might have been carrying a weapon and a few where no one goes armed. Satisfied, he stepped back again.

"All the way up," he said.

I straightened.

"Why are you looking for El?" I asked.

"I'm looking for all of them."

"Why?"

"What you do now is shut the fuck up and walk—slowly—into the living room. You walk to the door. You touch the door and I'll blow your head off. You go down the staircase. You try to run, I'll fire a warning shot into your spine. Stop at the bottom of the stairs. Let's go."

I was in trouble and I knew it. With amateurs, you could always count on a moment or two of hesitation before they pulled the trigger. That at least gave you a fighting chance. This guy, he wasn't going to hesitate. Not for a second. My only hope—he didn't actually want to shoot me, I told myself. He could have done that already. Instead, he wanted to take me somewhere. Along the way, who knows what might happen?

I stopped at the bottom of the steps as instructed. I glanced behind me. He had been momentarily distracted by the door with the flowers attached, probably wondering if danger lurked behind it. Yet he was too far away for me to take advantage.

"Eyes front," he said.

I turned toward the closed front door.

"I want you to open the door. Open it wide. You walk out onto the stoop away from the door and stop. No sudden movements. You don't need to look behind you. I'll be there."

Again I did exactly as he instructed.

I heard the door shut behind me. I felt his presence.

"Now what?" I asked.

"Which one is your car?"

"The Jeep Cherokee."

"You walk slowly down the steps, down the sidewalk to your car. You get in on the passenger side. Do not try to close the door. You get in and ease yourself across the seat until you're behind the steering wheel. You put both your hands on top of the wheel."

"Where are we going?"

"You'll know when we get there."

I took a deep breath, filling my lungs with winter air. I did not feel cold, though. I felt as if it were summer and ninety degrees in the shade.

"Now," he said.

I took two short steps. Before I could manage a third, I heard it—a sound like a man being punched hard in the chest followed instantly by the thud of weight being thrown against the duplex door; the sudden exhale of breath. I felt it, too—liquid spraying the back of my neck and head. I turned.

The gunman stood against the door as if he had been glued there. A spreading red stain in the center of his chest sopped the fabric of his winter jacket. His head faced the street, his sunglasses firmly in place. He coughed weakly and blood ran from the corners of his mouth and down his chin. His arms hung limply at his side. He dropped the gun and it clattered against the cement. The glue gave, and he slid slowly along the door, leaving a streak of blood behind, until he was sitting on the stoop, his knees up.

I dove off the stoop into the snow and rolled, rolled, rolled until I was lying against the foundation of the house next door.

A Minneapolis Police Department cruiser was on the street. Its brakes locked up and the car slid sideways on the icy pavement in front of me. Detective Jean Shipman came out of the passenger side, her Glock in both hands, using the car for protection. The driver, a uniformed officer, dove out of his door and found cover behind a car parked on the far side of the street. Together we scanned the houses, parked cars, trees, and snowbanks. There was no movement that any of us could see.

"McKenzie," Shipman said.

"Here."

"Where did the shot come from?"

"I don't know."

"Rifle?"

"Subsonic round. Something big."

"Stay where you are."

Sounds like a plan.

It seemed longer, yet only ninety seconds passed before the air was filled with the sound of sirens. Enough cops with enough guns appeared on the scene that you'd think they were storming the beaches at Normandy. They searched the area with great vigor and found nothing except a couple of kids walking home from the U. They interviewed every neighbor, including the old woman a block over whose backyard deck had a clear view of the front door of the duplex. She hadn't heard a thing but was pretty sure that the footprints in the snow leading to and from the deck weren't hers.

EIGHT

I was sitting on the bottom step of the staircase inside the duplex feeling numb, wondering what the hell happened and did I cause it. The Minneapolis cops seemed to think so. I was questioned a half-dozen times by both them and a Hennepin County assistant attorney. No one seemed satisfied with my answers. It wasn't personal, though. They weren't particularly thrilled by what the landlord had to say either.

Leon Janke lived in the ground floor of the duplex. He said he had been renting the top floor to college kids for over twenty years without a lick of trouble.

"These kids," he said, "were even better than most. Quiet. Respectful. Helped out with the snow shoveling and grass cutting. Good kids."

Janke said he received a check from them just last week. He had no idea they had moved without telling him, couldn't imagine they'd break their lease.

That's the part the Minneapolis cops had trouble getting their heads around: how they were able to move all of their belongings down that narrow, twisting staircase without him noticing.

In reply, the old man cupped a hand around an ear and said, "Huh? Speak up."

I was the only one who laughed. The cops looked at me like I was cracking wise at a funeral. The lead detective on the case was named John Luby.

"Shut up, McKenzie," he said.

"Are you done with me?"

"No, I'm not done with you. Sit there and shut up."

So I did while they continued questioning Janke. He explained that he had not been home when the shooting occurred because he was out for his daily walk.

"I do five miles a day come rain or shine," he said. "I never run. Oh, no. Satchel Paige said to avoid running at all times, and I agree with him. At my age you gotta keep the juices flowin' by jangling gently as you move, also what Paige said. I saw 'im pitch, you know. When I was a kid."

"Really?" I said.

"Saw 'im that time he was barnstormin' with Bob Feller," the old man said. "And later when he had a cup of coffee with the Moorhead Red Sox."

"Very cool."

Detective Luby and his colleagues made it known that they were upset that I had interrupted their interrogation, but Minneapolis cops were like that—unlike St. Paul police officers, who were reasonable all the time.

Yeah, right.

The cops became bored after a while. A third of them went upstairs—what they hoped to find there, I couldn't say. Another third went outside. The final third, led by Luby, commandeered Janke's downstairs apartment for a strategy session, leaving him alone in the foyer with me.

"The police don't like you at all, do they, son?" he said.

"Wouldn't seem so."

"Got anything to do with all that blood on ya?"

"Little bit."

"Can I ask . . ."

"I was standing next to the victim when he was shot."

"Cops act like you were the one what squeezed the trigger."

"Cops are like that."

"FUBAR."

"Got that right."

"Know what it means?"

"Fucked up beyond all recognition. It was something the old man used to say on occasion when things got out of hand."

"Your daddy, did he serve?"

"He was with the First Marines at Chosin Reservoir."

"Hell you say." The old man sat on the step below me. "I was with the Seventh Infantry. Your daddy and me, we ate some of the same dirt. He still with us?"

"He passed closing in on seven years now."

"Sorry to hear that. Not many of us left what did time in Korea."

"The Forgotten War."

"Lord knows I've been trying to forget it. So, what you doin' here—McKenzie, is it?"

"Looking for El and the others."

"You don't mean 'em any harm, do ya, son?"

"No, sir. Believe it or not, I'm trying to help them."

"How long you know them kids?"

"The only one I've met is El, and that was four days ago."

"Hardly makes sense you bein' here, then."

"That's the way the cops look at it, too. What can I say? You become attached to people, and how long you've known them doesn't always factor into it."

"No, it doesn't. These kids—I grew up in Cohasset. I haven't really lived there since I was drafted, but these kids come lookin' for a place to stay, I find out they're from Deer River what's ten miles down the road, I kinda adopt 'em, you know? Can't help but look out for 'em."

"What else did you know about them? What did they do for a living?"

"This and that. I guess El did some house-sitting. You know

how real estate agents have their tricks like puttin' out flowers and fresh-baked cookies, like makin' sure the closets are half empty so it looks like there's plenty of storage space? El says they sometimes also hire people to stay in a house that's for sale cuz an empty house is harder to sell but also because buyers come in and see these beautiful people livin' there and they want to be just like 'em. You believe that?"

"Who did El work for? Did she tell you?"

"You soundin' like the cops now."

"Sorry. I didn't mean to."

He patted my knee in response. A few beats later, Janke was called into his apartment. He patted my knee again before he left. It made me feel better, but not by much.

Footsteps on the stairs caused my head to turn. Detective Shipman sat next to me. I was aware of her careful and intense stare.

"How are you holding up?" she asked.

"I've been better."

"You should soak your jacket and jeans in cold water. I'm not sure the blood will come out, though. There's so much of it."

"Yeah."

"I might have known you'd get here before me."

"Honestly, Jeannie, I wish it were the other way around."

"When I saw you on the stoop as we were driving up, I thought, what a bastard. Then I saw . . ."

She didn't finish her thought, and I was glad.

"What about the kids?" she asked. "Do you think they're hiding?"

"You're asking me?"

Shipman slipped an arm through mine like we were the best friends in the world.

"Yes, I'm asking you," she said.

"I think they're hiding."

"From Elbers?"

"I don't know."

"Their friends Up North, do you think they know where they are?"

"No. The kids left before Cyndy Desler gave me their address. I think she would have told me if she knew they had moved."

"The gunman on the stoop, his name was Karl Olson. At least, that's what his driver's license says."

"I should have told you about him."

"Tell me now."

I did.

"I wasn't withholding evidence," I said.

"I didn't think you were. I mean, what could you have told me? You didn't know his name, and you didn't—hell, you didn't even know for sure he was following you along the river. If you had said anything about him, I probably would have laughed."

"We seem to have that kind of relationship."

"On the other hand, it would help explain why Elbers didn't feel safe in your condo. First Olson and then Howard? I would have been concerned, too. Did he know you, Olson?"

"Not at first. I was just a guy in the room doing what he was doing. Looking for the kids. Later he recognized my face. He didn't know my name, though."

"Where was he taking you?"

"Probably to the nearest shallow grave."

"We ran his prints. Took the FBI's computers all of twenty-seven minutes."

"Isn't technology grand?"

"Olson has no record that we're aware of."

"That surprises me."

"Why?"

"He was very competent. You don't just wake up in the morning with those skills. They're developed over time."

"A gifted amateur."

"It's possible, I suppose."

"Do you think Elbers shot him?"

"No. He was killed with a rifle. El didn't steal any rifles."

"She stole enough money to buy one."

"That's true."

"The fact Olson was shot while we were moving up on the scene makes me wonder if he might have been killed to keep us from taking him in, keep us from making him give up his friends."

"Makes me wonder, too."

"That's not why you're feeling gloomy, though, is it? You're feeling gloomy because it got very iffy there for a while. It got very iffy, and you're thinking whoever killed Olson probably also saved your life. That's why you're not your usual smartass self giving me crap, because it got so iffy."

True, very true, my inner voice said.

"Why him?" Shipman asked. "Why not you? Why not both of you?"

"You ask as if you expect me to have an answer. I don't."

"But you're going to keep at it until you do have one, aren't you?"

That's the way you're wired, my inner voice said. I kept the thought to myself.

"I met Nina Truhler, you know," Shipman said. "At Bobby's barbecue last August, remember? She has the loveliest pale blue eyes I've ever seen."

"Yes."

"Why don't you take her away from all this, take her someplace warm? Take her to Florida. Take her to Hawaii. You have more money than God, take her to Tahiti. I mean, what are you doing here, McKenzie? Why are you doing these things?"

"This is my home. I like to be useful."

"Once a cop, always a cop—is that what you're saying?"

"Something like that."

Shipman gave my arm a squeeze.

"Go home, McKenzie," she said.

It was past 3:00 P.M. when I finally returned to the condominium. How time flies when you're having fun. I parked in the underground garage and took the elevator to the lobby. I was hoping to transfer to the elevator that could take me to the seventh floor without being noticed, but Smith stopped me. Or was it Jones?

"Mr. McKenzie?"

I pivoted toward the desk where the security guard sat. He had a troubled expression on his face.

"A man showed up here this morning," he said. "He was looking for you. We never send anyone up without asking permission from the tenant first. He wouldn't give us his name, though. He said he just happened to be in the neighborhood and might come back later. We kept an eye on him when he left. Saw the car he drove. We ran his plate."

The guard slid a small sheet of paper off the desktop and handed it to me. It contained the driver's complete record.

"His name is Mitchell Bosland," the guard said just in case I couldn't read.

The name caught me by surprise. I guess I had been expecting to hear Olson's name instead.

"Do you know him?" the guard asked.

"No," I said. "I think I met his sister, though."

He was also one of the men El spent time with here in the Cities, my inner voice reminded me. *Assuming Cyndy M's recollection of El's Facebook posts could be trusted.*

"When was this?" I asked. "When did he show up?"

According to the guard—it was Smith, by the way—Mitch appeared at approximately the same time that Olson caught me in El's duplex. I waved the sheet at the guard.

"Thank you for this," I said. "I really appreciate it."

"It's our pleasure," Smith said. "Umm, Mr. McKenzie . . . your coat, your clothes—they're soaked with blood."

"You should see the other guy."

I thought about taking Shipman's advice and soaking my coat in cold water and decided against it. Instead, I balled it up and shoved into a garbage bag. The crinkling of paper reminded me of the flyers I had stuffed into my inside pocket. I hadn't mentioned them to the cops—honest to God, it had completely slipped my mind—and I wondered if they had found the copies that I left in the wastebasket.

I set the flyers on my dresser.

I removed the rest of my clothes and put them in the garbage bag, too—even the ones that weren't stained with blood. Afterward, I took a long, hot shower. I toweled off and stretched out on the bed, where I stared at the ceiling and contemplated my life choices. Shipman had asked why I did the things I did. Not long ago, I would have told her that I was merely trying to help people who couldn't help themselves. I might even have told her that I was making the world a better place; that's how arrogant I am. Lately, though, I've been wondering about that. How many favors have I done for how many people in the years since I left the police? Is the world a better place because of them? It sure didn't seem like it.

You're feeling sorry for yourself, my inner voice told me.

If I don't, who will?

What would the old man say?

Knowing Dad—the world doesn't stop spinning cuz you're unhappy with it. Get your lazy ass out of bed.

Well?

Ten minutes later, I was fully dressed and making a call on my smartphone.

"Hello," a woman's voice said.

"Hello. Cynthia M. Desler?"

Her voice sounded weary, as if hearing her formal name was cause for concern.

"Yes," she said.

"This is McKenzie."

"Oh, hi."

I noticed that hearing my name didn't improve her outlook any.

"You said you would check Ella Elbers's Facebook posts," I said. "I was wondering if you found anything."

"I didn't."

"You didn't check or—"

"I didn't find anything."

"What about Oliver Braun?"

"No."

"Are you sure?"

"I'm sure."

"Your friends, the Deer River tribe, they moved away from the address that you gave me. Did you know that?"

"No, I didn't."

"Then you don't know where they went."

"Why would I?"

"There have been no texts, no tweets, no status updates on their Facebook pages?"

"I need to go. My daughter is calling me."

"Wait. M, tell me. Is something wrong?"

"No. Nothing's wrong. Why would you ask?"

"You sound frightened."

"What? No, McKenzie . . ."

"You were happy to help last night. Now you're not. What's changed? Did someone threaten you? Who threatened you, Cyndy?"

"It's not like that."

"What is it like?"

"McKenzie . . ."

"Let me help you."

In the long silence that followed, I thought she might hang up. Instead, I heard her take a deep breath. She spoke with the exhale.

"Right after I started bartending," Cyndy said. "This was about a year before Ingvar made me manager. I was bartending and this guy came in, pleasant enough, bought a few drinks, bought dinner, paid with a one-hundred-dollar bill. I don't usually get hundreds, but okay. I took the bill and gave him his change. Ten minutes later, some cops came in—state cops, they weren't local. They said the bill was marked, that it was taken in an armed robbery. They accused me of laundering stolen money and said they had the legal right to shut down the bar and take me in. They said they would forget about it, though, forget it ever happened, if I told them about another guy who sometimes came into O'Malley's. They even made it easy for me. They told me what to say. I told them to go . . . entertain themselves. Maybe that was a stupid thing to do. I think about it sometimes, how much trouble I could have been in. I have a daughter, McKenzie. My God. Yet I did it anyway. Do you know why? Because they weren't from around here, and the guy they wanted me to rat on, he was."

"I understand."

"Do you?"

I flashed on Leon Janke, loyal to a handful of kids he had never met simply because they grew up ten miles from where he did.

"I think so," I said. "Tell me, have you heard from Ms. Bosland?"

Cyndy paused before slowly answering. "No. Why would I?"

"Because her brother Mitch lives in the Cities. He came to visit me today while I was out."

"Why are you telling me this, McKenzie?"

"The only way he would have known about me is if his sister told him."

"I get it. Don't worry, McKenzie. I'm being careful."

"Good girl. The story about the state cops—tell me what happened?"

"Nothing. Nothing at all. I never saw any of them again."

"Let's hope you're just as fortunate this time. One thing more, M, please, before you go."

"What is it?"

"Can Ella shoot?"

"What do you mean?"

"Can she shoot a rifle?"

"This is northern Minnesota," Cyndy said. "Everyone hunts up here. Everyone can shoot."

On that encouraging note, I went shopping. I returned thirty minutes later. My cell started playing "Summertime" the moment I came through the door. I answered just as Ella Fitzgerald's lush voice gave way to Louis Armstrong's trumpet.

"Hey," I said.

"Anything interesting going on?" Nina asked.

"Depends on what you find interesting."

"Humor me."

I told her about finding Oliver Braun in Highland Park, but not about Karl Olson.

"Does Bobby think Fifteen killed him?" Nina asked.

"I rarely know what Bobby thinks until he tells me, and even then . . ."

"What do you think?"

"If Fifteen wanted to kill Oliver, I think she would have used the gun, not a knife."

"Then why was the gun in the car?"

"It's a mystery."

Nina gave it some thought.

"Are you still there?" I asked.

"Yes. Are you coming down tonight?"

"I don't think so."

"Are you sure? We have Charmin Michelle and Joel Shapira in the big room."

"We also have the Wild on TV. If they win a couple of games down the stretch, they might actually get into the playoffs for a change."

"Okay. I'll see you later tonight. Maybe then you'll tell me what's really happening."

"What do you mean?"

"McKenzie, please. After all these years you don't think I know when you're holding out on me?"

There was a smile in her voice, and I thought, the thing with Nina, I could say just about any damn thing that popped into my head and she would either laugh, cry, agree, argue, accept, contradict, take offense, nod, shake her head, or say "Yes, dear" in that sarcastic way she has. Yet she would never hold it against me. Unless I said it twice.

"I'll have crème brûlée waiting when you get home," I said.

"Yum."

NINE

It was approaching 11:00 A.M. when Nina finally got up. She walked into the kitchen area wearing what she had worn to bed—gray gym shorts and a white tank top, except now it was beneath a frayed robe that she left untied.

"Morning," she said and went to the coffeepot without waiting for a reply.

"I remember, before we actually started living together, when you wore weapons-grade nightgowns and other assorted outfits from Victoria's Secret."

"That's when I was lucky if I saw you a couple times a week. It was more of an event back then. Now I see you every night."

"The excitement has gone out of our romance."

"I wouldn't say that. Besides, it's what's in the package that matters. Not the wrapping paper."

Still . . . my inner voice said.

There were bagels in a bag on the counter. She opened the bag, retrieved a blueberry bagel, and set it on a plate. Her hand hesitated as it reached toward a wooden block where our Chicago Cutlery was stockpiled.

"Where's the knife I like to use?" she asked.

"Probably in the dishwasher."

"The knives should be hand-washed. Honestly, McKenzie."

"Try the guillotine."

Nina shook her head like she thought it was silly—the miniature guillotine used to halve bagels and English muffins that I bought *before* we moved in together. Instead, she found a different knife, sliced her bagel in half, and dropped the halves into the slots of a toaster I acquired from France that she apparently had no misgivings about.

The excitement really has gone out of our relationship.

While the bagel toasted, she brought her coffee to the island and sat on a stool.

"I found these on the dresser," she said.

She reached into the pocket of her robe and withdrew the flyers I had taken from the duplex. She smoothed out the folds and slid them across the countertop.

"Yeah, 'bout that," I said. "What are you doing this afternoon? Do you have any plans?"

"Not in the afternoon, why?"

"How would you like to go to a garage sale in Arden Hills?"

"Wait. You want to take me to a garage sale? Voluntarily?"

"Why not?"

"I can think of a couple of reasons but yes, sure, if that's what you want to do?"

"It's scheduled from one till five. I'd like to get there around two. I figure that's when it'll be busiest."

"And less likely we'll be noticed."

"Something like that."

"Fine, but you have to explain what's going on first. I was going to ask last night, but I became distracted after you seduced me with your crème brûlée."

"You always hear people say that the way to a man's heart is through his stomach, but if I knew when I was younger how susceptible women are to homemade desserts . . ."

"McKenzie, I saw your new coat hanging in the closet when I got home. You left the tags on, for goodness sake."

"Can't a guy change up his wardrobe?"

"What happened to your old coat?"

"I threw it in the Dumpster."

"What was wrong with it?"

"It was stained with blood."

Nina took a long sip of her coffee and set the mug in front of her. She held it with both hands. She looked me hard in the eye. "I'm waiting," she said.

I told her everything.

"Why don't you just tell me these things?" Nina asked. "Why do you make me pull the stories out of you one paragraph at a time?"

"I didn't want you to worry."

"Too late. I've been worrying for the past five and a half years."

"I guess I didn't want you to know that *I* was worried. I have no idea what's going on or why. I'd like to help Fifteen—Ella—but right now I honestly don't know if she's the good guy or the bad guy."

"Or a little of both."

"Exactly."

"What does the garage sale have to do with it?"

"Maybe nothing, but the fact that the kids had so many copies of the flyers makes me think they were distributing them."

"So we'll be working undercover?"

"You could look at it that way."

The smile that crossed her face was so vibrant I had to look away.

"Fun," she said.

A full third of Arden Hills consisted of an abandoned and terribly polluted U.S. Army munitions plant that city and county officials had been trying to develop with little success for well over a decade. Beyond that, it was like any other middle-class suburb you've ever driven through, houses with all the personality of paper cups set in orderly rows. The paper cup we were looking for was located on a street near Round Lake. It was large and white, with an attached two-car garage and a plus-size yard. Both garage doors were open to the elements. I could see several cafeteria-style tables laden with goods inside as we drove past, as well as several more lining the snow-free concrete driveway. There were so many customers that we were forced to park Nina's Lexus a full block away. We had taken her car so if anyone ran the plates, her name would pop up instead of mine.

The warming trend had continued. It was a balmy forty degrees with the sun shining bright and many of the customers had gone gloveless and hatless with winter coats hanging open, including Nina.

"Spring has sprung," she said.

"It isn't spring in Minnesota until the first day of baseball season, and sometimes not even then."

"You can be so cynical, McKenzie. I don't even know how you make it out of bed in the morning."

"What I want to do—I'll go first. You come along a couple of minutes later. We'll pretend we don't know each other."

"Is there a reason for that?"

"If these people are connected to Fifteen, it's possible they might also be connected to Karl Olson, which means they might know who I am. Anyway, men flirt more freely with you when I'm not standing by your side. I've seen it."

"You want them to flirt with me?"

"I want them to talk to you."

"Okay."

I opened the car door, but left Nina a final word before I climbed out. "Doesn't mean you have to flirt back."

"Who? Me?"

I left the Lexus and walked to the driveway. The customers were in a festive mood, and I wondered if it was a product of the weather or the prices on the merchandise arrayed along both edges of the driveway—all of it offered at fifty to thirty percent of its retail value. One side had little-used lawn mowers and snowblowers, an arbor like the kind some people get married under, garden hoses and tillers, ten-speed bikes, a couple of air conditioners, an unassembled twenty-foot aboveground swimming pool, hammocks, benches, birdbaths, tools and toolboxes, auto parts, and even a 12-horsepower go-kart. On the other side were household items like microwave ovens, a George Foreman grill, KitchenAid mixers, waffle irons, coffeemakers, teapots, nonstick skillets, slow cookers, stereo equipment, and clock radios that played nature sounds when you hit the snooze bar.

A young man—I placed him in the midtwenties—was busy showing a fistful of customers that the remote-controlled cars, trucks, helicopters, and airplanes on display really did work. A woman close to his age was demonstrating an 850-watt Breville juice extractor that she said she'd let go for a hundred bucks. I lingered a moment to watch, telling myself I could use a juicer.

Out of the corner of my eye, I saw Nina passing a blue and white sign announcing that the house was for sale. She browsed her way up the driveway into the garage. I followed discreetly behind, making sure I was never more than a few yards away from her.

The garage was heated, and even though the doors were open wide, the blowers overhead were working hard enough to keep it toasty warm. Nina had draped her long charcoal coat over her arm, revealing the snug white turtleneck she wore beneath it. Which was probably why the young man standing behind the table was watching her so intently. She was examining a green silk blouse when he approached.

"This is very impressive," Nina said. "It reminds me of the rummage sale they hold every September in Minneapolis—the one conducted by the wealthy parents of the kids who attend that expensive private school along the river. People literally line up around the block and wait hours to be among the first to get a chance at their castoffs."

"That's pretty much our business model," the young man replied.

Nina's smile wasn't quite as dazzling as her pale blue eyes, yet it was close, so when she flashed it at the kid, he couldn't help but smile in return.

"You hold these a lot?" she asked.

"A couple times a month, usually," he said. "What we do, we gather high-value merchandise from people who don't want to bother with eBay or their own garage sales, but at the same time don't want to just give it away to Goodwill or some church. Think of us as a floating consignment store."

"I never heard of such a thing."

"We send out a few flyers, but mostly it's word of mouth. One customer tells another customer. We don't want a high profile. That's why we never hold a sale at the same place twice. The government, the IRS, they tend to ignore garage sales, but if they knew we were holding them regularly, they'd want us to take out a license; they'd want us to pay taxes."

Nina waved her hand as if it were a topic not worth another moment's consideration, which made the kid smile some more. She kept browsing. Designer clothes, denim jeans, handbags, cell phones, digital cameras and recorders, iPods and MP3 players, smartphones, GPS devices, HDTVs, laptops, tablets, and video game players, as well as an assortment of high-end cosmetics, electric toothbrushes, men's razors, pregnancy tests, and a couple of cartons of baby formula, were carefully arranged on the tables. While the list sounds impressive, there wasn't that much of it, and the merchandise looked as though it had already been thoroughly picked through. Still, there wasn't a mark on any of it. Not even a smudged thumbprint.

I followed closely behind as Nina searched through a pile of silk blouses.

"These are beautiful," she said. "Only I can't find anything in my size."

"What is your size?" asked the young man.

"Four to six, depending on how the clothes run." I detected a certain amount of pride in Nina's answer. Given the number of sit-ups she does nearly every night, her feet hooked under the sofa, it was a pride well-deserved.

"We can't control what merchandise comes in," the young man said. "It changes from month to month. But we're having another sale tomorrow afternoon in Woodbury, and there'll be plenty of different products, different clothes. Maybe we'll have what you're looking for then."

"Where in Woodbury?" Nina asked.

"Just a sec." The kid dipped down below the table, rummaged through a box, and came up with a flyer. He handed it to Nina. I glanced at it over her shoulder as I moved past. It was identical to the one in my pocket.

A woman pushing sixty was also listening to their conversation.

"Are you going to have more than what you have today?" she asked.

"Ma'am?" the kid said.

"You usually have a much better selection."

"Like I said, we can't control what comes in. And it is winter."

"Last February was winter, and you had more stuff."

"She's right," a man said. He was the same age as the woman, but I didn't get the impression that they were together. "You had much more merchandise the last time."

The kid spread his hands wide as if he didn't know what to say. The woman gave him a disappointed head shake and drifted away. So did the man. Nina kept browsing the tables until she came to a selection of jewelry—rings, watches, necklaces, pendants, and earrings. She found a teardrop pearl hanging from a white-gold chain. She read the price tag and examined the pearl some more.

"Two hundred and eighty dollars?" Nina batted those marvelous pale blue eyes.

"For you, two hundred and thirty dollars," the young man replied.

"I don't suppose you take credit cards."

"Sorry."

"Uh-huh."

Nina dipped into her bag and started pulling out bills—figuring something like this might happen, I had stopped at an ATM on my way to Arden Hills. She gave the bills to the young man, who gave the necklace to her.

"Do you have a Web site?" Nina asked. "Where can I find out about future sales?"

"No Web site. We do have a mailing list, though."

"How do I get on it?"

The young man asked for Nina's e-mail account. Nina supplied her personal address, not the one attached to her business.

"I hope to see you again, Nina," the young man said. Nina offered her hand and he shook it. "By the way, my name's Mitch."

Ella's Mitch? my inner voice asked. *Ms. Bosland's brother?*

"A pleasure to meet you, Mitch," Nina said.

He looked at her like he wanted to be friends. Nina turned and moved away. The eyes of the young man followed her until he was distracted by my presence.

"Good afternoon, sir," he said. "Have you found anything you like?"

His smile had lost most of its luster, but it wasn't personal. After Nina, I was a disappointing sight.

"A couple of things," I said.

"We're here to help."

He doesn't know who you are, my inner voice said.

I bought the juicer so I wouldn't look suspicious.

Nina didn't say another word until we were in her Lexus and driving away, with me behind the wheel.

"What do you think?" she asked.

"I think you did very well. We learned a lot without acting like we were trying to. Although, two hundred and thirty dollars? You couldn't buy something a little less expensive?"

"Says the man who paid a hundred for a toy he'll use twice a year if that. Besides, pearl is my birthstone. And . . . and—now they know we're big spenders."

"I'm sure that's what you were going for."

"Mitch—is he the one who came to the condo yesterday?"

"I think so."

"Why?"

"One of these days I'm going to ask him. For now, though, I think it's better that he doesn't know who I am."

"It was all stolen merchandise, wasn't it?" Nina said. "The blouses I looked at—some of them still had the manufacturer's fold lines."

"The used stuff on the driveway was probably loot taken in home and garage burglaries. The more expensive products in the garage were most likely shoplifted."

"I can understand stealing something that you can put in your pocket or a purse, but how do you walk out of a store with an HDTV or a KitchenAid mixer?"

"One way, you buy something, get a receipt, then you grab a product that doesn't fit easily into a bag and walk out the door with it under your arm while carrying the receipt in your hand for everybody to see. The staff will think you paid for it."

"What about the stuff with electronic surveillance tags?"

"There are a lot of gags you can pull. One thing, you get a shopping bag—they call them booster bags—that's lined with aluminum foil. It lets you take the products though the front exit without setting off the alarms."

"I am so naïve."

"Next time you go shopping, watch the people with baby strollers and umbrellas with handles that they can hook over their arms. Watch women with full skirts—they call them 'crotch-walkers.' "

"Because they carry merchandise out of the store between their legs?"

"Exactly. In fact, watch anyone who's wearing baggy clothes in general because they might have extra pockets and hooks sewn into the lining. Watch customers wearing bulky coats who seem always to have a hand in their pocket. More likely, only their sleeve is in the pocket. Their hand is hidden beneath the coat and free to snatch items off shelves without being noticed."

"All the clothes I looked at, none of them had those ink cartridges that the stores attach, not even the expensive sweaters."

"It's easy to get rid of those, even if you don't have a detacher, what the salesclerks use. Depending on what kind of cartridge you have, you can remove them with a hammer and nail, screwdriver, wire snipper, needle-nose pliers, magnets, even a rubber band if you know what you're doing. I knew this one guy, he'd put the clothes in a freezer and when they got cold enough, he'd just break off the cartridges. Ink can't spill if it's frozen."

"How do you know all this?"

"I used to be a cop for eleven and a half years, remember?"

Nina stared as if she weren't sure she believed me.

"The people at the garage sale, the customers—do you think they know all the merchandise was stolen?" she asked.

"Probably."

"Why would people buy stolen property?"

"Because they don't have the nerve to steal it themselves."

"You're being cynical again."

"Think about it. Shopping is second only to dining out as a way people give themselves a treat. Take it to the next step. Most nonprofessional shoplifters, the ones who aren't addicted—"

"People get addicted to shoplifting?"

"Sure they do. Anyway, to most nonprofessionals, getting

something for nothing is like giving themselves a reward for working hard, for making it through the day. Buying stolen property, usually at a substantial discount—it isn't the same thing, but it's close. Besides, you can always tell yourself, 'I didn't steal it.'"

"That's crazy."

"It's human nature. Nina, only three percent of shoplifters are professionals and they steal only ten percent of the stuff. The rest—over seventy-five percent are adults who have money in their pockets. Some studies claim that one out of every eleven shoppers is a thief."

"Hanging out with you can be so depressing sometimes."

"You want depressing? Next time you're on eBay, ask yourself how much of that merchandise is stolen."

"Stop it."

"I don't want to pick on eBay, but that's where a lot of it ends up, online auction sites. That and small businesses, flea markets, and garage sales."

"What about pawnshops?"

"Not so much anymore. Pawnshops are required by law to keep track of the merchandise that comes in; they have to record serial numbers and product descriptions. If the cops find a computer or snowblower or diamond ring that was stolen, shops have to be able to provide them with the name and address of the customer who sold it to them."

By then I had the Lexus on 35W and was driving south through Minneapolis.

"Where are we going?" Nina asked.

"To a pawnshop."

"There's no need for that, McKenzie. I'll take your word for it."

"Did you enjoy your little undercover assignment today?"

"Yes, I did, actually."

"Want to do it again?"

"What do you have in mind?"

Pawnshops have always gotten a bad rap as a desperate resource for desperate people, and maybe there was a time when they deserved it. Yet there was nothing desperate about Easy Cash. It was light and airy and clean and, at first glance, resembled any consignment store you've ever been in with its astonishing array of merchandise—over twelve thousand square feet of computers, DVD players, electric guitars, clothes, jewelry, tools, bicycles, lawn mowers, even motorcycles and snowmobiles. If a product had financial value, Easy Cash traded in it. The only exception was guns. There was a large sign next to the front entrance that read: EASY CASH DOES NOT BUY OR SELL GUNS OF ANY KIND. YOU ARE PROHIBITED FROM CARRYING A GUN ON THESE PREMISES. It made me think I should remove the nine-millimeter SIG Sauer holstered behind my right hip, but I didn't.

We were met at the door by a young man who wore a blue tie over a blue shirt—all employees of Easy Cash were required to wear dress shirts and ties. He asked how he could help me today, and I told him I wanted to speak to the owner. Before any other words were spoken, though, Marshall Lantry called to me.

"McKenzie, you sonuvabitch," he said.

"You're good friends, I can tell," Nina said.

Lantry was wearing a blue sports jacket to go with his shirt and tie. He was waving at me from behind a counter in the center of the store. The counter was on a foot-high platform. I had convinced Lantry to build the platform years ago in order to discourage miscreants from attempting to come over the top of the counter for either the cash register or him and his employees. Originally, we had mounted posters of Anna Kournikova, Taye Diggs, and Jennifer Lopez behind him. Now it was Maria Sharapova, Boris Kodjoe, and Jennifer Lawrence. Hanging right above the posters were security cameras. The way I had explained it to Lantry, the posters would encourage customers—male and female alike—to look up, which in turn would help the cameras to get a good shot of their faces.

As we approached, he came around the counter and shook my hand. "Damn, I haven't seen you for the longest time," he said.

"Good to see you, too."

"Who's this?"

"Marshall Lantry, meet Nina Truhler."

"Ahh, Ms. Truhler." Lantry took Nina's hand between both of his and smiled brightly. "You are way too pretty to be spending time with this loser."

"People keep telling me that," she said.

"So, to what do I owe the pleasure? What can I sell you?"

"Something high tech," I said. "Something, maybe, in the back room."

The sparkle in his eyes added to his smile.

"You want to talk s*erious* business," Lantry said.

"I do."

A few moments later, Lantry led me to a large metal door in his basement fitted with an electronic lock that he disarmed by inputting a code into a keypad. The door opened, and rows of fluorescent lights flicked on automatically.

"Wow," Nina said.

Metal shelves were pushed against each of the walls. Electronic surveillance gear of every shape and kind, both new and used, was stacked on the shelves. I was surprised by the number of cameras.

"It's a video age," Lantry said.

"Wow," Nina said again. She was running her fingertips over the face of one of Lantry's satellite dishes. "The places you take me."

"Are you looking for a nanny cam, Ms. Nina?" Lantry asked. "I have seventeen different varieties, including the cutest teddy bears."

"Actually," I said, "we need a wire. For the lady."

"We do?" Nina asked.

"And a receiver."

"Distance?" Lantry asked.

"A couple hundred yards, at least."

"Recorder?"

"Probably a good idea, but I need to listen in real time."

"You realize that it's illegal to intercept and record conversations without the consent of the folks involved, right?"

"It's also illegal to sell bugs for the purpose of intercepting and recording conversations without the consent of the folks involved."

"Just as long as we're both on the same page."

"Wait. What?" Nina said.

"So, you're looking for . . ." Lantry turned his back to me and was scanning his shelves. "People are going to say things to the lady and you want to listen in?"

"Exactly."

"What people?" Nina asked.

Lantry went to a shelf laden with computer keyboards, mouses, wireless routers, thermostats, smoke detectors, power strips, air fresheners, wall clocks, clock radios, picture frames, even baseball caps.

"Are all these bugs?" Nina asked.

"Listening devices, yes." Lantry spoke as he rummaged. "TV shows, you always see the hero wearing a wire, literally a wire, taped to his chest. That's just so the audience can wonder if the hero's going to get caught. It's for dramatic effect. In reality, there are so many less visible ways to do it. Hey, McKenzie, how 'bout this—a woman's silver watch that contains a high-definition miniaturized camcorder. Or wait, I have the same camcorder in a black pen"—he showed it to me—"and a key chain." He showed that to me, too.

"We don't need pictures," I said.

He took an earbud and held it up for everyone to see.

"Spy Ear III," Lantry said. "Two-way communications system."

"I didn't know these were real," Nina said. "I thought it was just something you see on TV."

"Oh, they're real."

"Except that you need to wear a neckloop," I said.

"What's that?" Nina asked.

"It's a coil of wire that you wear around your neck," Lantry said. "It's kinda like an antenna that plugs into an audio monitoring device."

Nina's hand went to her throat as if she were already wearing it.

"An actual wire like TV again," I said. "I'd like to avoid that."

"Sure, sure." Lantry held up a listening device that resembled a tiny flower—a light blue forget-me-not—attached to a needle about the length of a toothpick. "Lapel mic. Pin it to her coat. I'll configure your cell phone so you can listen in and record. One ninety-nine retail. For you, one forty-nine."

"Sold," I said.

Lantry set the forget-me-not in Nina's palm.

"Not as cool as the earbud," she said.

TEN

Unlike Arden Hills, Woodbury did not want for development. It wasn't even a city fifty years ago, yet now it was the tenth largest in Minnesota. *CNN Money* ranked it eleventh on its list of 100 Best Places to Live, and for the most part its homes reflected that position. They were large and opulent and looked as if they had been built yesterday. The house listed in the flyer was no exception. We found it near a Lutheran church at the top of a T-intersection. Like the place in Arden Hills, it was surrounded by vehicles. I was fortunate to find an open space about a block away at the bottom of the T with a clear view of the garage.

"You don't have to do this," I said.

"They'll speak to me more freely if you're not around," Nina replied. "You said so yourself."

"Actually, what I said is that they'll be more likely to flirt with you if I'm not around."

"And that'll help me get information."

"That's the plan."

Nina flicked the petals of the forget-me-not attached to the lapel of her charcoal coat. The sound of it rumbled off my smartphone speaker like a rifle shot.

"Will it be dangerous?" she asked.

"I wouldn't think so. On the other hand, we are dealing with a criminal enterprise."

She flicked the lapel mic again.

"Stop that," I said.

"Just checking to make sure it works. Should we have a code word in case something goes wrong?"

"I'll have eyes on you"—I held up a pair of binoculars—"as well as ears, so probably that's not necessary. On the other hand . . ."

"I could say 'broccoli.'"

"You could say 'help.' How 'bout that?"

"Fine."

"Call for help and I'll come running."

"Good to know."

Nina left the Lexus and started walking toward the house. The layout was the same, with "used" items lining the driveway and newer merchandise loaded on tables inside the garage, although the garage was larger. It had doors for two vehicles and a third for a boat and trailer. There were more customers as well. They seemed better dressed, too, which didn't surprise me. Woodbury had a median income of over one hundred and ten grand. Instead of saying WELCOME, the signs posted at the city limits read PLEASE WIPE YOUR FEET.

I watched Nina through the binoculars as she passed a blue and white real estate sign.

"Hey, McKenzie," Nina said. Her voice was perfectly calm. "Wasn't the other house for sale, too?"

"Yes, it was," I answered, although she couldn't hear me. I wrote the name of the Realtor in the little notebook I always carry.

Nina browsed her way up the concrete driveway. Like the day before, the temperature was touching the low forties, and the customers were in a jovial mood. I heard many happy voices. One guy said, "I bet we're playing golf by the end of the month."

I assumed it was the fellow standing just off of Nina's shoulder and handling a pitching wedge that he took from a golf bag belted to a hand-drawn cart.

"Don't jinx it," another fellow said.

The golfer returned the wedge to the bag and removed a putter.

"This year I'm finally going to break eighty," he said.

"Okay, now you're just talking crazy," his partner replied.

Nina kept moving along the tables. She paused to examine one of those flat, round vacuum cleaners, the kind that roam randomly across the floor, caroming off of furniture until, theoretically at least, it covers every nook and cranny. She held it up, I presume for me to see.

"I have a boyfriend who would love this," she said.

A young woman was standing behind the table—the same one who was demonstrating the juicer the day before.

"Would you like to buy it for him?" she asked.

"No. When it comes to housecleaning, he's lazy enough as it is."

"Hey, hey," I said.

Nina returned the vacuum cleaner and kept moving, seeming every inch the dedicated shopper. She stepped inside the garage, and my cell phone started broadcasting a steady moaning sound that competed with the voices. It was the sound of the overhead blowers working hard to keep the garage heated. I turned up the volume just in time to hear the young man.

"Nina, isn't it?" he said.

I could see Nina pivot slowly to find Mitch standing behind her.

"You made it," he added.

"Yes," she said. "Thanks for inviting me."

Mitch's smile was clearly visible to me through the binoculars, and I thought, Be very, very careful, pal.

"You showed some interest in pearls yesterday," he said. "I have something you might like."

Mitch led Nina to the cafeteria-style table where they had laid out the jewelry. He held up something for Nina that I couldn't see. Nina took it from his hand.

"Pearl earrings," she said.

"They're nearly identical to the necklace you bought yesterday."

"I can see that. How much are they?"

"Two hundred dollars for the pair."

"That's a very good price."

"A new customer, we like to keep your business."

"This is the way to do it."

Nina reached into her bag and produced the cash. If Mitch had been paying attention, he would have noticed that there was plenty more where that came from. The way he suggested, "Please, keep looking. I'm sure you'll find other merchandise that you'll like," made me think that he had. Nina wasn't about to let him go, however.

"Do you get a lot of pearls?" she asked.

"Depends."

"I love pearls."

"I gathered."

Nina allowed her voice to drop an octave or two.

"If you should come across a necklace made with Japanese Akoya pearls, I'd be interested in paying a buy-it-now price," she said.

"Buy it now?"

"Isn't that what they do on the Internet auction sites, give customers a chance to buy it now and avoid an auction?"

"It's not an auction, but—Japanese Akoya pearls, you say? It's possible we can do something for you."

"I'm also looking for pearl pendants."

"If we come across anything . . ."

"You have my e-mail address."

"Clever girl," I said.

"Mitch."

Over the smartphone, it was just a guy calling a name. The way Nina's and the young man's heads snapped around, it must have sounded much more fervid to them.

"Excuse me," Mitch said.

I followed him with the binoculars as he left Nina's side and moved toward an older man who was standing with his hands locked behind his back. A second man, younger, taller, thinner, with short brown hair and completely devoid of expression, stood a few feet behind him, his head swiveling slowly from side to side.

Bodyguard, my inner voice said.

Mitch said something that I couldn't hear, and the older man grabbed his arm. Mitch pulled it out of his grasp. The older man glanced about as if he were afraid of being overheard, took Mitch by the arm again, and guided him to the table stacked with cashmere sweaters. The bodyguard moved with them, keeping a respectful distance.

Mitch and the older man spoke earnestly, only I couldn't hear a word that they said. And then I did. Nina was moving slowly toward them.

"No, no, no," I chanted.

The two men ceased speaking.

"Excuse me," Nina said.

She fondled a couple of sweaters and moved on.

"What are you doing here?" Mitch said.

His voice was clear over my smartphone.

"Damn, Nina," I said. "Good move."

"Didn't you hear me?" the older man said. "Karl Olson is dead. Someone shot him."

"Yeah, I heard," Mitch said. "What has that got to do with us?"

"You could've told me."

"All I knew about Olson was his name. The Boss paid him to hang around during the sales to make sure nothing went sideways; he wouldn't even talk to us. Which made me think he wasn't here to watch the customers, he was here to watch us. Only he didn't show yesterday."

Mitch threw a thumb at the bodyguard.

"Now we have this guy," he said. "Are you hearing everything okay? Are you sure you don't want to stand a little closer?"

The bodyguard didn't move, didn't even acknowledge that Mitch had spoken to him.

"What's your name, anyway?"

He didn't reply.

Mitch lowered his voice and spoke to the older man. "What's his name?" he asked.

"Peter Troop, I think, but I don't know. I barely knew Olson. You could've told me about him. Why did I have to read about it in the *Star Tribune*?"

"It's not my job. Look, John. We had an arrangement."

John, my inner voice said. *His name is John.*

"Yes, we did," John said. "I handle the outside and you handle the inside. Except you're not doing a very good job with your part."

"We're doing fine."

"Hell you are. You think I don't hear the complaints? You haven't brought in any merchandise worth selling in over a month, and that's starting to affect my side of the business."

"Whose fault is that? Everything was fine until you got greedy."

"It wasn't me. How many times do I have to say it? I'm just doing what I was told."

"Sure you are."

John jabbed a finger in Mitch's face.

"The Boss says—"

Mitch pushed the finger down. "Don't do that," he said.

"The Boss says to get that so-called expert crew of yours back into the stores. If there isn't an improvement by next week, there'll be consequences."

"Fuck the Boss." Mitch's voice was defiant, yet I noticed he glanced over his shoulder at the bodyguard when he spoke. "As far as I know you're the Boss. You invented this unseen persona to keep me in my place."

"You know that's not true."

"We were doing fine before the Boss came along."

"C'mon, Mitchell. That's not true either. We were driving around the Midwest working flea markets—and only when it wasn't winter, and when isn't it fucking winter up here? Now look at us. The Boss got us working together—"

"The Boss that I've never met. How 'bout you?"

"I never met him either. Dammit, Mitch. We went from penny ante to big time." John gestured at the large crowd rubbing elbows in the garage and driveway. "Business is good."

"Except now we're in a different line of business, aren't we? That's why you're really here. Not to deliver a message. You're here to claim another victim for the Boss."

"I'm doing what I'm told. You should do the same."

"This was supposed to be a three-way partnership. Do you feel like a partner? Cuz it looks like you're an employee."

"Whatever, it has nothing to do with you."

"Hell it doesn't. El was right about that."

John started pointing fingers again.

"I don't want to hear her name again," he said. "She's gone. And good riddance, too, bitch trying to ruin our lives."

"Is that how you justify what happened? By blaming her?"

"If she had just . . . kept . . . quiet."

My hands gripped tightly to the binoculars. I forced them to relax.

"You should do the same," John said.

"Is that what the Boss says?" Mitch asked.

"You get the same e-mails that I do."

It was as good an exit line as any, yet John didn't exit. Instead, he moved out of the garage and down the driveway, stopping in front of the young woman who tried to sell the vacuum cleaner to Nina. Peter Troop moved with him, again maintaining a respectful distance. The young woman watched Troop as he donned a pair of sunglasses. She seemed uncomfortable in his presence. If the security guard noticed, he didn't care.

"Mitch," a man said.

I angled the binoculars to look back inside the garage. The young man who had been demonstrating the remote-controlled toys in Arden Hills was now also standing next to the cashmere sweaters.

"What did Kispert want?" the young man asked.

Kispert, my inner voice said. *The man's full name is John Kispert.*

"Hell, Craig. What do you think he wanted?"

Ella's Craig?

"We should never have gone into business with these people," he said.

"They made us an offer we couldn't refuse, remember?"

"I remember that we were doing better on our own. At least we were happier."

Disgruntled employees, my inner voice said. *You can use that.*

"I know, I know," Mitch said. "Sometimes I wish we had never left Rochester."

Ms. Bosland came from Rochester.

"Got that right," Craig said.

"Look at him. He's here to claim another victim for the Boss, I know it."

"Yeah, and sooner or later it's going to come back on us."

"Like it hasn't already?"

"Did Kispert ask about Olson?"

"That was topic number one."

"What did you say?"

"I said Olson wasn't our problem."

"Not anymore, anyway. Did he say who he thought killed him?"

I could see Mitch shaking his head through the binoculars.

"I thought he might blame El because of what happened," Craig said.

"He thinks she's long gone. I don't know, maybe she is."

"What about the other kids? Do you think they went home?"

"My sister would have told me if they had."

"We need to replace them. We need to do it soon."

"I know. It won't be easy, either. How long did it take us to teach El and them their trade? And now we have to start over?"

Craig didn't speak for a long time, and when he did, he said, "How could things go so badly?"

"Maybe we should get out—like the kids," Mitch said.

"Do you think the Boss will let us?"

"If we found someone to take our place . . . I don't know."

"It might not matter."

"What do you mean?"

"Olson. If Kispert and the Boss think he was killed because someone is trying to move in on our business, they might fold it up. We could become free agents again, just like we talked about."

"That'll take more than Olson getting shot, I think."

The two young men stopped chatting and simply stood next to each other, comfortable in the silence that followed the way that good friends sometimes are. I started searching for Nina. I found her in the driveway, squatting next to an eighteen-inch-by-three-foot high hexagon-shaped glass terrarium with a hook on top so you could hang it from the ceiling. She was examining it as if she were actually planning to buy it and I thought, C'mon, Nina. Where in our condominium do we have room for a terrarium, and who's going to take care of it anyway?

A woman moved past Nina to the mouth of the garage. Despite the springlike weather, she was dressed in a black wool coat buttoned to her throat, black gloves that disappeared beneath her sleeves, black boots, and a black short-brimmed cloche hat with a red-ribbon hatband and side bow. She reminded me of a femme fatale from a 1930s gangster movie. It was difficult to make out her features even with the binoculars, yet her body language suggested there wasn't a place anywhere on earth that she wouldn't rather be than where she was.

Kispert approached her. He locked his hands behind his back and rocked on the balls of his feet as if inspecting an ice sculpture at the St. Paul Winter Carnival. She put her hand in her pocket. He shook his head and spoke slowly. His words made her flinch. He walked off. The expression on his face gave me the impression that, like the woman, he wished he were somewhere else, too.

The femme fatale looked around, saw the table piled with silk blouses, grabbed one in a gloved hand without bothering to check the size, and returned to Kispert. He took the blouse and folded it neatly, frowning all the while. She reached into her pocket and produced a white number-ten envelope. Kispert took the envelope and stuffed it into his own pocket. At the same time, he returned the blouse. She gripped it as if it were something she used to dust her knickknack shelves and walked away— walked as if she wanted to run but was afraid people would notice.

The woman headed down the block to a gray car. She opened the door, tossed the blouse inside, and climbed in after it. From the angle where I was parked, it was impossible to make out the license plate—or the make and model of her vehicle, for that matter. Given the cookie-cutter appearance of automobiles these days, it could have been anything manufactured in the past decade, both foreign and domestic.

I retrained the binoculars on the garage sale. Kispert had moved to the mouth of the driveway. Peter Troop joined him there. Kispert spoke; the security guard listened. Mitch and Craig had separated, and both were now assisting customers. I found Nina. She had drifted back into the garage.

"All right, sweetie," I said. "Time to go."

As if she had heard me, Nina started walking down the driveway. I could see the blue forget-me-not pinned to her lapel. She reached Mitch and said, "Send me an e-mail about your next sale. I'll bring friends."

"You and your friends are always welcome," Mitch said.

It was because I was watching her that I didn't see the car that drove up in a hurry until it filled the lenses of the binoculars.

I heard gunshots—over the cell phone they sounded like the pop-pop-pop of someone playing with Bubble Wrap.

The car drove off. The lenses cleared. I saw half the customers flinching and ducking at the unexpected noise. The other half turned their heads and looked around as if wondering what they had missed.

Another car passed in a hurry, yet I didn't follow that one either. Instead, I kept the binoculars focused on the driveway.

Kispert was lying across a mound of snow at the entrance and looking in the direction the two cars had gone. He seemed to be fine.

Troop was also down, sitting on the concrete apron, his hand gripping his thigh just above the knee.

Nina was standing twenty yards behind him.

Broccoli, my inner voice said.

I left the Lexus in a hurry and started running toward the garage. At the same time, I reached for the SIG Sauer holstered beneath my zippered coat. My feet became tangled and I slipped on the ice. I fell, shoulder first, and skidded next to a parked car.

I cursed and pushed myself to my knees.

I didn't realize I was still carrying the cell phone until I heard Nina's voice.

"What are you doing?" She might have been asking if I was putting extra peppers in my spaghetti sauce for all the emotion that she displayed.

I looked up. Even from that distance I knew she was looking directly at me.

"Are you all right?" she asked. "Seriously, what's going on?"

My answer was to brush the snow off and return to the Lexus, although I wasn't happy about it. I retrieved the binoculars.

Kispert was up now. He and Mitch were helping the security guard walk the length of parked cars until they reached a Honda Accord. They opened the door and helped him sit, his leg outstretched.

Craig was speaking to his customers.

"What was that?" someone asked.

"I don't know," Craig said. "Kids with their car stereo up too loud, or maybe a backfire."

C'mon, my inner voice said. *When was the last time you actually heard a car backfire? It's become so rare it's almost an urban legend now.*

"The guy was startled and slipped on the ice," Craig added. "He'll be all right."

Nina was looking directly at the Lexus when she said, "Huh."

Once I assured myself she was safe, I trained the binoculars on Craig. He moved along the parked vehicles until he reached the Honda. Mitch said something, and Craig hurried to a second car, popped the trunk, and retrieved a red and gray satchel. The soft-sided bag contained a wide array of emergency supplies including jumper cables, folding shovel, tools, tape, fuses, flares, flashlight, and survival blanket, plus a forty-five-piece first aid kit—I had carried one just like it in my dearly departed Audi. Craig gave the bag to his friend. Mitch wrapped the blanket around Troop's shoulders and began ministering to his leg while Kispert looked on.

Craig returned to the driveway to pacify his customers some more, although none of them seemed terribly concerned. The crowd was thinning out, however. He spoke to his assistants, and they quickly began packing up merchandise and collapsing tables.

Mitch finished attending to the security guard. He patted his shoulder; Troop nodded in reply. Kispert slipped behind the steering wheel of the Honda and drove off, leaving Mitch standing in the middle of the street.

Nina reached the Lexus, opened the passenger door, and slipped onto the seat.

"Are you all right?" I asked.

"I'm fine. Are you? I saw you fall. What was that all about?"

"You don't know?"

"I heard a noise, I saw a man slip and fall, I saw people trying to help him up, and then I saw you running toward the driveway. Well, actually, I saw you tripping—what happened?"

I started the car. Several white panel trucks had appeared. They stopped in front of the driveway. I drove around them.

"McKenzie, what happened?"

I explained.

Nina closed her eyes and rested her head against the back of the seat.

"Well, that was unexpected," she said.

"I'm sorry. I didn't think."

"The man who was shot . . ."

"He was working security for someone called the Boss. From what I saw, it looks like he'll be okay."

"I was five feet from him when the shooting started."

"Actually, you were farther away than that."

Nina cocked her head as if I had ruined a perfectly good story. Neither of us spoke until we put a full mile behind us. Nina opened her eyes and grinned slightly.

"At least I got some pearl earrings out of the deal," she said. A block later, she asked, "Who was the other man, the one who dove into the snowdrift?"

I explained.

"For what it's worth, you were wonderful," I told her. "You were great. Stashing the bug in the sweaters so I could hear those guys, masterful."

"Do you think it was Fifteen in the car? Do you think she's the one who shot Karl Olson? I hope she did. I mean—it would prove she's alive. I've been worried ever since your gun showed up in Highland Park. I don't want her to be a murderer. On the other hand . . ."

Nina's words pretty much captured the mixed emotions I was feeling, too, so I kept quiet.

"Was the drive-byer trying to hit Kispert and the security guy, or just shooting randomly?" she asked.

"Drive-byer?"

"You know what I mean."

"He might have been trying to scare everyone and Troop just got in the way."

"Yeah, well, mission accomplished because now I'm plenty scared. The gun wasn't very loud."

"Probably something small."

"Like a .25 caliber Colt?"

"Like a .25 caliber Colt."

"One of the handguns Fifteen stole."

"It might be unconnected to her. Rival criminals fighting over turf. Craig seemed concerned that someone might be moving in on the operation."

"I like that theory better than Fifteen shooting up the place."

"So do I. Unfortunately, she's our primary suspect until we can find someone we like better."

"Speaking of suspects—McKenzie, buying the pearls just now, how big a crime is that?"

"Gross misdemeanor punishable by ninety days in jail and/or a seven-hundred-dollar fine. 'Course, in your case, it's two counts."

"That's not funny."

"Assuming the county prosecutor can prove you knew the merchandise was stolen when you bought it."

"Of course I knew—"

I put an index finger to my lips. "Shhhhh."

"What about when I told Mitch I wanted a Japanese Akoya pearl necklace? How bad would it be if he actually stole one?"

"Aiding and abetting felony theft, five years, ten thousand dollars."

Nina stared at me for a moment before resting her head back against the seat and closing her eyes again.

"Will you visit me in prison?" she asked.

"Every Wednesday between six and eight P.M."

We were on Radio Drive heading north toward I-94 when I saw the flashing lights in my rearview mirror. The lights came from the grille of an unmarked police car. I might have said "Uh-oh" as I pulled to the side of the road.

Nina turned her head to look.

"Should I throw the earrings out the window?" she asked.

"Why? Are they stolen?"

Nina gave me a hard look as I stopped the car. She settled back in the seat and stared straight ahead.

"This isn't nearly as much fun as I thought it was going to be," she said.

A moment later, Detective Shipman walked up to the driver's-side window. I powered it down.

"Is something wrong, Officer?" I asked.

"I don't even know where to begin," she said. "Hello, Nina."

Nina leaned forward and turned her head to see past me.

"I'm Jean Shipman. We met at a barbecue last August."

"I remember," Nina said. "You're Bobby's girl."

"There's a Caribou coffeehouse a couple of blocks up. Meet me there. We have much to talk about."

"No," Nina said.

"Excuse me?"

"Ward 6 on Payne Avenue. Do you know it?"

"Yes . . ."

"Meet us there instead."

Shipman hesitated for a few beats before agreeing. I powered up the window as she returned to her vehicle. Nina held out her hand, and I turned my head to look at it. The hand was trembling.

"The last thing I need right now is caffeine," she said.

Ward 6 was a small yet highly regarded bar and restaurant located in a 130-year-old building in the Dayton's Bluff neighborhood of St. Paul, about three minutes' drive from police headquarters on Oak Street. Before Prohibition, it had been a "tied house," one of those neighborhood taverns that was owned by Hamm's Brewery and served only Hamm's products, and it still boasted the original bar. None of that seemed to interest Nina, though. She was concerned only with the shot of amaretto that she threw down in one gulp and chased with one of the joint's notorious adult milk shakes. I might have said something about the danger of drinking alcohol that tasted like candy, except the look in her eye told me it'd be best to keep my opinions to myself.

I ordered a beer, and Shipman had black coffee. She seemed fascinated by Nina and kept watching her even while she spoke to me.

"If you show me yours, I'll show you mine," she said.

"You first."

"I was at the garage sale. I didn't see you, but I saw Nina."

I had no doubt that Nina was listening intently, yet she did not react to the sound of her own name.

"What else did you see?" I asked.

"I saw the drive-by shooting. Rather, I should say, I heard it. I was looking down at the time. It took me a moment to figure out what happened. I pursued the car, only by then it had too much of a lead. I lost it."

"Butterfingers," I said. "Did you at least get a license plate number?"

Shipman shook her head.

"By the time I returned to the scene, the circus was packed

up and gone," she said. "I sent a bulletin to the hospitals. What do you think the chances are that the shooting victim will seek treatment in an emergency room?"

"From what I saw, his wound didn't seem too serious."

"I'm working with a detective out of the Minneapolis PD named John Luby. Know him?"

"I met him at the duplex the other day."

"We put together a kind of an informal task force. We think that my killing and his killing are connected, yet we have no evidence to prove it. It'll become a formal joint operation once we find a way to tie them together. In the meantime, Luby's working his side of the river and I'm working mine. So far he's found nothing about Karl Olson that we don't already know."

"What about Oliver Braun?"

"Everyone we've talked to said he was a good kid, and I have no reason to doubt it. He worked as an intern for Merle Mattson— she's a Ramsey County commissioner. The job satisfied a requirement for his political science degree, but it ended last November right after the election. The last time Mattson saw Oliver was when she gave him a glowing letter of recommendation. That was over three months ago. She wept when we told her about the kid."

"I don't trust tears, especially from politicians."

"Neither do I, but hers were genuine."

"Girlfriends?"

"His parents think Oliver might have been dating someone, but he had a habit of keeping his relationships to himself. Something about an unfortunate incident that occurred when he brought a date to a family wedding a couple of years ago."

"They can't confirm that he was seeing El?"

"No. We asked his friends about her. They don't seem to know much either, except that they haven't seen Elbers around since Christmas. Apparently they broke up—like your Deer River source suggested. Truth is, we've found nothing definitive to connect Elbers and Braun since Christmas except your gun and the telephone call. Which brings me to the flyers we dug out of the trash at the duplex. I'm guessing you found them, too, since you were at the garage sale in Woodbury as well as the one yesterday in Arden Hills. So, McKenzie, what do you know that I don't?"

"I think the garage sales are being conducted by a shoplifting and burglary ring," I said.

"I could have told you that. How are the kids living in the duplex connected? How is Elbers connected?"

"Except for the flyers, I honestly don't know."

"C'mon, McKenzie."

"I was told that El posted the names Craig and Mitch on her Facebook page. Mitch and Craig are the names of two of the people involved with the garage sales. I don't know if that makes El their acquaintance, friend, customer, or colleague."

"What about Oliver Braun? Has his name ever popped up on Elbers's page?"

"Not since Christmas."

"What do you make of the drive-by?"

"What do you make of it?"

"Could be your girl looking for some payback. Someone threw her off the back of that damn truck. Maybe it was Mitch and Craig."

"Or it could be a rival gang."

"What makes you think so?"

I couldn't answer honestly without revealing that we had been conducting electronic surveillance. Probably Shipman wouldn't have cared. On the other hand . . . Nina must have understood my predicament, because she jumped in without a moment's hesitation.

"I overheard them talking," Nina said. She spoke without touching the mic still pinned to her lapel or even glancing at it—a mistake others might have made. "They also said something about getting out of the business while the getting's good, so if you're going to arrest them . . ."

"I might do just that, or at least get Woodbury to do it for me since the sale was held outside of my jurisdiction. Craig and Mitch wouldn't be the first to try to deal themselves out of the jackpot. I don't suppose you know who they are or where I can find them?"

I considered handing over the intel Smith had given me in the lobby of the condo two days earlier, yet kept it to myself.

"Sorry," I said.

"Uh-huh. What about the time and location of the next garage sale?"

"If I hear anything, I'll let you know."

Shipman thought that was fair enough and said she'd be in touch. She left, leaving me to pick up the cost of her coffee. Nina watched her through the window. She didn't speak until Shipman was driving away.

"You didn't tell her everything."

"She didn't tell me everything either," I said.

"But why didn't you tell Shipman about Kispert and the Boss and all the rest?"

"I have a plan. She wouldn't approve."

"It's not because you don't like her, is it? It's not because you want to prove that you're smarter than she is?"

"Of course not. You have to understand, Shipman just wants to close her case. That's fine. That's her job. I'm willing to help, too. First, though, comes Fifteen. We're trying to protect her, remember? At least until we know if she's guiltless or not. That's why we got involved in the first place."

"If you say so."

"Oh, and for the record—I *am* smarter than Shipman. If I was still in harness, I'd be Bobby's partner, not her."

"As long as we have our priorities straight."

Nina ordered a second adult milk shake.

"I can see why Fifteen likes these things," she said. "I'm feeling much better already."

ELEVEN

Monday morning and the sun was shining bright in a cloudless sky, yet it gave no warmth. At least not much. We were experiencing another setback in our march toward spring—a high of twenty-eight degrees. The weather geek on Minnesota Public Radio said we should be happy about it, though, because it was a mere ten degrees below our average for that date in March. Which gave you an idea of how our winter was going—that we would be thankful when the temperature dipped ten degrees below normal.

I figured Kenwood Real Estate must have originated in Kenwood, one of the most expensive neighborhoods in Minneapolis, and branched out from there, because it now had offices scattered all over the place. The one I wanted was located in a converted white colonial on Rice Street in Roseville, not far from Steichen's, the now shuttered family-owned sporting goods store where I used to buy all of my equipment starting when I played peewee hockey and Little League baseball. It had been driven out of business after sixty years by the all-things-to-all-people discount giant down the street that I have never set foot in—not that I'm bitter. Yet the sight of Steichen's empty, unplowed parking lot was the reason I was in a surly mood when I stepped inside the colonial and asked for Emily Hoover.

It hadn't been hard to learn her name. All I needed to do was Google the addresses of the houses in Arden Hills and Woodbury to learn that they were indeed for sale through Kenwood Real Estate—they of the blue and white signs—and Hoover was handling the transactions. It hadn't occurred to me that Mitch and Craig's garage sales were being held without permission from the owners until I saw the signs at both locations, yet it made perfect sense. I remembered arresting a suspect years earlier who dealt drugs out of a fourplex that he had been hired to convert into condominiums. The only reason we caught him was that the owner dropped by one day to check on the contractor's progress and discovered him plastering over bullet holes in a wall.

The pretty young thing manning the reception desk led me deeper into the building. The ground floor was laid out like a bank. There were a half-dozen desks, each with a computer terminal on top and a couple of chairs in front. The desks were separated only by a few yards of empty carpet. It was easy to hear the conversations going on around you. I figured that would work to my advantage.

The receptionist led me to Emily Hoover's desk. She was a handsome woman in her late fifties with a trim figure and streaks of gray running through her otherwise auburn hair. She rose to greet me. I shook her hand and told her my name was Nick Dyson and I was interested in purchasing the property in Arden Hills near Round Lake. She offered me a chair and began working her computer. The receptionist returned to her own desk near the door. I leaned forward and informed Emily that I was also interested in the property in Woodbury. Her fingers froze above the keyboard. It told me all I needed to know.

"I have three questions, Ms. Hoover." I spoke softly, yet her eyes flew across the room to see if someone was listening just the same. "Question one—do the owners of the homes know what happened there this weekend? Question two—does your employer know? Question three—do you want me to tell them?"

"Who are you?"

Her voice was that of a woman who was scared silly. I wanted her to be frightened; I needed her to be frightened. Yet at the same time I felt like the biggest jerk.

"I told you. My name is Dyson." I leaned forward and spoke softly. "I'm sorry if it sounds like I'm threatening you. Actually, I'm not sorry, because I am threatening you. But I mean you no harm, I promise. If you answer my questions, Emily"—I used her first name on purpose, speaking it as if we were friends—"I will leave you alone."

What a sonuvabitch you are, my inner voice said.

Her eyes flitted over the trophies arranged on her desk: a gold figure of a female athlete, her arms stretched over her head, mounted on a black cube with a tiny plaque that read TOP CLOSER VOLUME AGENT OF THE YEAR; next to it, a pair of crystal wings carved with the words CONGRATULATIONS! 1,000 HOMES SOLD.

"I've been in real estate for thirty-five years without a mark against my name," Emily said.

"We can speak privately. Or we can speak here. You decide."

She replied so softly that I nearly missed it when she said, "In private."

"There's a coffeehouse down the street. Do you know it?"

Emily nodded.

"Meet me there. Don't make me wait too long."

I did a survey back when I was living in Falcon Heights and discovered that there were thirteen coffeehouses within a two-and-a-half-mile radius of my front door. How they all stayed in business, much less thrived, was a mystery to me. With a couple of notable exceptions, they seemed identical. Certainly the café mocha I was served ten minutes after I left Kenwood Real Estate tasted no different than any other café mocha I've ever had. It had been served in a paper cup with a plastic lid. The name Nick had been scrawled on its side although there weren't enough customers in the coffeehouse to cause confusion.

There really was a career criminal named Nicholas Dyson who specialized in robbing banks, jacking armored cars, and burgling the occasional jewelry store. Google his name and you'll find all kinds of information about him, along with photographs of me. In one I'm clean-shaven; in the others I'm wearing long hair and a scraggly beard. A couple of friends with the FBI and ATF coerced me into going undercover as Dyson to look for weapons along the Canadian border; they had edited the files and uploaded the photos to support my disguise. That was nine months ago, and although the case was now closed, they forgot to remove them. I never said anything about it because, well, there were times when a guy might want to pretend to be someone else. Like when there was a distinct possibility that his real name was known to the friends and colleagues of a dead gunman, a murdered college kid, and a young woman who might or might not have killed them both.

I sat at a small table next to a gas fireplace that wasn't lit and watched the door, all the while trying to remind myself that I was the good guy. It was hard to believe, especially when Emily Hoover entered, clutching her bag to her chest as if it were the most valuable thing she owned. It took her a moment to find me. She came to the table and sat down, moving as if in slow motion. Her face no longer looked handsome, merely old.

"I'm here."

From the sound of her voice, she could have been a condemned prisoner declining the blindfold offered by her executioner.

"May I get you something to drink?" I asked.

She shook her head.

A young man entered the coffeehouse; a chime that sounded

like it came from an ancient clock rang when he stepped through the door. That coupled with the sight of him caused Emily to flinch. There was nothing about his appearance that was cause for concern, unless it was the Where's Waldo stocking hat that he wore. Yet Emily's eyes kept moving from me to him and back again as he ordered his beverage and set up a laptop on a small table near the door while he waited for it to be made.

"Friend of yours?" I asked.

"I thought he was a friend of yours," Emily said.

She's paranoid, my inner voice decided. 'Course, if I were her, I'd be paranoid, too.

"I don't mean to put you on the spot," I said. "What I said before is true. I'm not trying to mess up your life."

"Men have told me that before. Yet, here I am."

"Tell me about them—the men using your properties. From your reaction, I'm guessing that you didn't give them access willingly."

My remark seemed to surprise her. Her eyes flitted to Waldo. He had retrieved his drink and was now sipping from the cup while he stared intently at his laptop. Not once did I notice him glancing at Emily. Her gaze came back to me.

"Who are you?" she asked again. "Are you the police?"

"Hardly."

"Who, then?"

"Let's just say I'm an interested third party and let it go at that. Your houses—"

"Not the police?"

I held up my cell phone for her to see.

"I could call them," I said.

"They forced me."

"How?"

"They have pictures. Videos."

Ahh, hell, my inner voice said. At the same time, I had to ask.

"Videos of what?"

"I bought computer equipment," Emily said. "At one of their garage sales. Later, they sent an e-mail. It said they had a TV for sale. The exact kind that I told them I wanted. They have a video of me buying it. The TV was stolen. They said if I didn't do exactly what they told me, they'd send the e-mail and the video to the police and to Kenwood. They said they'd post them on the Internet. I'd lose everything. My license. My career. My reputation. They'd send me to prison for five years."

I was actually relieved to hear it. When she said "video," my mind went somewhere else entirely. Still, blackmail was blackmail—there was nothing I hated more.

"Who are they?" I asked.

"I don't know his name. At least not the first man."

"Describe him."

She gave me a pretty good *portrait parle* of John Kispert.

"What did he make you do?" I asked.

"I have houses for sale. Some of them are unoccupied. I was forced to make them available for their garage sales. They'd use them for just one day and then . . ."

"Do you know when the next garage sale takes place?"

Emily didn't reply.

"Tell me," I said.

"Why should I trust you?"

"Because I didn't ask these questions in a loud voice in your office surrounded by your friends and colleagues."

Emily set her bag on the table and let her arms drop to her side. She appeared utterly defeated.

"I always knew this day would come," she said.

"When does the next garage sale take place?"

"Saturday."

"Where?"

Emily recited an address in Apple Valley that I wrote into my notebook.

"This man who is blackmailing you, how does he make contact?" I asked.

"He doesn't. Not anymore. Not after that first meeting. After that, he made me deal with two other men."

"What are their names?"

"Mitch and Craig. That's all I know. They're the two that sold me the computer and the TV in the first place. They probably took the video, too. We've never spoken of it. We haven't actually met since then, since they sold me the TV."

"How do you communicate?"

"Cell phone."

"Do they call you or do you call them?"

"Little of both."

"The number that you call—is it the same number or does it change?"

"The same number."

"Give it to me," I said.

She read it off her cell phone log, and I inputted it into mine.

"Ms. Hoover, after I left your office just now, did you call them?"

She didn't answer.

"That's okay," I said. "I don't mind. They probably want you to call back and tell them what I wanted. Go 'head and do that. Tell them my name is Nick Dyson, if you haven't already. Tell them I forced you to give up their cell number. Tell them that I have a mutually beneficial proposition for them and that I'll call soon to set up a meeting. Will you do that, Emily?"

She nodded.

I wanted to give her something to hang on to, words of encouragement. I wanted to let her know that it was all going to work out and that she would be okay. Yet that would have been out of character. Nick Dyson was a sonuvabitch.

I stood, put on my coat, and started for the door. If Waldo noticed that I was preparing to leave, he didn't show it.

Emily called to me.

"Why are you doing this?" she asked.

"Nothing personal, lady. It's strictly business."

You're sure it's Dyson who's the sonuvabitch, right? my inner voice asked.

Rosita called my name and gave me a hug just moments after I walked through the front door of Tres Hermanas Mexican Restaurant and Grocery. I admit it made me feel special even though I knew she greeted many of her regular customers the same way.

"*Estoy feliz de verite, mi amigo,*" she said. "*¿Cómo estás?*"

"*Bueno, bueno. ¿Cómo va el negocio?*"

Rosie flicked her hand at the nearly full restaurant behind her.

"I can' complain," she said. Which was how she always replied when someone asked how business was. Rosie can't complain. Good, bad—she was one of the Three Sisters, and she had been living the dream ever since she and her family moved to South Minneapolis from Puerto Rico thirty-five years ago. I asked her once, since she was Puerto Rican and she and her sisters served Puerto Rican food, why they called Tres Hermanas a Mexican restaurant. She said when they first immigrated, she discovered that most people in the Midwest thought Puerto Rico was in Mexico, a part of Mexico, and they didn't think it would be good business to contradict them. The customer, after all, is always right.

"Has Herzy been around?" I asked.

Rosie's eyes narrowed and she began wiping her hands on her apron even though they weren't soiled—it could have been the same apron she had been wearing when I first met her.

"I like ju," she said.

"Thank you. I like you, too."

"I like Herzy."

"I like him, too."

"Ju bad for 'im."

"Me?"

"Ju get 'im in trouble, and he been tryin' so 'ard to stay outta trouble."

"Are we talking about the same guy?"

"I mean it, Mc'enzie."

I held up both hands in surrender.

"Ningún problema, señora," I said. "I promise."

From her expression, I didn't think she believed me. Still, she led me through the gate that separated the grocery store from the restaurant. I didn't need to work hard to find him. Herzog was African American and the largest man I had ever seen in person. He made the table for four near the bar look like a TV tray. The remains of an order of fried pastry stuffed with beef and chicken and a half-finished bottle of Tecate were set in front of him. Rosie picked up the plate.

"Ju two play nice," she said before she left.

I sat at the table without asking permission.

"How you doin', Herzy?" I asked.

He reached for the Tecate and brought the bottle to his lips without removing his eyes from the Spanish-language version of *SportsCenter* playing on the TV suspended above the bar. There was no way my Spanish was good enough to watch ESPN Deportes. Herzog, though, could speak it fluently. He also loved jazz and baseball, probably the only things we had in common.

"No," he said.

"No, what?"

"No to whatever you're gonna ask."

"Herzy . . ."

"Uh-uh, McKenzie. I'm outta the life. I ain't hurtin' nobody no more."

"Who asked you to?"

Along with size, Herzog was the most dangerous man I had ever known. He'd done time for multiple counts of manslaughter, assault, aggravated robbery, and weapons charges. He'd been out on parole for two years with another three to go.

"Oh?" Herzog said. "You come here to invite me t' party at your new crib? Chopper told me about it. View of the river. Sounds nice."

"There's a couple of bucks in it."

"Don't need money. Been workin' for Chopper. Sitting at a computer terminal all day buyin' up tickets to concerts and such, then scalpin' 'em. Well, brokerin' they call it now since they made it legal."

"Sounds like a lot of fun."

"No one gets hurt, McKenzie. That's the thing."

"I'm glad you found religion, Herzy. I really am. But I need your help."

"You ain't listening, McKenzie."

"There's this girl . . ."

I explained about El, how they rolled her off the back of a pickup truck onto the freeway, how she'd gone missing. The thing about Herzog that I knew and Rosie knew and maybe one or two others knew was that, despite his checkered history, he had a kind heart.

"You're not lookin' to scramble these guys?" he asked. "Put 'em down?"

"I'm just trying to keep from getting hurt myself. Who's going to start trouble with you standing behind me looking like, well, looking like you?"

"What I like about you . . ."

I wasn't sure that you did, my inner voice said.

"What I like about you, McKenzie, you got a code. Lives by it. You tell a brother you gonna do a thing, it gets done. You tell 'im no one's gonna get shot, he believes it."

"I can only promise that I'll be the one carrying a gun, not you."

"That's good, cuz I ain't violating my parole."

"So, how 'bout it?"

"Your Nina, she took care of me that one time at Rickie's.

Cécile McLorin Salvant came to town, and she got me a table right up front, me and my date. Even introduced us after her set. That was sweet."

"She'll give you hell if something bad happens to me."

"What do you want me to do?"

I called Craig and Mitch on a $19.99 burn phone that I bought at Target—I sure as hell wasn't going to use my cell. Emily Hoover must have contacted them as I suggested, because they were waiting for the call. I told them I wanted to meet. When I gave them the choice of venue, they answered without hesitation. Red Lobster. I'm not making this up. A family restaurant surrounded by customers and an attentive waitstaff—I guess it made them feel safe. We arrived early because I wanted to feel safe, too. Herzog and I sat in the Jeep Cherokee and watched as they drove up. We could see them as they took a booth against the window in the bar.

"I don't know," Herzog said. "Is this the dumbest move I've ever seen or the smartest?"

"Dumbest. Have you eaten here?"

"What are you talkin' about? This place has great food. You just a spoiled rich boy."

Herzog might have been on to something. Eating regularly from Monica Meyer's menu at Rickie's had ruined chain restaurants for me. 'Course, I would never tell her that.

"Once the boys know that you're with me, I want you to find a place at the bar where they'll have no problem seeing you," I said. "Look menacing."

Herzog opened the door, then hesitated.

"You buyin', right?"

"Of course."

It took us less than a minute to reach the lobby. A huge door opened onto the restaurant area. A smaller door opened onto the bar. I assumed the bar was primarily for customers waiting for a table during peak hours. I mean, who drinks at the Red Lobster?

Herzog and I went into the bar. It was nearly empty. We went up to the booth where Craig and Mitch sat across from each other.

"I'm Dyson," I said. "Say hello to my little friend."

The eyes of the two young men grew wide with alarm at meeting Herzog for the first time. I might have laughed except I had seen the reaction before and I was prepared for it. Without speaking a word, Herzog retreated to the bar. He sat at the corner where Mitch and Craig could watch him watching them without turning their heads. I pulled a chair from an empty table and sat facing the booth.

"Gentlemen," I said. "You're probably wondering why I called this meeting."

Before they could reply, a waitress appeared with a pretty smile and two tap beers. She set the beers in front of the boys and pivoted toward me.

"May I get you something?" she asked.

I pointed at the tap beers.

"I'll have one of those."

"Back in a jif," she said.

The moment after she left, Mitch spoke.

"I've seen you before," he said. "Where was it?"

"I'm not here to reminisce."

"What, then?"

"I have a business proposition."

"That's what you said over the phone. How did you get our number, anyway?"

The question surprised me.

"Your contact," I said.

"What contact?" Craig asked.

I didn't know if he was playing cute or if he was genuinely mystified by my remark. Mitch reached across the table and set a hand on Craig's arm to keep him from saying more.

"What do you want, Dyson?" Mitch asked.

Before I could elaborate, the waitress reappeared carrying a tap beer that she set in front of me.

"Can I get you anything else?" she asked. "Would you like to see a menu?"

"No, we're good for now," I answered.

She left. I took a sip of the beer.

"Jeezuz, what is this?" I asked.

"It's a light beer," Craig said.

They seemed offended when I pushed the glass away.

"Where was I?" I asked.

"You said you had a business proposition," Mitch said. "Get to it."

"You're starting to annoy us," Craig said.

I turned in my seat and looked toward Herzog. The waitress was placing a platter of food in front of him.

"Hey, Herzy," I said. "They're annoyed."

"Happens all the time," he said.

I turned back.

"Contain yourselves," I said.

"What do you want?" Mitch asked.

"I have been aware for some time that you and your partners are using a floating garage sale to dispose of . . . new and used property, shall we call it that? It's also come to my attention that you're running low on inventory and have no way to replenish it. I, as luck would have it, have plenty of merchandise on hand. Unfortunately, due to circumstances beyond my control, I no longer have the means to market it."

"We don't know what you're talking about," Craig said.

"'Course you do."

"I remember now," Mitch said. "I saw you in Arden Hills. You bought a juicer."

"Think of it as a fact-finding mission."

"How do you know about the garage sales?"

"The same way I know you."

"How's that?"

I didn't answer. A wise man once said that knowledge is power. I wanted Craig and Mitch to think that I possessed more than I actually did.

"What kind of merchandise?" Craig's voice was assertive. "Be specific."

I gave him a list of products available in high-end stores.

"I don't bother with electric toothbrushes, baby formula, disposable razors—the stuff any amateur might boost," I said. "I deal only in merchandise that appeals to a discerning customer base. Like the kind you had in Woodbury, yesterday. Oh, and gentlemen—I can provide this merchandise on a regular basis."

A glance passed between the young men; they were trying hard not to smile. I was offering them exactly what they needed. They could see the future and it was bright and shiny.

"Perhaps we can do business on a trial basis," Mitch said. "If everything works out . . ."

"We need to make sure you can deliver what you promise," Craig added.

"Fair enough," I said. "I need to make sure you can deliver what I need as well."

"Apparently you're already familiar with our operation," Mitch said.

"Familiar enough to know that you lost your crew. Why was that?"

"That's none of your business."

"There's the drive-by shooting yesterday in Woodbury. You did a good job containing that, by the way."

"That's none of your business either. Once we take possession of the goods, you're out of the loop. You will not be involved in distribution."

"I'm looking for a long-term relationship. I don't want to have to find a new customer tomorrow because you don't have your shit together. More important, I don't want any of your shit blowing back on me."

"If you're afraid of doing business with us—"

This time it was Craig who reached across the table to touch his friend's arm.

"If things work out, once we know you're dependable, we can talk more," Craig said.

I knew exactly what he was thinking; I replayed the conversation he had with Mitch the day before in the back of my mind.

Maybe we should get out—like the kids.

Do you think the Boss will let us?

If we found someone to take our place . . .

I spread my hands wide as if I didn't care one way or the other.

"We would like to inspect the merchandise before we buy," Mitch said.

"Of course," I said. "I believe your next sale is Saturday in Apple Valley."

"You know a lot about our business," Craig said.

"*Our* business," I said.

"Not yet," Mitch said.

"Does Friday work?"

"Wednesday would be better."

"I'll call with a time and place. Oh, and let's keep it to ourselves. I deal with you two. I see friends or friends of friends, the deal is off."

The expression on their faces suggested that they wouldn't have it any other way.

A few moments later, they were gone. I picked up the tab for the beers and drifted to the bar and Herzog. He was eating from a platter heaped with a variety of deep-fried fish. I snatched a scallop and popped it into my mouth.

"Git your own," he said.

"That went well. See, I told you no one would get hurt."

"Where are you going to steal all that stuff you promised?"

"I'm not going to steal it. I'm going to buy it. I'm going to Mall of America for a shopping spree. After that, I'm going to Easy Cash and buy some of Lantry's merchandise, too. Want to come with? It'll be fun."

"Nah."

"You're afraid I'm going to put you to work carrying stuff."

"I'll just get in your way if I go to the mall. Security types gonna be watching me every minute I'm there, follow every step I take. Happens all the time."

"Really?"

"You okay, McKenzie, but you know nuthin' 'bout being a brother. Walk with me down the street someday and you'll hear the sound of locks clicking shut in every car I pass. People say Minnesota loaded with liberals; ain't no racism up here. C'mon. High school graduation rates for blacks is the lowest in the country. Cities got the highest economic gap between blacks and whites of all the big towns. Only six percent of the population in Minnesota is African American, except in Minnesota's prisons it's like thirty-seven percent. Think it's all a coincidence? Minnesota Nice—fuck that."

"I'm sorry, I really am," I said to be saying something and not just sitting there looking dumb. "I didn't realize."

Herzog patted my shoulder like he felt sorry for me.

"Could be worse," he said.

For two consecutive days it had been warm in Minnesota; it felt almost unnatural. Herzog and I were able to stand comfortably outside at night and lean against the hood of my rental van in the parking lot of a mini storage facility, one of those places that lease what amounts to an extra garage. My feet were warm even though the snow packed on the asphalt had turned to a thin layer of slush, and so were my ears in spite of the fact that I wasn't wearing a hat. When I took a deep breath and let it go, there wasn't even a hint of mist rising up from my mouth. I glanced at Herzog to see if he had noticed. He was busy studying his watch.

"They're late," he said.

"Actually, they're early," I said. "They drove by twice already to make sure we weren't setting an ambush."

The mini storage units were located alongside 280, the highway that more or less separated the northern reaches of St. Paul and Minneapolis. We were on the Minneapolis side, and from where we stood, we could observe the service road that provided access to the businesses located along the highway, the hill that rose up behind it, and the highway on top. Drivers pushing their vehicles along the highway could easily look down and see the storage garage as well. Which was precisely why I chose it.

I watched Mitch's car move along the service road for the third time. It slowed as if a decision had been made and pulled into the lot. Mitch maneuvered so that the vehicle was between the road and us with the nose of the car facing out. He and Craig left the car, separated, and walked toward us at angles, their hands visible and empty.

"Trusting, ain't they," Herzog said.

"Must be my frank and forthright personality."

"That's what I was thinking."

Mitch and Craig came close enough to speak without shouting and stopped. Herzog stretched, causing them both to flinch, which the big man seemed to enjoy. He folded his arms across his chest and half-closed his eyes as if he were bored. Mitch watched him intently even as he spoke to me.

"You have something for us?"

"This way," I told him.

I led Mitch and Craig to a large maroon garage door that I unlocked with a key. I rolled the door up and switched on an overhead light. Some of the merchandise was stacked on shelves provided by the storage company; the rest was displayed neatly on the floor.

"Oh my," Craig said.

Mitch gave him a sharp elbow in the ribs; I presume he was afraid that Craig's exclamation would raise my price.

Shopping had been much harder than I expected. Nina and I hit the Mall of America at nine thirty in the morning when most of its stores opened and had kept at it until I reached my twenty-thousand-dollar limit at about eight that evening. 'Course, we had to pause for lunch. And dinner. And then there was all that time we spent hauling merchandise to the van I had rented and parked in the north garage—the mall's five hundred and twenty stores were scattered over ninety-six acres, and moving between them wasn't exactly a walk in the park. Well, actually, it was more like a walk in several parks.

Between the two of us we covered most of the upscale stores from Abercrombie & Fitch to Zales, with visits in between at Aveda, the Gap, Macy's, Old Navy, Aéropostale, Ann Taylor, Best Buy, Helzberg Diamonds, Kay Jewelers, Rogers & Hollands, Swarovski, Williams-Sonoma, and the Apple Store. Suspicious store managers asked us what we were doing. We told them we were shopping for a charity auction. They thought that was generous of us, yet kept checking our identities against our credit cards just the same. Twice I had to talk to my bank, carefully answering its security questions to prove I wasn't ripping myself off (which I appreciated very much, although it was a pain in the ass). Even without Herzog present, security guards swarmed us. I anticipated their interest and brought my passport along. Nina thought I was being silly. "Who brings their passport to the Mall of America?" she asked. Turned out, lots of people. Most from outside the country, but still . . .

That was Tuesday. On Wednesday, I brought the van to Easy Cash and bought a couple thousand dollars' worth of Marshall Lantry's better merchandise. Now it was all carefully arranged in the garage, which was rented, by the way, under Nick Dyson's name.

Mitch and Craig perused each product carefully—HDTVs,

laptops, designer clothes, gourmet cookware, high-end cosmetics, and just about everything else that Nina and I thought was worth stealing. I had left the price tags whenever possible, yet had been keen on removing any and all receipts.

"I have to admit," Mitch said, "I'm impressed."

"We aim to please," I said. "Oh, one more thing."

I directed their attention to a box on the shelf near the light switch. Craig opened the box and discovered an eighteen-inch Japanese Akoya pearl necklace with an eighteen-karat white gold clasp. He showed it to his partner. Mitch's eyes lit up like he was gazing at the Holy Grail.

"How much?" he asked.

"Eighteen," I replied. "For the lot."

"Don't be ridiculous. Five."

"Now who's being ridiculous? Sixteen."

"This is a business. We're trying to make a profit. Eight and a half."

"Fourteen. And I'll throw the pearls in for free."

"Who are you kidding? Ten."

"Twelve—but only because we're doing business for the first time. Don't expect me to be this generous in the future."

"Done."

"I presume you have the cash on you?"

"C'mon, Dyson," Craig said. "Who carries that kind of money?"

"You had better be."

"Yes, we have the money," Mitch said.

He stared at Craig as if wondering what he had missed. Craig gestured with his head at Herzog, who had moved to the mouth of the garage. I did a little gesturing myself, and Herzog retreated back to the rental van. Craig let out a nervous sigh.

"Just a sec," Mitch said.

He and Craig returned to their own vehicle and popped the trunk. At the same time, I closed the door to the storage unit and locked it. I turned from the unit and crossed the parking lot, key in hand. Mitch slammed the trunk lid closed and started toward me. He was carrying a wad of bills held together by a thick rubber band.

"Pleasure doing business with you, Dyson," he said.

Above us on the highway, I watched a car slow until it came nearly to a stop.

"Get down," I yelled.

At the same time, I grabbed Mitch by the shoulder and pulled him to the asphalt.

Craig was standing next to Mitch's vehicle. He turned to see what I had been looking at.

Muzzle flashes appeared in the rear passenger window of the car on the hill, followed almost simultaneously by the pop-pop-pop of a semiautomatic.

Craig dove behind the vehicle even as the bullets tore into its body and splashed off the asphalt.

Out of the corner of my eye, I could see Herzog crouching next to the rental like a basketball coach anxious to see how well his team executed the play he had just choreographed.

I pulled out the nine-millimeter SIG Sauer that had been holstered to my right hip, but that was mostly for show.

The shooting stopped as abruptly as it began.

The car on the highway sped off.

A kind of unhealthy silence fell across the parking lot.

"What the hell was that?" I asked.

Mitch hopped to his feet and dashed across the lot to Craig's side.

"Are you okay?" he asked.

Craig rose slowly, brushing the slush off his knees. At the same time, I turned toward my own partner.

"You okay, Herzog?" I said.

He grunted his reply.

"Who were those guys?" I asked.

"I don't know," Mitch said.

"What do you mean, you don't know?"

"This had nothing to do with us."

"What are you talking about? You get a drive-by at your garage sale Sunday and now this? Of course it's all about you."

"No one knew we were going to be here," Mitch insisted. "Just Craig and I knew we were going to be here."

"Then you must have been followed, because it sure as hell wasn't me."

Mitch and Craig stared at each other as if they were running different equations yet coming up with the same solution.

"Gentlemen," I said. "I told you before I didn't want your crap coming back on me."

"We can fix this."

"Fix it, then, because if you don't, I'll find someone else to do business with."

"Don't worry about it."

"Yeah, right. Give me my money."

Mitch handed over the wad of bills. I gave him the key to the storage unit in return.

"Is your car good to drive?" I asked.

Mitch got behind the wheel and started it up while Craig looked beneath it.

"I don't see anything leaking," he said.

"I'll call you later," I said.

Craig climbed into the vehicle, and he and his partner drove off. I drifted back to the rental. As I did, I counted out a number of bills from the wad Mitch had given me.

"Was that necessary?" Herzog asked.

"I want to keep them motivated." I handed the bills to him. "For your friends."

"Much obliged."

"Tell them the next time I say use fucking blanks they had better use fucking blanks."

"They couldn't find any."

"What do you mean they couldn't find any?"

"No one carries them. I can get you armor-piercing rounds for a .50 caliber machine gun, but man, go into a gun shop and ask for blanks sometime. Man looks at you like you're up to no good."

TWELVE

I don't like funerals. But then, who does? Funerals for young people are the worst. It's as if we're not only burying them, we're burying the future—theirs and ours. We're interring everything that might have been. Oliver Braun's parents, for example. They weren't just saying good-bye to their son, they were laying to rest all the hopes and dreams they'd ever had for him, as well as the daughter-in-law they'd never meet, the grandchildren they'd never see, the continuation of their line, the remembrance of their name, the world made better by their heirs. The fact he died not of accident or illness but by the hand of an unknown other only made it more unbearable. There was no celebration of life. Only a deep mourning of loss. And the question—why?

There was no graveside ceremony, which would have been unendurable in the polar vortex that enveloped the Twin Cities— yes, another one. Oliver's parents chose cremation instead, so following the church service, mourners gathered in the church's large community room, where an early lunch was served mostly by relatives glad to be doing something besides just sitting there feeling sad.

Nearly everyone present had been drawn to the funeral out of love for Oliver or some other personal connection, and most embraced the attitude that if you were a friend of his then you were a friend of mine, at least for the morning. At the same time, cliques formed. Close family members settled in one area, extended family in another, and friends, classmates, and co-workers in yet others. A group of college-age kids banded together around a cafeteria table far from Oliver's parents as if they wanted to grieve their loss but didn't want to share their profound pain. I took my plate of sliced ham on a bun, potato salad, and three-bean casserole and sidled up next to them. No one questioned my presence in word or manner. Perhaps they thought I was one of Oliver's college professors. Conversation whirled around me.

"I can't believe it's so cold."

"I guess the medical examiner wouldn't release his body. That's why it took so long—the funeral. Said he had to maintain control of the remains until the forensic work was completed."

"That means they cut him up, doesn't it?"

"I thought we had turned the corner."

"What was Oliver even doing in Highland Park? Does anyone know?"

"The cops aren't saying."

"That's cuz they don't have a clue."

"It'll never be spring. We're gonna go from winter straight to summer."

"I just hate it."

"What do you hate?"

"Everything."

I spoke as casually as I could. "I'm surprised El isn't here."

"Where is El, anyway?"

"She moved back home after she and Oliver broke up."

"Some cop from St. Paul asked about her."

"What did you say?"

"That she moved back home after she and Oliver broke up."

"Who's El?"

"Girl Oliver met at a bar in Dinkytown."

"Is she a student?"

"No, but holy mackerel is she pretty. Long blond hair . . ."

"She was crazy about him."

"Do they think she did it, the cops?"

"Who knows with cops?"

"I heard the high tomorrow is supposed to be forty-eight degrees."

"I heard it was going to snow."

"You'd think she'd come back for this, breakup or not."

"Would you stop talking about the damn weather?"

"She might not even know what happened."

"He liked older women."

"Who?"

"Oliver. He broke up with El because he liked older women."

"You're crazy."

"I bet the Twins wish they had built a roof on Target Field now."

"You're worse than Mark Twain, always complaining about the weather, yet never doing anything about it."

"He was seeing an older woman. It's true."

"Mark Twain?"

"Wait. What?"

"Her."

A finger was pointed at a woman dressed in a black wool coat and a black short-brimmed cloche hat with a red-ribbon hatband and side bow. She was hugging Oliver's parents each in turn.

It's the femme fatale from Woodbury, my inner voice reminded me.

"Who is she?" someone asked.

"Ramsey County Commissioner Merle Mattson."

"The woman he worked for over the summer?"

"Here I thought it was an unpaid internship."

"Stop it."

"If you want to fuck a MILF, that's the MILF to fuck."

"She's not a mother. She's not even married."

"That takes some of the fun out of it."

"You two are disgusting."

"Did you tell the cops?"

"Cops didn't ask."

"How come it's okay for an old man to sleep with a young woman yet people go crazy when an old woman sleeps with a young man?"

"How old is she?"

"Old enough to know better; young enough not to care."

"Stop it. I mean it this time."

I drifted away from the kids.

There was a table loaded with soiled plates, so I added mine to the pile. I moved to a different table closer to the door and found a seat. I wanted to be in position to intercept the commissioner when she left the gathering, even though I was unsure how to approach her. Asking why she didn't tell the police she was sleeping with Oliver came to mind. Simply blurting out the question seemed combative, however, and if she was any kind of politician, she'd know how to deal with it. At the same time, the fact she was a politician made gaining her trust, her confidence, problematic at best.

It was because of the internal debate that I didn't feel Jean Shipman's presence until she pulled the chair next to me out from under the table and sat down.

"What are you doing here, McKenzie?" she asked.

"Apparently the same thing you are, Detective."

"Shhhh."

"You don't want the mourners to know a police officer is hanging around, conducting surveillance, hoping to see or hear something that'll help close the case?"

"Quiet."

"I'm sure the family would embrace you heartily, especially since you already arrested the suspect who killed their child—oh, wait."

"That's what I mean."

We sat silently, Shipman surreptitiously scanning the guests while I more or less studied the county commissioner. A college-age kid thought she was old. I was twice his age and I disagreed. Older, maybe, but old? Her eyes were bright, and the lines on her face looked as if a very considerate and generous sculptor etched them there. When she opened her coat, she revealed a body that was familiar with exercise, and when she removed her hat I saw waves of red-brown hair without a hint of gray—whoever colored it had done an expert job. She appeared to be taller than I was, but that might have been the heels on her black dress boots talking.

A late mourner arrived; a burst of icy wind followed him inside the room, causing those of us closest to the door to revolve in our seats to gaze at him. He was young, tall, and thin, with brown hair, and he wore sunglasses and a neutral expression. He walked with a limp.

He stopped just inside the doorway and glanced about, his head rotating slowly as if on a swivel—just like it had at the garage sale. Now, as then, I didn't think he was looking for anything specific, just getting the lay of the land, as it were, until he found the county commissioner, and his head stopped turning. At the same time, Mattson saw him. She closed her eyes and opened them again as if she were hoping he was a mirage that would vanish as quickly as he appeared. When he didn't, she deliberately involved herself in the conversation of the mourners around her, pretending he wasn't there. He found an empty table and moved to it, all the while watching the commissioner as if afraid he'd lose sight of her. He unzipped his coat, yet did not remove it; nor did he take off his gloves.

"I've done this many times," Shipman said. "Intruding on the grief of a victim's family, and nothing good has ever come of it. How 'bout you?"

"You mean besides today?"

"Do you have something to say, McKenzie? Or are you just giving me the business, as usual?"

"The man who just walked in—see him sitting there, blue-green jacket?"

"What about him?"

"He's the one that was shot in the leg Sunday at the Woodbury garage sale."

"I don't believe it."

"What's not to believe?"

"That you would actually be useful to me. What's he doing here?"

"No idea."

"Name?"

"Peter Troop."

"And you know this—how?"

"I'm psychic."

"Yeah, well, when you see a pig fly you're not disappointed if it doesn't stay airborne all that long."

"Are you calling me a pig?"

"You take the right, I'll take the left."

Shipman and I moved to the table where Troop was sitting. As instructed, I sat in the chair to his immediate right, Shipman to his left.

"Terrible tragedy, isn't it," Shipman said. "A boy so young."

If Troop was surprised by the intrusion, he didn't show it.

"Did you know Oliver personally or are you just a friend of the family?" I asked.

Only his head turned, looking first at Shipman, at me, and back to her again.

"Are you trying to kid me?" he asked.

"Do we look like we're kidding?" Shipman asked.

"Leave me alone."

"Seriously," I said. "Who crashes a funeral? The food is lousy."

"If you're not a friend of Oliver or his family, why are you here?" Shipman said.

"Who wants to know?" Troop asked.

Shipman gave him a look at her badge, neatly cupped in her hand so no one else could see. He stiffened at the sight of it.

Dammit, she's leaving, my inner voice warned.

I had been half-watching the county commissioner while I sat with Troop and Shipman. She seized my full attention when Mattson replaced her hat, buttoned her coat, made her good-byes, and headed for the door. I wanted to follow her, yet I was committed to Shipman's play.

"I didn't do anything," Troop said.

"No one said you did, Peter," Shipman told him.

Troop's eyes widened with alarm at the sound of his own name. "You can't arrest me," he said.

"Why would I want to?"

"I just came in to get warm."

"As good an excuse as any."

"What do you want from me?"

"Let's go outside and chat for a sec."

"Why should I?"

I set my hand on his outer thigh about six inches above his knee and pressed down hard.

"Because it's so much easier than the alternative," I said.

Troop winced in pain and knocked my hand away. Afterward, he rested his hand on his thigh and rubbed gently.

"That hurts," he said.

"I bet it hurt a lot worse last Sunday when you were shot."

He stopped moving—except for his head, which jerked toward me.

"Do you wear sunglasses indoors because your eyes are sensitive to light or because you're the worst poker player in the world?" I asked him.

"C'mon, Peter," Shipman said. "We don't want to disturb the mourners."

She stood and I stood, and after a moment's reflection, Troop stood as well. We turned in unison and headed for the door. Troop zipped his coat shut. And then he did something that should have tripped all of my internal alarm systems, yet didn't, probably because I was busy tending to my own jacket—he removed the glove from his right hand.

Shipman held the door open for him. He stepped across the threshold, she followed him, and I followed her. We were immediately assaulted by frigid air and hard wind, yet Troop didn't seem to notice. He tramped angrily down the sidewalk away from the door until he reached the edge of the parking lot.

"That's far enough," Shipman said.

Troop stood on the edge of the curb and gazed out at the lot. I had no idea who or what he was looking for. I thought for a moment that Mitch and Craig or even John Kispert might have been out there. If they were, I didn't see them.

"Let's see some ID," Shipman said.

"You have no business harassing me."

Troop made no move to fetch his wallet, nor did he turn to face us. Instead, he hid his hands in front of his body and tilted his head as if he were trying to locate us in his peripheral vision. He adjusted his stance, dropping his right foot back slightly, preparing to turn.

Troop's words, the sound of his voice, and the posture of his body caused Shipman and me to react the same way. She moved slowly to his right while dropping her hand into the open bag hanging from a strap over her shoulder. I went to his left, unzipping my jacket as I went. Our field training officers would have been proud.

"I didn't do nothing," Troop said.

"It's okay, Peter." Shipman's voice was soothing, almost maternal. "Relax. We're just talking here."

"You got no right."

"Nothing bad is going to happen today."

"I just wanted to get out of the cold."

"Let me see your hands."

Troop screamed—it wasn't a word, just a bunch of consonants strung together. His ungloved right hand pulled a knife from under his left sleeve. The blade was thin but long. He pivoted toward Shipman. She lifted a Glock from her bag and brought it up swiftly with both hands.

"No, no, no," she chanted.

Troop brought the knife up as if he were going to throw it.

She sighted on his chest.

Troop ceased moving.

By then I had a gun in my hands as well.

Like Shipman, I was in a Weaver stance, the sights of the SIG Sauer settled on his core.

"Please drop the knife." Shipman's words were consolatory, yet there was no mistaking the command in her voice.

"It wasn't my fault," Troop said.

"Please. Drop. The knife."

I couldn't see his eyes because of the sunglasses, and I wanted desperately to see his eyes. I was sure they would tell me what he was thinking.

Shipman screamed at him. "Drop the fucking knife."

Troop flinched as if he were startled.

He opened his hand.

The knife slipped out.

It bounced against the concrete sidewalk at his feet.

Thank God, my inner voice said.

"I'm sorry," Troop said.

Shipman gasped like a woman who had been holding her breath for far too long.

"Step away from the knife," she said.

And we heard the crack of a rifle shot.

Troop's chest exploded outward.

We were showered with his blood.

All in the same instant.

It took a moment before Shipman and I realized what had happened. When we did, we both dove to the ground. I ended up on the asphalt parking lot. Shipman found a mound of snow. I thought I heard the sound of a car driving off in the distance, yet I would never be sure. I crawled forward until I was behind an SUV. I came up and searched the lot behind the sights of the SIG. Shipman rolled to her right, went to her feet, and dashed behind a different car. She held her Glock steady with one hand while fumbling for her phone with the other. At the same time, she turned her head to look at Troop, sprawled face first on the sidewalk. He was still wearing his sunglasses. The warmth of his body escaped through the wound in his back and mixed with the cold air, creating a mist. Instead of floating upward, though, it was snatched away by the wind.

None of the mourners had come to the heavy door or windows. They didn't yet know what had happened. Hell, I didn't know what had happened. I heard Shipman speaking into her cell.

"Shots fired. Officer needs assistance."

She kept staring at Troop's body.

To this day I have no idea what she was thinking.

Shipman got her task force after all.

Nine people crowded into the small conference room. Bobby stood at the head of the table. I sat against the back wall and tried to make myself invisible.

Little Canada was an inner ring suburb with a population of just under ten thousand people. It didn't have its own police department. Instead, emergency calls were answered by the Ramsey County Sheriff's Department, whose deputies were the first to arrive at the scene. That was several hours ago. Now we were all gathered in the James S. Griffin Building, headquarters to the St. Paul Police Department, located northeast of downtown. It was part of the Ramsey County—St. Paul Criminal Justice Campus, which also included the Ramsey County Law Enforcement Center and the Adult Detention Center. It was a fifteen-minute trip for Detective John Luby and his partner from the Minneapolis Police Department. Everyone else just walked across the parking lot.

"Okay," Bobby said. "What do we have? Keith."

Keith was a firearms examiner—actually a forensic scientist who specialized in firearms and tool marks for the Minnesota Bureau of Criminal Apprehension. Minneapolis and Hennepin County had their own examiners, but St. Paul farmed the work out to the BCA.

"The bullet passed through our victim and pancaked on the concrete," Keith said. "We tried to pull it apart, but . . . We can tell you it was a caliber .30-06, the same as the round that killed the victim in Minneapolis. It was so badly damaged, though, that we can't identify the specific manufacturer or say conclusively that it was fired from the same weapon."

"Okay, you're no good to me. Doctor?"

The assistant Ramsey County medical examiner stood and cleared his throat as if he were about to deliver a lecture to a roomful of premed students.

"As requested, we compared our measurements of the wounds suffered by Oliver Braun—our victim in Highland Park—against the size and shape of the blade of the knife that was recovered in Little Canada," he said. "After careful analysis, we have concluded that they are consistent."

"Are you saying it's a definite match?" Bobby asked.

"It's never definite, Bobby. You know that. However, we did find a trace amount of blood on the hilt. Give me seventy-two hours and I will give you a profile."

"Make it forty-eight."

"Seventy-two, and that's with someone working it full time."

The ME sat down. He seemed disappointed there wasn't applause.

"Okay. Deputy Sergeant?"

The deputy sergeant was a member of the General Investigations Unit of the Ramsey County Sheriff's Department. The department didn't get many murders. It investigated only those committed in the seven small contract cities like Little Canada for which it was paid to provide services, so I was a little surprised that someone with a higher rank wasn't in the conference room acting all large and emphatic.

"We canvassed the area, interviewed the mourners," said the sergeant. "No witnesses. The church had never installed security cameras, so there's no film to look at either. My deputies did find a shell casing at the far end of the parking lot. Federal .30-06."

"Ahh," said Keith.

"We sent it to your office. You should have it by now."

"Ahh," said Keith again.

"Prints?" Bobby asked.

"We lifted a partial," the sergeant said. "That's why it took so long to get it to the BCA. Not enough points to run it through the system, though."

"Did you find any brass at the first shooting?"

Bobby was speaking to Luby, who squirmed slightly in his chair.

"No," he said.

"Did you look?"

"I—I don't know. There was a lot of snow."

"Okay."

"I'll get someone back out there with a metal detector."

"Okay."

"In the meantime, we've been trying to work up a history on Karl Olson, our victim," Luby said. "So far with little success. We don't know much more about him than what we found in his wallet. Family, friends, who he worked for, where he's from—nothing. So far. We've also been trying to get a line on the kids who lived in the duplex. We know a great deal about them except, well, where they are at the present time. I went up to Deer River myself. I was able to confirm everything that McKenzie told us. Beyond that . . ."

"Okay. Jeannie."

Shipman had a notebook open in front of her. She knew this moment would come and had prepared what to say. She spoke of the flyers that were found in the duplex and the garage sales that they led her to. She related her suspicions that the sales were a front for a shoplifting and burglary ring and that they were operated by two young men named Craig and Mitch—that was all the ID she had—and that Ella Elbers had been tentatively linked to them. She said she was sure that Peter Troop was also involved in the garage sales and that he had been shot in the leg during a drive-by shooting on Sunday.

"So that's where the wound came from," the ME said.

But, Shipman said, she had no information about the shooters or their motives.

"Could the drive-by shooter in Woodbury and the sniper in Little Canada be the same person?" the deputy sergeant asked.

"My opinion, I want to say no," Shipman said. "Unfortunately, I have nothing to base it on except that the sniper seems very competent and the drive-by shooter not so much."

"Let's assume for a moment that the blood on Troop's knife matches Braun's . . ."

"Unless the good doctor tells us otherwise," Bobby said.

"That raises the question—what the hell was Troop doing at the kid's funeral?"

"I don't know," Shipman said.

"Guilty conscience," said a second deputy. "He did say he was sorry."

"Puhleez," said Luby's partner.

"My question," said Luby. "McKenzie, what were you doing at the funeral?"

"McKenzie," Bobby said, "speak up."

I felt a twinge of panic when the room full of officers turned their undivided attention on me. I sat straighter in my chair.

"I'm trying to find Ella Elbers," I said. "With permission from the commander." I added that last part to remind Bobby that I wouldn't be there at all if he hadn't sent El to my condominium in the first place. "I went to the funeral in case she showed up."

"Why would she?" Luby asked.

"She and Oliver Braun used to date. They broke up around Christmas. Braun's friends at the funeral, none of them have seen her since."

"Why did they break up?"

My shrug didn't satisfy anybody.

"What else can you tell us?" Bobby asked.

I had seen the look in Bobby's eyes before. He was wondering how much of what I had told him was the truth and how much wasn't. He was also debating whether or not I was holding out on him, and given our past history, he was leaning heavily toward not. I needed to give him something more. If I didn't, two things were going to happen. Thing one—his anger would probably reach biblical proportions. I didn't mind that so much. It wouldn't be the first time he was upset with me, and after all these years, I figured our friendship could withstand pretty much anything—after all, I was best man at his wedding and godfather to his eldest daughter, and his daughters were heirs to my estate, such as it was. But thing two—he'd cut me off from the investigation now and forever, and I didn't want that.

I reached into my wallet and removed the sheet of paper that Smith, the security guard at my condominium, had given me. I unfolded it and set it on the conference room table. It was passed from one hand to another until it reached Bobby.

"Mitchell Bosland," I said. "From Rochester, Minnesota. El made a reference to him on her Facebook page. He's one of the three men operating the garage sales, as Detective Shipman said earlier. The sheet contains all of his driver's license information."

"McKenzie," Shipman said, "why didn't you tell me?"

"Honestly, Detective, I thought you already knew."

What a liar you are, my inner voice said.

From her expression, whatever earlier opinion Shipman held of me took a catastrophic nosedive. I thought she was about to give me an idea of how much it had sunk when Bobby interrupted her.

"What else?" he asked. His voice made it clear that I had better have something else.

"The second man is named Craig. I don't have a last name, but I'm sure he's from Rochester, too."

"And . . ."

"And the third man is named John Kispert. I know nothing about him, although I'm pretty sure he operates the home and garage burglary end of things."

I heard Shipman's harsh whisper—"Bastard."

"Okay," Bobby said. He passed the sheet to Shipman and started assigning tasks to nearly everyone in the room. When he finished, he announced, "First priority—Karl Olson, Oliver Braun, Peter Troop. Somehow, somewhere their lives collided. Connect the dots, people."

The officers made ready to evacuate the conference room, but he halted them.

"Up until now we've been able to operate below the radar," he said. "That's going to change. A murder suspect killed at the funeral of his alleged victim—you know the media's going to be all over this one. No leaks. I mean it. I want this case airtight. Any journalists start asking questions, you refer them to me."

"Especially if the reporter is Kelly Bressandes," Keith said.

The remark caused a snicker to ripple through the room. Bressandes had the nicest legs and best come-hither smile on local TV.

"Damn right," Bobby said. "If anyone is going to give Bressandes an exclusive, it's going to be me."

The ME slapped Bobby on the shoulder as he passed out of the room. "Rank does have its privileges," he said.

I was the last to leave. Bobby intercepted me at the door.

"McKenzie, do you know why I let Shipman take the lead on this investigation instead of doing it myself?" he asked.

"Because you're a desk-bound bureaucrat?" I said.

"It's because I didn't want to put you in a position where you would lie to my face. And I didn't want to put myself in a position where I would have to do something about it."

"I understand."

"Do you?"

"Shipman knows everything that I know."

"See, that's exactly what I mean."

"Trust me, Bobby."

"Uh-huh. One more thing. If you tell Shelby what I said about Kelly Bressandes, I will shoot you where you stand."

THIRTEEN

Later that evening, I went to Rickie's. Joey DeFrancesco and his trio had just begun their first set in the upstairs performance hall—I could hear his Hammond B-3 organ singing—yet instead of listening, I went to Nina's office. I knocked on the door and stepped inside without waiting for permission. Nina was sitting at her small desk, her feet up, and drinking Scotch. She did not look happy.

"What happened?" I asked.

"You don't know? It's been on the news."

The shooting, my inner voice said.

"Yeah, I know," I said.

I sat in the chair opposite her. She studied me long enough for it to become uncomfortable.

"What?" I asked.

"You were there."

"How do you know?"

"You were standing close when it happened. That's why you have bloodstains on your new jacket, isn't it? Because you were so close when it happened."

I hadn't noticed the stains.

"I have some old jackets I can wear," I said.

"Do you want to talk about it?" Nina asked.

"Not particularly."

"So, what else is new?"

"Talking won't change anything."

"It always makes me feel better."

"It just makes me feel sad."

"That's because you think Fifteen did it. You like her, and it bothers you to think she killed that man. Him and the one in Minneapolis."

"You like her, too. If I recall, you said you wanted to adopt her."

"I still don't believe she did it."

"Why are you drinking alone in your office, then?"

Nina didn't reply.

"I don't know what I think," I told her.

"McKenzie, there were three men in that truck. If it is Fifteen, and I'm not saying it is, but if she is trying to get revenge on the men who hurt her, who dumped her on the freeway— there's one left."

"At least one. If it was a man. We don't know for sure."

"Who?"

"I have no idea. Maybe Kispert."

"Should we warn him?"

"Do you think he needs warning?"

Nina took a long pull of her Scotch.

"It's my own fault," she said. "I wanted to involve myself in your adventures. Before that, I hardly ever drank. Now look at me."

"Do you have any more of that?"

She did. We sat together drinking silently.

"Oh, I forgot to tell you," Nina said. "I received an e-mail just before you walked in."

"From whom?"

"Our friend Mitch. Actually, it wasn't just to me. It was to his entire mailing list. The garage sale set for Saturday in Apple Valley? Postponed indefinitely."

"I was afraid something like this would happen. With all the heat from the shooting, they decided to go dark. I bet Shipman has Mitch under the bright lights even as we speak."

"Forgetting the mixed metaphors—you sold him twenty-four thousand dollars' worth of merchandise for fifty cents on the dollar."

"It was my money."

"We're not going to have that discussion right now, the one about joining our finances. The point is, the investment was supposed to tie us in with these guys, right? Get us close so we can find out if they're the ones that tried to kill El and then decide what to do about it. Now what?"

"I don't know."

"I thought you had a plan?"

"Can't imagine what gave you that idea."

We drank some more.

"Do you want to go upstairs and listen to Joey?" Nina asked.

"Actually, I was thinking of taking you home."

We started making out before we even opened the door. Nina had her hands around my neck and was nibbling my ear—which I really, really liked—while I fumbled with my key card, trying to slip it into the lock. I realized that we were on camera; Smith and Jones were probably watching us on their security monitor. I didn't care.

They said they were bored, my inner voice reminded me.

I managed to open the door and we spilled into the condominium. I closed the door and had Nina pressed back against it. My fingers were working the buttons of her long coat. I stopped when I heard what sounded like a polka played on a xylophone.

"What the hell?" I said.

"Is that you?" Nina asked.

"No, that's not—wait." I rummaged through my pockets until I found the burn phone I had used to contact Mitch. Now he was trying to contact me. I pressed the button that allowed the cell to accept the call.

"This is Dyson," I said.

Nina's eyes grew wide at the name.

"Dyson, this is Mitch."

"I was just going to call you," I said. "What's this shit I hear about you canceling the garage sale? I told you I need a reliable distributor."

"That's why I called. I'd like to meet with you. You and Mr. Herzog."

I flinched at the sound of his name. Nina must have noticed, because she leaned toward me, a concerned expression on her face.

You used Herzog's name at the storage garage, my inner voice told me. *Damn, he's going to be pissed.*

Mitch filled in the silence that followed.

"We checked you out, you and Mr. Herzog," he said. "We believe you can help us."

"Help you what?"

"That's what we want to meet about."

"When?"

"Now, if it's convenient."

I was watching Nina when I answered.

"It is most certainly not convenient," I said.

I agreed to meet him anyway. Nina leaned away from me after I finished the call and folded her arms across her chest, a defensive gesture.

"Dyson?" she said. "Nick Dyson?"

"Yeah, about that . . ."

"I need another drink."

Herzog was even more unhappy than Nina, especially when I explained that Craig and Mitch knew his name and apparently accessed his record. It took a lot of fast talking and the guarantee of a sizable payday to convince him to accompany me to the meeting. Even so, he remained in a foul mood. When we arrived at Cafe Latté, a gourmet cafeteria specializing in exotic desserts located in St. Paul, he marched to the table where Mitch and Craig were nursing coffees and announced, "I don't like to drink caffeine at night, it keeps me awake." From the expression on their faces, you'd have thought he threatened to set them both on fire.

"I'm sorry, Mr. Herzog," Craig said. "They serve—I could get you green tea. That has only a little caffeine."

"Japanese cherry," Herzog said. "With honey. And while you're at it, I could use a slice of that raspberry torte they got."

Craig was quick to his feet, pausing only long enough to ask, "Mr. Dyson?"

Mister, my inner voice said. *I like that. Means they're frightened or impressed, probably both.*

"I'm good," I said aloud.

We remained at the small table while Craig left to serve Herzog. I said, "What do you want?" Mitch said, "We should wait," even as he gestured toward his partner's empty chair. So we did. Quietly. Meanwhile, a steady stream of customers flowed around our table as if it were an obstacle in a creek. No doubt that's why Craig and Mitch chose the place, I told myself—for its loud, crowded, and breezy atmosphere. As for me, I prefer privacy when I conspire to commit a major felony.

The wait was long enough that Mitch grew restless.

"We Googled you," Mitch said, just to make conversation. "Both of you. Is your name really Glen?"

"Think that makes me happy?" Herzog said. "You checking up on me?"

"I was just saying . . ."

"You call me Glen again, I'll fuck you up."

"Yes, sir. Sorry, Mr. Herzog."

"Fuck the Internet."

Mitch avoided Herzog's stare after that. He found my face. He smiled slightly as if he were hoping to find an ally. I glared at him.

You don't see me calling him Glen, do you, numb nuts? my inner voice said.

Mitch looked away.

Craig returned a few minutes later. He served Herzog from a plastic tray.

"Will there be anything else, sir?" Craig asked.

Herzog sipped the tea while Craig hovered above him.

"You waiting for a tip?" Herzog asked.

"No. No, no." Craig sat down, setting the tray in front of him. "No."

"Start talking," I said.

"We have been forced to suspend operations," Mitch said. "We won't resume until . . . until certain matters are dealt with."

"What matters?"

"The police are onto us."

Herzog spoke around a forkful of raspberry torte.

"What do you mean, us?" he said.

"Us, us," Mitch said. "Well, not you. I mean us."

"Better not be me."

"What happened?" I asked.

"A St. Paul detective named Shipman brought me in for an interview. She wanted to know about the garage sales. I don't think she had any evidence, and I gave her nothing. Kispert, he didn't say anything either."

"Who's Kispert?" I knew the answer, but Dyson didn't.

"John Kispert," Mitch said.

"He's our . . . associate," Craig said.

"The detective didn't arrest either of us, so we figure we're okay. But now that we know they're looking . . ."

"Why are they looking?" I asked.

Both Mitch and Craig took a deep breath and exhaled slowly. It was as if they had practiced together.

"There have been . . . incidents involving a former employee," Mitch said. "Things that have nothing to do with you."

"Then why am I here?" Herzog asked.

"We're hoping you can help us," Craig said.

"Help you what?" I asked.

"The former employee, a woman, a girl really, she needs to be found," Mitch said. "She needs to be . . ."

"Dealt with?"

"Uh-huh."

"We should start at the beginning," Craig said.

"They don't need to know all that."

"You're right, you're right."

"No, you ain't," Herzog said. "You wouldn'ta called us here unless you want us to do somethin' untoward."

Untoward? my inner voice said. *Herzy, listen to you.*

"We won't even consider it unless we know everything," Herzog said. "We don't walk into a room without our eyes wide open." The big man pivoted in his chair to look at me. "Right?"

He seemed so earnest it was all I could do to keep from laughing.

"Eyes wide open," I said.

"You got till I finish my torte," Herzog said. "I eat fast."

Mitch and Craig both took another deep breath and exhaled, except this time they were out of sync.

"The girl is named Ella Elbers," Mitch said. "El for short. She was part of our crew—"

"Your crew of shoplifters," I said.

"Yes. She was very good at it, too. A real professional. But she found out that we—not us, not Craig and me, but our associates, Kispert and the Boss—they were blackmailing some of our customers."

"Wait," Herzog said. "The Boss? Who the hell is the Boss?"

Craig looked down at Herzog's plate. He seemed relieved that the big man had stopped eating.

"We don't know," he said.

Dammit.

"That requires explanation," I said aloud.

"It has nothing to do with what we're asking," Mitch said.

Herzog pointed two fingers at his own eyes, pointed them at Mitch's, and repeated the gesture a couple more times.

"We maintain a list of customers, an e-mail list," Mitch said. "Someone on the list, we don't know who, sent us a message over a year ago saying we had a business rival, but not to worry. The sender, whoever he was, said he could arrange a merger of our operations, combining our resources, so that instead of competing for customers we would both profit by appealing to the same customer base. He said he could also furnish security as well as rotating venues, which would make it more difficult for the cops to catch us—all this in exchange for a third of the take. The e-mail was very convincing. Anyway, the sender—he signed the e-mail as the Boss—brought us together, and yeah, it worked out pretty well. Even though we've never met. We'd get the location for the garage sales a week in advance by e-mail and snail-mail his share to a PO box. It went great. Until we discovered that both Kispert and the Boss were targeting some of our customers for blackmail."

"Women," Craig said. "Usually women who were single. Always women who were vulnerable because of what they did for a living."

"Buying stolen property, what is that?" Mitch said. "You get caught, most of the time it doesn't amount to much more than a fine. For some women, though, women who have jobs that require them to be above reproach . . ."

"Teachers. Ministers. Lawyers."

"Women whose careers would be totally screwed if they were

arrested, if news got out that they knowingly bought stolen property—yeah, they pay."

"Like a real estate agent?" I asked. "Someone who's invited into people's homes?"

Both Mitch and Craig seemed confused.

"I suppose," Mitch said.

You suppose?

"Anyway, El discovered what was going on," Mitch said. "She found out before we did."

"She's the one who told us," Craig said.

"She said that boosting overpriced iPods was one thing, but this was where she drew the line. She said if we didn't stop, she'd rat out the entire operation."

"We were upset, too," Craig said. "It wasn't what we signed up for, either. You should know that."

Why should I know that? Are you trying to assuage your guilt?

"We confronted Kispert," Mitch said.

About the blackmail or El?

"He told us he'd take care of it."

"Take care of it," Craig repeated.

"We convinced ourselves that he meant to frighten her. Make El rethink her position. When she disappeared, we figured his threats must have worked, that she took off. Maybe she went home, we thought. Only I have people up there who could check, and she never . . . After a while we thought the worst."

"The worst," Craig said.

"Now, we're not so sure."

"Why aren't you sure?" I asked.

"Because a little while ago her friends, the rest of the crew, they disappeared, too," Mitch said. "Without warning, poof, they were gone."

"Along with our ability to replenish inventory," Craig said.

"Then people started getting shot."

"What people?" I asked.

Craig mentioned Karl Olson in Minneapolis.

"Olson worked for the Boss," he added.

"Then Peter Troop was shot this morning," Mitch said. "He was killed outside a church, do you believe that?"

"He also worked for the Boss," Craig said. "Not us. We barely knew him."

"The drive-by shootings Sunday in Woodbury and last night at the storage facility, we think that was her, too."

"What about Oliver Braun?" I asked.

"Who's he?"

"Are you talking about the kid in Highland Park?" Craig asked. "That has nothing to do with us." Craig looked at his partner. "Does it?"

Mitch shrugged.

"You thinking that somehow a little girl done all that?" Herzog said. The way he said it, it was clear that he thought Mitch and Craig were the little girls.

"We don't know for sure," Craig said.

"The Boss thinks so," Mitch said.

"The Boss, whom you never met," I said.

"He sent us an e-mail. Sent it to Kispert and us after what happened to Troop. It said we should hire—we should approach you both with an offer."

"The Boss sent you to hire us?"

"You and Mr. Herzog, yes."

"How did the Boss know who we were?"

"We told him about our business arrangement, and then when this other thing happened . . ."

"That makes me very unhappy," Herzog said.

"We had no choice," Craig said. "We're the ones holding the stick. If it all goes sideways, we're the ones the cops are going to pin it on. If we try to make a deal, tell them about the Boss, put it all on him, the cops are going to laugh at us."

"We have no real evidence," Mitch said.

Serves you right for engaging in such a one-sided relationship, my inner voice said.

"Doesn't answer my question," Herzog said. "Why would this little girl try to whack you?"

"Revenge," Craig said. "For what the Boss tried to do to her."

"What did he try to do?" I knew, of course. I was merely seeking confirmation.

"Kispert wouldn't tell us; made it sound like he was innocent in all this," Mitch said. "An innocent bystander. But whatever it was, Olson and Troop, you can bet they were in on it."

"Screwups," Herzog said. He didn't specify whom he was referring to; I was pretty sure it was an all-inclusive insult.

"Where does the Boss get the names of his blackmail victims?" I asked.

Mitch and Craig glanced at each other as if it were the first time the question came up.

"From our e-mail list, I guess," Mitch said.

"You're telling me he chooses them at random?"

"Not exactly. I mean—what happens, Kispert asks us to identify customers who purchase certain kinds of merchandise, who're inclined to spend a lot of money . . ."

"That's all we do," Craig said. "Honest. Everything else, that's on them."

Sure it is, my inner voice said.

"What about video evidence?" I asked aloud. "Do you get your customers on tape?"

"Why would we do that?" Mitch said. "That'd be evidence against us, too."

"You haven't said exactly what you want from us," Herzog reminded everyone.

"Stop her," Craig said.

"You mean kill her? Say it."

Yet neither of them would.

"What's in it for us?" Herzog asked.

"Twenty thousand dollars," Mitch replied. "Is that fair?"

"But, but," Craig said, "you know, maybe you won't have to . . . I mean, if you could just get her to stop without . . . Then we can all just get back to business."

"The price, though. Is it a fair price?"

"We have no quarrel with the price," I said. "It's a very fair price,"

"We want half up front," Herzog said. "Old bills, nonsequential serial numbers."

"Cash?" asked Craig.

"Fuck yeah, cash. What you think? We subscribe to PayPal?"

"Yes, of course, of course. It's just—we've never done this before."

"It'll be a day or so before we can get the money together," Mitch said.

"Take your time," Herzog said. "Just so you know—we don't even get up in the morning 'less we have cash in hand. Right?"

"Right," I said.

"There might be another problem, though," Craig said.

Mitch looked at his partner in a way that suggested he wanted him to remain quiet. Craig kept talking anyway.

"There's someone else looking for El."

"Who?" Herzog asked.

"Some guy named McKenzie."

Herzog started laughing.

"Fuck you say," he said.

"My sister called from Deer River, where El used to live," Mitch said. "She warned us about him. Do you know McKenzie?"

"Yeah, I know 'em. Used t' be a fuckin' cop, now just pretends."

"He claims to be El's friend, that's what my sister says. All I know is that he lives in an expensive condo in Minneapolis."

"That sounds right."

"Should we be worried about him?" Craig asked.

"McKenzie? Fuck no. He's a pussy."

We hung around, pumping Mitch and Craig for additional information, most of which I already knew. Afterward, Herzog and I walked to my Jeep Cherokee. Snow was falling; a half inch had already accumulated, and while there was plenty of traffic negotiating the crowded intersection, the weather muffled the noise.

"What's going to happen when the clown patrol finds out you and Dyson are the same guy?" Herzog asked.

"Clown patrol—is that street?"

"How should I know what's street? I don't listen to rap."

"The clown patrol doesn't interest me. It's the ringmaster I want words with."

"The Boss. What kinda self-important asshole goes around calling hisself the Boss?"

I flashed on Donald Trump, yet let it slide.

"We're gonna split the money, right?" Herzog said.

"Even though you called me a pussy, yeah, you can take half."

"I was just keepin' it real."

"Thanks, Herzy. That makes it a lot better."

"We're not going to do anything to earn it, right? The twenty G's? I mean, we're not really going after that little girl, are we?"

"We?"

"You—unless you need help, then, yeah, we."

"Herzy, my man. Yes, we're going after El, but—like I said before, we're trying to save the girl."

"Seems to me those two pussies in there, they're the ones need saving. Why should we interfere?"

"You could say we're protecting El from herself. If they're now recruiting professionals to kill her, the girl's in way over her head. Besides, what she's doing is wrong."

"Who says?"

"If El killed these guys when they tried to hurt her, hell, we'd erect a statue in her honor and put it in Rice Park. Hunting them down six, seven weeks later, though—no. That's not self-defense. That's premeditated murder. She could have picked up a phone. She could have called the cops."

"Call the cops?" Herzog thought the suggestion was amusing. "That's not how it works where I come from."

"I thought we came from the same place."

"C'mon, McKenzie. We may be living in the same city in the same state in the same country, but no way we come from the same place."

Nina was waiting up for me when I returned to the condominium, which wasn't as noble as it sounds. She rarely goes to bed before two in the morning, even when she's not working.

"That didn't take long," she said.

"After you conspire to commit murder, you don't hang around for chitchat."

"Murder?"

"They wanted to hire Dyson to find Fifteen and make her stop disrupting their business."

"What did Dyson say?"

"Just what you'd expect him to say. The man has no scruples whatsoever. Besides, the money was very good. Twenty thousand dollars. I know guys who would do it for five."

"Then Fifteen *is* responsible for the killings."

The disappointment in Nina's voice was startling. At least I was startled. I knew she cared about the girl; nevertheless . . . Her eyes closed and she became very still.

"They seem to think so," I said. "I remain unconvinced."

Nina's eyes snapped open.

"We're dumping it all on Fifteen because she's gone missing," I added. "That's not evidence. That's conjecture."

"What about the gun in Oliver Braun's car?"

"I'm gonna go talk to someone about that tomorrow. In the

meantime, instead of chasing her, maybe there's a way we can get Fifteen to come to us."

"How are you going to manage that?"

"Did you reply to Mitch's e-mail?"

"No."

"Do it now."

"What am I supposed to write?"

"Ask him—does this mean I'm not going to get my pearls?"

Nina went to the computer. She called up Mitch's e-mail, wrote a reply, and hit SEND.

"Now what?" she asked.

"We wait. I don't expect to wait long. They'll be concerned about income now that their business has gone dark. I think the boys'll jump at the chance to make some easy cash."

I was correct. Mitch responded as we were getting ready for bed. Nina read the e-mail aloud.

"He says, 'As luck would have it, I have come into possession of an eighteen-inch Japanese Akoya pearl necklace with an eighteen-karat white gold clasp that I can let you have for four thousand dollars.'"

"You're kidding me," I said. "I paid only thirty-seven hundred for that sucker. The man is trying to rip you off."

Nina stared like I was the one with criminal intent.

"What should I tell him?" she asked.

"Ask him where he got the necklace."

Nina did. Mitch must have been waiting for her reply, because his response came quickly.

"He says he doesn't ask questions of his suppliers," Nina said.

"Tell him, in that case, neither will you."

Nina typed in the message and hit SEND. The reply came in less than a minute.

"He said his schedule is up in the air right now," she told me. "Can he contact me tomorrow to arrange a meeting?"

"Write that you look forward to hearing from him."

She did.

FOURTEEN

The media hadn't paid much attention to the first two killings. The *St. Paul Pioneer Press* gave Oliver Braun only four paragraphs under the headline OFFICERS INVESTIGATE HOMICIDE IN HIGHLAND PARK and didn't even identify the victim, referring to him instead as "a Little Canada man." Karl Olson's murder was summed up in six paragraphs in the *Minneapolis Star Tribune* under the headline: POLICE SEARCH FOR SNIPER NEAR UNIV. CAMPUS, and the article dealt more with the manhunt involving eight squads, one ambulance, and one fire truck than the actual shooting. KARE-11, the only TV station to cover the crime, used the same hook. Over sixty seconds of its ninety-second piece were devoted to neighbors telling the camera how surprised they were by the police presence.

However, the murder of a man in the parking lot of a church during a funeral, coupled with allegations that the victim might himself be a murderer? Now that's something a news organization could get excited about.

The *Pioneer Press* announced on its front page:

LITTLE CANADA MURDER VICTIM
LINKED TO ST. PAUL HOMICIDE

SUSPECT WAS SHOT AT FUNERAL
OF ALLEGED VICTIM

The *Star Tribune* proclaimed on the cover of its local section:

HOMICIDE SUSPECT KILLED
WHILE IN POLICE CUSTODY

As for the local TV stations that actually broadcast the news, each gave the shooting as much as two and a half minutes of airtime.

Still, all of the stories were appallingly inaccurate, probably because journalists were only able to quote unnamed authorities and "sources close to the investigation." No one who had been sitting in the conference room at the Griffin Building was identified, including Bobby and myself—which pleased me no end.

Nor did anyone mention the name of Ramsey County Commissioner Merle Mattson.

Which, I thought, gave me leverage.

I bought two hours of time from a meter in front of the St. Paul Public Library. I could have rented a stall in a parking garage and walked to the courthouse using the city's elaborate skyway system, a network of second-story boulevards and enclosed pedestrian bridges that connect public buildings to one another, yet thought better of it. The purpose of the skyway was to allow people to travel between buildings without forcing them to brave the elements, be it the snow and freezing temperatures of Minnesota's winters or the heat and humidity of its summers. It had reached the point where often people would go to and from work without actually stepping outside; the skyway allowed them to commute from their attached garages to one of downtown's many enclosed parking ramps in nothing more than shirtsleeves. Given the overall brutality of our winter, who could

(216)

blame them? Yet at 10:00 A.M. the temperature was a giddy forty-five degrees, and I was reveling in it.

"Enjoy the pleasant weather while you can," a TV meteorologist told us before predicting a weekend of plunging temperatures and rain turning to sleet turning to snow and ice. The evening news anchor—no, it wasn't Kelly Bressandes—was so incensed by the forecast, she tossed her script into the air and stormed off the set, the weather-bunny calling after her, "Don't blame me, I'm only the messenger." The anchor returned after the commercial break and said, "Normally, I love winter, but this has been too much," which wasn't an apology, merely an explanation that prompted the rest of us to nod our heads and say, "Got that right."

So I walked the two blocks, thinking with each step, Nature, you mother, bring it on.

The Saint Paul City Hall/Ramsey County Court House—that's its actual name—was eighty years old, a twenty-one floor monument to what was considered American Art Deco architecture at the period it was built. It had bronze elevator doors, light fixtures, and stair railings, gold leaf ceilings, glass murals, polished marble, and an astonishing array of domestic and foreign woods—American black walnut, Cuban mahogany, Indian rosewood, Mexican prima vera, English brown oak, and African avodire, to name just a few.

As the name suggested, it housed most of the offices for both governments, including the St. Paul mayor and city council and the Ramsey County Commission. Except that wasn't the reason the security detail at the door forced me to empty the contents of my pockets into a plastic bin, step through a metal detector, stand with arms extended while a security wand was passed over my body, or lift my pant legs to the height of my boots. It was because of the Second Judicial District courtrooms located on the upper floors. I had testified enough times in those courtrooms against suspects who would do anything to escape that I knew better than to carry a gun into the building.

I climbed the steps to the second floor. The first thing I saw when I entered suite 220 was a wraparound reception desk. A stern-looking woman sat behind the desk. I told her I had an appointment to see Commissioner Mattson. I told her I was early. She directed me to a clutch of comfy leather chairs. I sat in one of them and passed the time studying the black-and-white photographs spaced artistically on the walls. Nearly every one featured a member of a minority group; I decided they had more representation in the photographs than in our government.

Ten minutes later, the receptionist spoke to me. "You're here to see Commissioner Mattson, correct?"

"Yes," I said.

"At ten thirty?"

"Yes."

She looked at the clock on the wall, confirmed the time, picked up a phone, and told the person on the other end that I had arrived.

She didn't tell them you had come early, my inner voice said. *She waited until the exact moment of your appointment.*

I was both impressed and appalled at the same time.

A couple of moments later, Merle Mattson entered the lobby. She introduced herself, shook my hand, and ushered me down a silent corridor. I was able to look through open doors into the offices of the other commissioners as we passed them. They were neat and orderly, and I wondered if they were used for actual work. Mattson's office, on the other hand, seemed in disarray.

"You'll have to forgive the mess," she said. "Unlike my colleagues, I've been having a hard time going paperless."

The commissioner excused herself and stepped into the adjoining office and issued a few instructions in a soft voice to her assistant. It gave me time to peruse her space. Besides the stacks of reports and files, there were many books, two white hard hats, a golden sledgehammer, several empty coffee cups, a couple of college degrees, a map of Ramsey County with her district highlighted, and dozens of framed photographs. In most of those, she was posing with one or more people in a professional setting. I spotted only one photo of her alone. In it, a much younger Merle Mattson was dressed in the crisp uniform of a Ramsey County sheriff's deputy and clutching a trophy from the National Police Shooting Championships. I recognized the trophy because I had come *this*close to winning one myself.

A moment later, the commissioner returned to the office, closing the door behind her. She settled behind her desk, and I sat in front of it.

"What can I do for you, Mr. McKenzie?" she asked.

"I'd like to ask you about Ella Elbers."

"I don't know her."

"Yes, you do."

I had just called her a liar, yet nothing in Mattson's facial expression or body language told me what she thought about it. No nostril flare or lip compression to indicate anger or frustration; no grin, grimace, lip pout, canine snarl, brow raise, or downward gaze. Her pupils did not expand or contract, nor did she cover her mouth, tug at her ear, or shift her weight in her chair. Instead, she stared straight ahead, and I was reminded of something my FTO told me back at the academy—remember, while you're studying a suspect's body language, he might be studying yours.

"Let me rephrase," Mattson said. "I met El, but I don't know her. I meet a lot of people in my job that I don't know."

"She was Oliver Braun's girlfriend."

"He introduced us. I don't recall him using the term 'girlfriend.'"

"El *was* Oliver's girlfriend. She's disappeared. There's evidence that suggests she was involved in his death. I'm trying to help sort it out."

"What evidence?"

I was glad of Mattson's question. Most people would have asked why I was involved, and I wasn't sure I could provide a satisfactory answer.

"A gun was found in Oliver's car," I said. "The gun belonged to El."

Actually, it belonged to me, I reminded myself, but why complicate the story.

"I read the newspaper account very closely," Mattson said. "There was no mention of a gun."

"No, there wasn't."

Mattson leaned back in her chair and looked up to the right as if she were searching inside herself for information stored there.

"The *Pioneer Press* speculated that Peter Troop killed Oliver," she said.

"I read the piece, too. It's probably correct. Yet it didn't explain the gun or El's disappearance or answer the big question—why?"

The commissioner gazed down for a moment as if distracted. When her head came up, she said, "I was glad when I read that the man who murdered Oliver was killed. I hoped the person who murdered Troop got away with it. I might even have said so out loud."

"I can't blame you for that."

"Now you tell me Ms. Elbers might have had a hand in it."

"No. What I meant—I believe the people who killed Oliver also tried to kill her."

"Who would that be?"

"The people she used to work for."

"I don't know who that is."

"Sure you do."

"Mr. McKenzie . . ."

"I saw you in Woodbury, Commissioner. I saw you pay off John Kispert. What stolen property did you buy that they're now holding over your head?" I gestured at a flower-filled vase sitting on the corner of her desk. "Crystal?"

"It's possible I resemble someone you saw in Woodbury,

Mr. McKenzie. I'm pretty sure, though, I can prove to everyone's satisfaction that I never left my home office on Sunday."

"Who said it was Sunday?"

Mattson's pupils enlarged, and I thought her fight-or-flight instinct was kicking in—either that or she was sexually aroused by my aggressive manner.

"I'm sure you must have mentioned it," she said. "How else would I have known?"

Her answer was so straightforward and confident, I half believed it myself.

You're not very good at this body language thing, are you? my inner voice asked me.

"Commissioner Mattson," I said aloud, "I'm not with the police. I'm not a reporter. I'm not a spy working for your political rivals. You don't need to be afraid of me."

"I didn't know that I was."

She sure as hell isn't behaving like she is.

"You aren't the first woman they blackmailed," I said.

"I'm not being blackmailed, but since you brought up the subject, Mr. McKenzie—I agree that blackmail is about fear. However, I have nothing to be afraid of. The next election is in three and a half years. I'll be sixty-two. I'd like to serve one more term before I retire. I could live without it, though. I've lost elections before. I was voted into the State House of Representatives because I was tough on crime." She gestured at the photograph of her in uniform. "The party faithful voted me out in the primary two terms later because I wasn't tough on gay marriage. So it goes.

"Besides, what would a blackmailer get? Money? It's true that as a part-time citizen legislator I made thirty-three thousand dollars a year, and now as a full-time county commissioner I make eighty-three. Still, it hardly seems enough to make it worth the effort. It can't be about government contracts, either. We've been removed, the board has, from the selection process in order to eliminate favoritism and nepotism, any allegation of impropriety. Other departments do the grunt work now. All we do is vote yes or no. But tell me, McKenzie—not police, not a journalist, what's your interest in all this?"

There's that question after all.

"El," I said aloud. "I once saved her life."

"Now you feel responsible for her. The old Chinese curse. That's something I can appreciate. I used to be a deputy sheriff."

"I used to be a cop, too."

"We're probably thinking the same thing, then."

"Are we?"

Instead of answering, Mattson stared some more. Again her expression and body language gave me nothing. After a few moments, she leaned forward and rested her elbows on her desk.

"I met El at the party after we won the election," Mattson said. "In November. Oliver had worked for me as an intern throughout that summer and most of the fall. He came to us in the usual way. He called and asked for an opportunity. We don't advertise these things. There are no job postings, no formal process. Oliver contacted my assistant, said he lived in the district, said he was a poli-sci major at the U, and asked if there were any summer internships to be had.

"I liked him right away. He was very smart and very enthusiastic. We put him to work around the office. It was an election year, so there was more to do than usual, and he was happy to do it—whatever we asked. Occasionally I sent him to take notes at meetings I was unable to attend—seventy percent of my job is meetings. Often he would accompany me on door knockings. We'd roam the neighborhoods, knocking on doors, introducing ourselves, passing out campaign literature. A lot of legislators rely on social media these days. My experience, McKenzie, nothing beats the personal touch. Tip O'Neill was right when he said all politics is local. That doesn't mean just city or state, though. It means the street where you live.

"You have no idea how much I appreciated that—Oliver being with me when we did the knockings, taking notes when voters voiced their concerns, and often writing the follow-up letters and e-mails we would send back to them. Also, there were safety concerns. Some people aren't as nice as you would hope. Standing in someone's yard, in the corridor of an apartment building, talking to voters who are clearly angry, listening to them vent over issues that more often than not are well beyond my control, telling them, 'Here's my home address, here's my home phone.' Sometimes I couldn't believe I was giving them my personal information, yet that's what you do when you want to get elected on a local level. Having Oliver there made it much easier.

"After the election, there wasn't as much for him to do, plus he had classes to attend. However, I made sure he was present at our victory celebration. That's when he introduced me to Ms. Elbers. I had not met her prior to that, yet I knew her name. Oliver spoke of her often. Clearly he was smitten, and when I met her I could see why. She is a lovely young woman and perfectly charming."

"Did El invite you to a garage sale? Is that how you first got on the hook?"

"Garage sale?"

"Like the one in Woodbury that you didn't attend."

"You can repeat the allegation as often as you like, Mr. McKenzie. My response will remain the same."

What did Einstein say about insanity? my inner voice said. *It's doing the same thing over and over again and expecting different results.*

"How 'bout Oliver?" I said aloud. "Why didn't you tell the police you were having an affair with him?"

I thought the question would jolt her. It didn't. Instead, Mattson answered as if she knew it was coming.

"I've been accused of many things in my political career, Mr. McKenzie," she said. "I have to admit, this one is new."

"Are you saying it's not true?"

"Of course it's not true."

"Yet you wept when you found out he was killed."

"Yes, I did. I get emotional when people I care about are brutally murdered. Who suggested I had a sexual relationship with Oliver?"

"His friends."

"Hormone-rich college students? I wouldn't say that's an entirely reliable source of information, would you?"

"As reliable as any."

"McKenzie, please. I'm old enough to be his . . . I met Oliver's mother. I'm a decade older than she is."

"What difference does that make? You're an attractive woman."

"Are you deliberately attempting to embarrass me? Put me in a position where I need to explain why a young man is not going to come knocking on my door? The odds a single woman my age will find a mate—I'm *reliably* informed it's more likely that a vending machine will fall on me. I understand and accept this reality; that doesn't mean it's something I like to contemplate. Be fair, McKenzie."

Spoken like a politician who used to be a cop—oh, she's very good.

I left Commissioner Mattson's office feeling as if I had been played by a certified expert. In a few short minutes, the woman had discovered nearly everything I knew or suspected. Yet I still had no idea what she knew.

Bobby Dunston would be appalled, I told myself.

There's no reason why he should know, my inner voice said.

As if on cue, my cell started playing "Summertime." The caller ID told me Bobby was calling.

"I was just thinking of you," I said.

"I'd say that great minds think alike except you don't have a great mind."

"I just discovered that for myself. What's up?"

"Buy me lunch."

"Where?"

The Blue Door Pub was located on Selby and Fairview in Merriam Park, the St. Paul neighborhood where Bobby and I grew up together—home of the Blucy, a burger stuffed with blue cheese and garlic that was just fabulous. Bobby and I sat across from each other in an old-fashioned wooden booth, the kind with high backs that you can't see over. I was halfway through both the burger and my second Summit Ale when he got to the point.

"Luby recovered the .30-06 shell casing from the shooting in Minneapolis," Bobby said.

"Good for him."

"It had a partial that we were able to couple with the print we took off the casing in Little Canada. Apparently they both came from the same right index finger . . ."

I stopped chewing, my mouth full of burger, and held my breath.

"If you recall, we took Fifteen's prints when she was brought into Regions after the freeway incident."

I held my breath some more.

"The BCA hemmed and hawed all over the place; said it couldn't make a conclusive determination because the data was too weak, you know how they are. Yet even though there weren't enough points to positively ID a suspect, I thought there might be enough for me to eliminate one. At least for the time being."

I exhaled around the burger, chewed quickly, and swallowed.

"El didn't do it," I said. "She didn't shoot those guys."

"She didn't load the rifle, anyway."

"I feel so much better than I did a little while ago."

"It doesn't let her off the hook. There's still Oliver Braun's murder to explain. There's still the shoplifting . . . Problem is, we can't find her. Elbers doesn't have any credit cards, so we can't track her movements through her purchases. Her friends can't help us because they've disappeared. She has no known criminal associates besides Mitch and Craig, who are denying everything, which means our CIs are useless. We finally located her missing Ram truck carefully hidden in the impound lot where it had been towed six weeks ago during a snow emergency, so we don't know what she's driving. We can't brief patrolmen to look for a specific make and model of a car, for her license plate."

"Someone must be hiding her."

"You think?"

Bobby picked up his burger and dropped it back on his plate without taking a bite as if he'd suddenly lost his appetite for it.

"Kispert," he said. "John Kispert. He's been busted several times for residential burglary; finished a thirty-eight month jolt in Stillwater for aggravated robbery two years ago. Nothing since then."

"That's because he moved up to management."

"Jean questioned him but got nowhere."

"I might have something for you."

I told Bobby everything I knew about Commissioner Mattson.

"Why didn't you tell Jeannie all this?" he asked.

"She didn't ask."

"Dammit, McKenzie—it's not a competition."

"You're right, it's not," I said aloud, although my inner voice was smirking.

She's not even in the same league.

"A former deputy sheriff who's now a sitting county commissioner—just what I need," Bobby said.

"If it's her, think of the interview you could give Kelly Bressandes."

"Funny. Mattson has a trophy from the National Police

Shooting Championships, you say. Didn't you win the individual handgun competition once?"

"I missed my last two targets."

"Oh, that's right. Kinda hard to shoot when you have both hands clutching your throat."

"So you've told me. Many, many times."

"You never even made it into the top ten after that, did you?"

"No, I didn't."

"Jeannie did. Twice."

"Good for her."

Bitch.

I was driving back to my condominium and feeling pretty good about myself when my cell sang a second time. I don't like it when other people talk on the phone while driving, yet I found myself doing it more and more often.

"McKenzie," I said.

"Hey," Nina said. "Why don't you come over and talk to me?"

"At the club?"

"Where else?"

I found Nina in her office. She was sitting at her desk and poring over a pile of what looked like receipts and invoices when I entered. She looked at me over the top of a pair of black-rim reading glasses. There had been a time when she would have been embarrassed to be seen wearing them. Until one day she announced, "I have a daughter in college. Who am I kidding?"

I said the glasses gave her a sexy-librarian vibe.

"Even better," she said.

There was a white coffee mug at her elbow. I reached for it as I sat and gave it a sniff.

Hazelnut, my inner voice told me.

"Really?" Nina said.

I returned the mug.

"Just checking," I said.

"I never mix caffeine and alcohol—unlike some people I could name."

"Why not?"

"Caffeine is a stimulant. It jazzes the body, increases blood pressure and heart rate. It's the equivalent of an adrenaline rush. Alcohol, on the other hand, is a depressant. It slows the brain and impairs your ability to walk, talk, and think clearly."

"I've noticed that."

"Some people think when you drink the two together, they cancel each other out, only it doesn't work that way. Instead, the caffeine masks the effects of the alcohol; people end up drinking way beyond their limits. That's why you should never buy those alcoholic energy drinks. People call them a blackout in a can. It's why Irish coffee is not on our menu."

"You're a damned good man, sister."

Nina gave me a baffled what-the-hell-are-you-talking about expression. It wasn't the first time I had seen it.

"It's what Sam Spade told Effie Perine in *The Maltese Falcon*," I said.

The expression remained on her face.

"No one reads the classics anymore," I said.

"What do you want, McKenzie?"

"You called me, remember?"

"Oh yeah. Yeah, yeah, yeah." Nina searched the top of her desk, found a sheet of paper, and handed it to me. It was the printed copy of an e-mail sent to her by Mitch.

If you still want the necklace we discussed, I can meet you today at the Como Park Pavilion at 3 PM. The asking price is $4,000. This must be an all-cash transaction. Please, no checks.

"What do you think?" Nina asked.

"You should know, things have changed since last evening."

I explained how they had changed.

"Fifteen isn't trying to kill them," Nina said.

"No, but they're still trying to kill her."

"Should we go through with the transaction?"

"I think so. The original plan is back in play. Get in close, see if we can discover who the Boss is, and take it from there."

"Just tell me one thing—is this going to be a gift from you to me?"

"I'll come up with the cash for the necklace, if that's what you mean."

"Can I keep it?"

"Sure."

"You're a damned good sister . . . Oh, never mind."

Nina replied to the e-mail, agreeing to meet Mitch and promising to bring cash, although—and I liked this touch—she said if she wasn't wowed by the necklace she'd take her business to Jared. Afterward, I gave her my best Groucho eyebrows and asked how she wanted to spend the next ninety minutes.

"I need to go back to the condo anyway, to pick up a few things," I told her.

Nina gestured at the pile of paperwork on her desk. "You know, McKenzie, some people actually have jobs," she said

I told her my job consisted solely of making her happy.

She suggested I wasn't working at it as hard as I could.

I would have argued the point, except for the lousy music that the burn phone in my pocket was playing. I checked the ID before answering. It was Mitch.

"This is Dyson," I said.

Once again Nina's eyes grew wide at the sound of the name.

"Mr. Dyson, this is Mitch. I have the money you requested. At least I will have it. Can you meet me at three thirty this afternoon?"

"Where?"

"The Como Park Pavilion in St. Paul. You know it?"

"I know it."

"See you then."

"Mitch, I appreciate why you want to meet in a public place, but you need to know—it won't protect you if you screw me over."

I ended the call.

"Do you believe it?" I said. "The man is going to use the money that you pay him for the necklace to help pay me and Herzog."

"This is why I don't want to combine our bank accounts."

Como Park in St. Paul is one of my favorite places. It has a large zoo housing all manner of creatures large and small, including Sparky the Sea Lion and twin polar bears named Neil and Buzz. Next door, the Marjorie McNeely Conservatory displays an astonishing array of plants and exhibits such as a Japanese garden and a fern room that always reminds me of Mirkwood. There is an amusement park with eighteen rides and a mini-donut stand, a hundred-year-old carousel, pony rides, an eighteen-hole golf course, athletic fields, a swimming pool, tennis courts, picnic shelters, and in the summer, paddleboats for rent that you can use to explore Lake Como.

Nina stood at the second-floor railing of the lakeside pavilion where two hundred and fifty visitors often sat on benches to hear music and watch amateur theatricals and dance recitals. I studied her with the binoculars from my Jeep Cherokee in the lot south of the pavilion. Many vehicles were parked around me, their occupants scattered along the plowed path that circled the lake and the park's three miles of hiking trails. Some of them gathered on the pier piled with snow and ice that jutted into the lake below where Nina was standing. Others moved up and down the ramp leading from the parking lot to the second floor, while even more people visited the coffeehouse—yes, another one—built into the structure's first floor.

I didn't have to guess what Nina was thinking, because she told me.

"I remember skating here when I was a kid." Her voice, transmitted by the forget-me-not pinned to the lapel of her charcoal coat, was clear over my smartphone. "They'd scrape the snow off the lake, do something to the ice to make it smooth and fast. Olympic speed skaters trained here. There was a green shack right over there where you could rent skates and cross-country skis . . ."

"Pay attention," I told her. Of course, she couldn't hear me.

"Now they have the oval in Roseville that's suppose to have the best ice in the Cities, better even than the Xcel Center, but I don't know. You have to be serious to skate there, and you have to pay. Seems to me you could skate here for free."

I saw Craig and Mitch long before Nina did. They parked near the gentle ramp that led to the pavilion. They carefully glanced around them as they exited their car, and kept at it as they climbed the ramp.

"You guys don't look suspicious at all," I said to no one in particular.

They had no trouble finding Nina. They moved to within twenty feet of her before she felt their presence and turned to greet them. From where I was positioned, I could only see the three of them from the waist up even with the binoculars.

"Nina," Mitch said as if greeting an old friend. "Good to see you."

"Mitch," Nina said "I don't believe I've met your friend."

"My partner, Craig. Craig, this is Nina."

Hands were shaken all around.

"Can you believe this weather?" Craig said. "Cold, warm, cold, warm. It's enough to give you whiplash."

"Yes, but mostly it's been cold," Nina said. "I read where this is our worst winter in over a hundred years."

"Kinda refutes all that talk about global warming."

"I don't know about that. Global warming leads to climate change, and our climate lately has been pretty screwy."

"Excuse me," Mitch said. "I don't mean to be rude, but we have another appointment to get to."

Craig glanced at his watch. "We have a few minutes yet," he said.

"That's all right, I understand," Nina said. "Business is business. I need to get back to mine, too."

"What do you do?" Craig asked.

"Let's talk about a Japanese Akoya pearl necklace," Mitch said.

"Sure, sure."

"Why did you want to meet here anyway?" Nina asked.

Dammit, honey, don't improvise, my inner voice said. *Pay the money, take the pearls, and get the hell out of there.*

"Since the garage sale in Apple Valley was canceled, we couldn't meet there," Mitch said.

"Why was it canceled?"

Nina . . .

"Circumstances beyond our control," Craig said. "We would have waited until we rescheduled, except we knew you were anxious about your pearls."

"It all just seems so . . . criminal."

Ahh, c'mon!

"Would you have preferred that we meet at your home or office?" Mitch asked. From the sound of his voice, he seemed as frustrated with Nina as I was.

"I guess not," she said.

"Do you have the money?" Craig asked.

Nina reached into the bag hanging by a strap from her shoulder, hesitated, and removed her hand.

"May I see the pearls?" she asked.

I heard Craig chuckle.

"Certainly," he said.

He handed Nina the box the store clerk had placed the pearls in when I bought them at Mall of America. Nina opened the box.

"These are nice," she said. "Four thousand dollars, though— I'm not sure about that."

I shouted, "Dammit, Nina, you're haggling?" so loudly that I didn't hear what Craig said in reply.

"This is our buy-it-now price," Mitch said. "If you want to take your chances when we make it available at our next sale . . ."

"No," Nina said. "I guess not."

She closed the box and tucked it under her arm. At the same time, she reached into her bag and withdrew an envelope. She held out the envelope for Mitch, yet he did not take it. Instead, all three of them turned to look at something I couldn't see.

A confusion of sounds and voices poured from the speaker of my smartphone.

"What are you doing?" A woman's voice.

"You . . ."

"It wasn't our fault."

"Wait."

"No, no, no."

Pop-pop-pop—the sound of Bubble Wrap bursting.

Nina disappeared from view.

"McKenzie, I'm shot," she said.

I dropped both the phone and binoculars and flew out of the Cherokee, not bothering to shut the door behind me. The SIG Sauer was in my hand as I crossed the parking lot. There was no slipping or sliding this time. I ran with purpose.

As I moved to the ramp that led to the second floor of the pavilion, I saw her.

Fifteen.

She came down the ramp in a hurry.

She was carrying a gun. My nine-millimeter Beretta.

She saw me and stopped.

I stopped, too.

She brought the gun up with both hands and sighted on me, a pyramid stance—one foot in front of the other with about twenty-four inches between heel and toe, arms outstretched at the same level as her shoulders, leaning into the shot. Whether she knew what she was doing or just slid into it, I couldn't say.

I, on the other hand, knew exactly what I was doing when I went into a Weaver stance and sighted on the center of her chest with the SIG.

We stood like that, two samurai waiting for the other to make a move.

One beat.

Two beats.

You don't have time for this, my inner voice screamed. *Nina's been shot.*

Fifteen lowered her gun and started running in the opposite direction.

I lowered mine and let her go.

I sprinted up the ramp.

Mitch and Craig were coming down.

They had guns in their hands, carrying them like they didn't know what they were for.

"Dyson, Dyson," one of them said—I don't know which. "Thank God you're early."

"Did you see her?" said the other. "She tried to kill us."

I might have told them to shut the fuck up. I don't remember. I remember only that I didn't care if I blew my cover or not.

The floor of the pavilion was crowded with benches. I dashed around them, making my way to the rear. I found Nina sitting down, her back against the railing, her legs stretched out in front of her. The box of pearls and the envelope filled with cash were lying next to her. Mitch and Craig had left them both.

They left her, too, the bastards.

I went to Nina.

Knelt at her side.

Set the SIG on the concrete floor next to the pearls and cash.

Nina's eyes were wet and shining, yet her face was pale. She smiled, an amazing thing to do, I thought.

"It doesn't hurt at all," she said.

I examined her wool coat. There was no blood, but I could see the hole on the right side—the worst side to be shot, because that's where so many major organs reside. The heat of the bullet had singed the material as it cut through it.

I cautiously unbuttoned the coat.

"I'm really sorry about this," Nina said.

"Shhh," I told her.

"You didn't want to involve me in your quests, but I insisted. What did I say? I liked living the devil-may-care? Serves me right getting shot."

"Don't talk."

I finished unbuttoning the coat and gently peeled it back. I expected to find plenty of blood. Instead, her white blouse was unblemished where the wound should have been.

I pulled the coat farther back and found a second hole.

Somehow the bullet had entered the front of the coat and gone out through the back without actually touching her.

Nina looked down.

Her hand went to her side.

She caressed it as if she wanted to see damage and was surprised that there wasn't any.

"I'll be a dirty name," she said. "The way the bullet pulled at my coat . . . It actually knocked me down."

I sat back and pulled my knees up. I rested my face against my knees.

"Hey," Nina said. "Hey, McKenzie. Are you crying?"

FIFTEEN

It started drizzling at sundown. A half hour later it turned to sleet. Twenty minutes following that it became snow. The weather demanded my full attention as I drove my Jeep Cherokee north along Highway 169 at a cautious 35 mph—which was a good thing. It helped me get my head back in the game.

I was as surprised by my reaction to Nina's non-shooting as she had been. I hadn't wept since my mother died, and that was when I was in the sixth grade; my father forbade even the appearance of tears at his funeral, and I had followed his instructions. Yet there I was, all misty-eyed, my throat closed, my hands shaking, and Nina hugging my heaving shoulders and telling me in a soothing voice that she was perfectly fine; better than fine, she was exhilarated by the experience. When the cops arrived, they thought I was the one in trouble.

Explanations were made; Commander Dunston and Detective Shipman were summoned. Shipman smiled at my behavior but said nothing. Bobby, on the other hand, kept staring as if I were an old friend whose name he couldn't remember.

Nina insisted that El hadn't actually shot *at* her. She had been walking toward them, said, "What are you guys doing?"— something like that. All of a sudden, Mitch and Craig had guns. And El had a gun. Nina didn't know who fired first, but she was pretty sure it wasn't El, and if it was El, she was *defending* herself. She was shooting at Mitch and Craig and hit her by mistake, probably didn't even know Nina was standing there. Neither Bobby nor Shipman could see what difference that made. Neither could I. Nina thought there was a *huge* difference and said she would refuse to testify against El if she was arrested.

"No harm, no foul—isn't that what you guys always say?" she told us.

This caused Bobby to throw up his hands like a parent dealing with a child who won't eat her green beans. He thought—aloud—that she must be suffering from shock. Nina buzzed his cheek and said, "Sure."

Meanwhile, Shipman wanted to arrest both Mitch and Craig and sweat Elbers's location out of them.

Except that Mitch and Craig don't know where she's hiding, I told her.

At least we could convince them to file a complaint against Elbers for assault with a deadly weapon, she said.

But, I said, given the reason they were soliciting money from Nina in the first place, it was highly unlikely they would press charges. Besides—and I was looking at Nina when I said it—there's a question of who shot at whom.

"We'll hold them for possession and sale of stolen property," Shipman said.

"About that . . ."

I told her that the necklace wasn't actually stolen. I had the receipt and the credit card statement, and the jewelry store more likely than not had video footage of me making the purchase.

Shipman demanded an explanation.

I gave her one, although I omitted both Herzog's involvement and the staged drive-by shooting.

She asked what the hell I had hoped to accomplish by pretending to sell stolen merchandise to a couple of thieves.

Use Mitch and Craig to find El, I replied.

"Congratulations," Shipman said. "Your plan worked. You must be very proud."

Around and around we went. The money, pearls, and SIG Sauer were eventually returned to me and the responding officers were dismissed. I gave the money and pearls to Nina. She stuffed them into her bag and moved to the edge of the pavilion. She set the bag at her feet and rested both hands on the railing. Bobby joined her there. He whispered something. Nina hooked an arm around his and rested her head against his shoulder. Together, they both gazed out at Lake Como. Shipman and I decided to give it a rest and drifted to the railing as well, standing on either side of the couple. Nina took my hand and squeezed hard.

"Ever since you entered my life, I've been having the most fun," she said. "Before that I was just a lowly, boring nightclub owner."

"Lowly?" Shipman said.

"Boring?" Bobby said.

"No more," I said. "I'm done putting you at risk so I can play cops and robbers."

"Amen," Shipman said.

Nina released Bobby and wrapped both of her arms around mine. She kissed my cheek the same way she had kissed his earlier—like it was the punch line to a joke.

"Sure," she said.

"I mean it."

"He had better mean it," Bobby said. "Next time I'll arrest him."

"For what?" Nina asked.

"Contributing to the delinquency of a minor."

Nina thought that was hilarious. Bobby was serious, though. So was I. Nina didn't believe it. She quoted Sally Field's second Oscar speech.

"You like me, you really like me."

No one seemed to know what to say to that, so we all remained quiet for a few beats. It was Shipman who broke the silence.

"Got any more bright ideas, McKenzie?" she asked.

"One or two."

"Any of them legal?"

Bobby asked, "What *are* you going to do, McKenzie?"

"I'm going back to Deer River."

"When?"

"Tonight."

Neither Shipman nor Bobby asked why I was going or what I hoped to accomplish when I arrived there. I don't think they wanted to know.

Bobby patted my shoulder and said, "Call me when you return." He took a few steps away, then turned and came back. He hugged Nina hard.

"Dammit," he said.

"Best to Shelby and the girls," she told him.

"They're going to be so mad at you."

"Blame McKenzie."

"I will. I do."

A few minutes later he disappeared. So did everyone else. Nina and I stood alone at the railing.

"I know you're embarrassed," Nina said, "about crying the way you did when you thought I was shot and then found out I wasn't. I need to tell you, though—that was the best gift you've ever given me. And you've given me a sixty-thousand-dollar piano."

"You're welcome." What else was I going to say?

"It would bother me, though, it really would, if I couldn't help out on your cases anymore."

"We'll talk about it later."

Nina kissed my cheek and said, "Sure."

"I wish you'd stop doing that."

"Do you have something else in mind?"

I did, yet it had nothing to do with sex—the second time I surprised Nina that day.

"You really are discombobulated, aren't you?" she asked me.

"No, but you soon will be. That's why I'm going to take you home. Right now you're high on adrenaline, except it's going to wear off. You're going to crash and burn—maybe get the shakes, dizziness, nausea, exhaustion. I'm going to take you home and wrap you in a blanket, set you in front of a fire, and force-feed you hot chocolate until you relax and fall into a long and untroubled sleep."

"McKenzie, this isn't the first close call I've had since we've been together."

"It's going to be the last."

"I thought we were going to talk about it."

My burn phone started playing its ridiculous song, interrupting the conversation.

"This is Dyson," I said. "What the hell do you want?"

"I just wanted . . . this is Mitch. I wanted to find out what happened. Should we be afraid?"

"The girl was unhurt, if that's what you mean."

"How is that possible? I saw her shot."

"Just dumb luck, man. The bullet grazed her. I got her out of there before the cops came, which is what you should have done."

Nina moved in front of me and pointed the fingers of both hands like they were guns.

"Phhew, phhew," she chanted.

I turned my head.

"We were under fire," Mitch said. "The girl—you saw the girl."

"I saw her."

"Why didn't you kill her?"

"Gee, I don't know. Maybe it was the thirty or forty people standing around going duh . . ."

"There weren't that many."

"Besides, I haven't been paid yet."

"We were going to pay you, except—now we're a little short. The woman, Nina, she owes us four thousand dollars."

"Stay the hell away from the woman."

Nina stuck her tongue out, and I turned away from her again.

"But our money . . ." Mitch said.

"Forget the damn money. Listen to me. Right now the woman's high on adrenaline with an interesting story to whisper to her friends when there's no one else around to hear. If you start leaning on her, there's a chance she'll freak and go to the cops. Here're the pearls, here's the money; here're the guys that tried to shoot me."

"But we didn't."

"What's the name of that cop, the female detective you told me about? Shipman? Think she'll buy that?"

"I get it . . ."

"Whaddya think she's going to do?"

"I said I get it."

"Leave the woman alone."

"Fine, fine, fine. What are we supposed to do now? The Boss wants the job done."

"Who knew you were going to be in Como Park?"

"What? No one."

"El knew."

"She must have followed us like she did the other night."

I came *this*close to explaining that I was responsible for Wednesday's drive-by shooting.

"Think about it," I said. "You must have told somebody."

"Just the Boss," Mitch said. "And Kispert. We sent them e-mails saying we were meeting with you and Mr. Herzog. Where is Mr . . . ?"

"E-mails? You sent e-mails?"

"Yes."

The silence that followed while I attempted to reason it out must have spooked Mitch.

"Do you think Kispert arranged it?" he asked. "Or the Boss? Why would they do that?"

"Let me think about it."

"Dyson, what are we going to do?"

"I don't want you to do anything. Leave it to me."

"What are *you* going to do?"

Nina placed her thumbs on her temples, wiggled her fingers, and crossed her eyes, forcing me to turn away again. It's because she distracted me that I blame her for the catastrophic mistake I made, although I wouldn't realize it until much later—I answered Mitch's question.

I said, "I'm going up to Deer River to see if I can get an idea where the girl is hiding from her friends."

"Thank you, thank you. We'll get you the money as soon as we can."

"In the meantime, you and your partner might want to reconsider your choice of occupations, because I don't think this one suits you."

"You're a funny guy, Dyson."

"Don't call me. I'll call you."

I slipped the phone into my pocket. Nina was smiling brightly while grooving to a melody in her head as if she were about to break into dance.

"Remember the cartoon *Underdog*?" she asked. "I loved that show. *Speed of lightning, roar of thunder, fighting all who rob or plunder . . .* "

I took her home and did exactly what I said I would do despite her entreaties, which, let's face it, were difficult to resist. It took a while before she fell asleep.

As a result of all this, I was a few hours later getting out of town than I had planned. Then there was the blizzard to contend with. It should have been a three-hour trip to Deer River, yet I spent nearly two and a half just driving to Lake Mille Lacs, about halfway. Fortunately, I was able to put the snowstorm behind me as I rounded the lake. After that, it was smooth sailing—if you didn't mind sailing in subfreezing temperatures. Spring might have been flirting with the Cities, but it was still giving the northland the cold shoulder.

It was nearly 10:00 P.M. when I pulled into the plowed parking lot of a motel near Blueberry Hills Golf Course just north of Deer River. The man who operated the motel was getting ready to leave his office just as I entered.

"He'p yeah?" he asked.

I think he thought I was going to ask for directions, because he was openly surprised when I requested a room for the night.

"Well, now, son, we don't get many visitors this time a' year," he said. "Fact is, we're as empty as a politician's promise, so you got your pick."

The motel consisted of a dozen cabins with two rooms per cabin; the cabins were spaced about twenty yards apart.

"Farthest from the road," I said.

"Not a problem."

He rounded his desk, produced a registration form for me to fill out, and swiped my credit card.

"During the summer and hunting season, we're always full up," the manager said. "Fact is, if you don't already have a reservation, you ain't stayin' here. The winter we get some snowmobilers, some cross-country skiers, not many, though, especially this winter. What brings you to DR? Not lost, are ya?"

"I'm going to meet a few friends tomorrow to do some snowmobiling before the snow melts."

"Hell's bells, son, snow ain't never gonna melt."

"It sure seems that way."

"Lucky you came in when you did. I was just about to call it a night myself. As it is, you need something, ice, microwave popcorn, whatever, now's the time to get it. I was just going off to my own place up the road. You're gonna be all alone down here.

Hope that's not a problem. There's a number you can call if there's an emergency."

"If you're not going to be here—the cabins, you say there are two rooms per. Are they adjoining?"

"Yep."

"Why don't you rent me both rooms, then, in case my friends come up early? You're not going to be here at the crack of dawn, are you?"

"Not if I can avoid it."

The manager installed me in cabin 9, and gave me two sets of keys for 9A and 9B, plus keys that opened the adjoining doors.

"Anything else?" he asked.

"That should do it," I told him.

He stayed in his office while I parked the Cherokee in front of 9A; mine was the only vehicle in the lot besides his. There were two doors—a metal-and-glass storm door that opened outside and a thick wooden door that opened inside. I pulled the storm door open, unlocked the inside door, stepped inside, shut the doors behind me, turned on the lights, and closed the drapes. It was warm inside the cabin. I checked the thermostat—sixty-eight degrees. 'Course, I was dressed for a Minnesota winter, including boots that would have kept my feet warm in the Arctic Circle. I unzipped my coat, though I didn't remove it. I made sure the adjoining door was unlocked so that I could move easily from A to B, although I purposely left the lights off in room B.

I waited until the manager departed about ten minutes later, leaving me completely alone. There was a card next to the phone that listed the motel's number and explained how to make local calls. I shoved it into my pocket, checked the SIG Sauer, returned it to the holster on my right hip, rezipped my coat, and left the cabin.

O'Malley's was only a five-minute drive from the motel, yet I managed to stretch it to ten while I figured out how I was going to do this. My cell phone started singing. I read the caller ID before answering.

"Hey, sweetie," I said.

"Where are you?" Nina asked.

"I just pulled into Deer River."

"I hate it when I wake up and you're gone and I don't know where."

"How are you feeling?"

"Exhausted. I feel more tired now than when I went to sleep. You were right about going through adrenaline withdrawal."

"It happens sometimes. Not always."

"I woke up with a song in my head that I can't get rid of. A song Madeleine Peyroux sang when she was last in town about her Daddy teaching her *'bout how warm whiskey is in a cold ditch and one more thing about good and evil: you can't tell which is which.*"

"The woman knows how to turn a phrase."

"It's a far cry from *Underdog,* I know. I think it's my subconscious telling me to tell you to come home. Turn your car around and come home. To heck with Fifteen. I brought her into my home and dressed her in my daughter's clothes. I let her play my piano. What does she do? She shoots me."

"I thought you said it was an accident."

"Accident my Great Aunt Matilda Mountbatten. She almost killed me, whether she intended to or not. As it is, she ruined a perfectly good virgin wool overcoat. I loved that coat. I spent twelve hundred dollars on it two years ago. It was a special treat from me to me because I had finally paid off all the notes on my club."

"I remember."

"So, McKenzie, I'm saying forget her. I mean, I still don't want anything awful to happen to Fifteen, but this has nothing to do with us, you and me. Let Bobby and Shipman deal with it."

"I can't do that."

I heard her yawn over the cell.

"I bet you could if you put your mind to it," she said.

"I'm here."

"What do you mean?"

"O'Malley's. I can see the lights just down the road."

"Even if you weren't . . ." I heard her yawn again. "Never mind. I just thought I'd give it a try. I'm going back to bed now, and I'm not going to leave it until you return."

I liked the sound of that so much I nearly did turn the car around.

I was fortunate to find an empty space in O'Malley's crammed parking lot. When I opened the front door, people nearly tumbled out of the building like they did in that Marx Brothers movie, so many of them were waiting for a table in the restaurant area or a place at the bar. I squeezed inside, to the annoyance of the customers who were already crowded there, and looked around. To my great surprise, I saw an empty seat at the end of the bar directly beneath the mounted head of the twelve-point buck. I figured that its owner had retired to the restroom, yet when no one claimed it after a while I realized the stool was unoccupied. It made me wonder if O'Malley's patrons were superstitious, if they believed sitting in the shadow of the dead deer somehow brought them bad luck. Certainly my life had been less than sunshine, lollipops, and rainbows since I last sat there—I quoted the Lesley Gore song because that's what was playing on the jukebox when I settled onto the stool.

There were two bartenders working the rail, an older woman and Cyndy M. It was Cyndy who turned to greet me and take my order. Her smile disappeared and her vibrant eyes became gray and cloudy at the sight of my face. I pointed at nothing in particular.

"Believe it or not, Marvin Hamlisch wrote this song when he was first starting out," I said.

"I don't know who that is," Cyndy said.

"Quincy Jones was the producer. Please tell me you know who he is."

She shook her head, and I thought, McKenzie, you are so old.

Cyndy excused herself to serve a couple of customers as far away from me as she could get and still be standing behind the bar. I turned in the stool and surveyed the room. My friends from the Northern Lights Inn—I knew them as tall and small—were sitting at their usual table near the jukebox. Neither of them seemed happy to be there. The taller of the two raised his glass in mock salute while the smaller pointed at the jukebox. I followed his finger until I found Tim Foley leaning against the machine. He was staring straight at me, a kind of panicked expression on his face, while speaking on his cell phone.

Cyndy must have decided that I wasn't going anywhere anytime soon no matter how much she ignored me, because a few moments later, she filled a twelve-ounce mug with Grain Belt Beer and set it in front of me.

"Would you like to see a menu?" she asked.

It occurred to me that I hadn't eaten since lunch with Bobby.

"What's the daily special?" I asked.

Cyndy sighed the way people do when they want you to know they're pissed off.

"Walleye deep fried in beer batter, fries, and coleslaw," she said.

"I'll have that."

She stared at me for a few beats, turned, and placed my order. She did not speak to me or even glance in my direction until my food was up. She set the plate in front of me.

"Tartar sauce?" she asked. "Ketchup?"

"Thank you."

She retrieved a bottle of each.

"Why are you here?" Cyndy asked.

I ate a french fry. While I chewed, I pulled my smartphone

from my pocket and called up a pic of Nina. I set the cell on the bar so that Cyndy would have no trouble seeing it.

"Her name is Nina Truhler," I said. "She had been very kind to your friend. Gave her a place to stay after she left the hospital; tried to take care of her as best she could. About eight hours ago, El shot her."

Cyndy took a couple of steps backward, although her eyes never left the smartphone.

"She wouldn't do that," Cyndy said.

"Maybe not on purpose. She did squeeze the trigger, though."

Cyndy's head came up; her expression was that of a child who had just learned there was no Easter Bunny and was now wondering about Santa Claus.

"I don't believe it," she said.

"Eight hours ago I probably would have said the same thing."

"Now you want to get back at her?"

At that moment, my burn phone started playing its preposterous melody. I held up a finger and told Cyndy, "Hold that thought," as I pulled the cell from my jacket pocket and checked the caller ID. It was Mitch. I answered by saying, "What?"

"Dyson?" he asked.

"What now?"

"Where are you? Are you in Deer River?"

I couldn't think of a single reason to tell him the truth, so I answered, "Why do you ask?"

"McKenzie's in Deer River—the guy we told you about who's also looking for El."

"He is?"

"My sister called. She said someone she knows saw him in a place called O'Malley's. That's where El's friend works. Cyndy Desler. She's the bartender. Manager. Something like that."

"Good to know."

"Where are you?"

"The Wagon Wheel next to the Holiday Stationstore on Highway 2."

"O'Malley's is on the other side of town."

"I'll find it."

"Good luck."

I ended the call without wishing him good luck in return.

"You carry two phones?" Cyndy asked.

"Occupational hazard," I said.

"I'm sorry about your friend, I really am."

"She's fine, by the way. Thanks for asking. She won't press charges against El, either. Something about that girl instills outrageous loyalty, damn if I know what it is."

"I won't speak with you."

"See? That's what I mean by outrageous loyalty. Still, you and I are going to have a conversation, M, whether you like it or not. If not now, then later. But we will have a conversation, I promise."

She ground her fists against her hips. "I'm not afraid of you," she said.

"There's no reason why you should be, but you're afraid of something. I saw it in your eyes the moment I sat down." I gestured at tall and small. "I see it in the faces of your friends."

She refused to reply. I took a chance.

"What do you know about a man named Nick Dyson?" I asked

Cyndy grimaced, took a step backward, and folded her arms across her chest.

Those are all defensive gestures, my inner voice said. *She is afraid, and now you know why—assuming your body-language training wasn't completely useless.*

It's all starting to make sense now, I told myself.

"Look, M," I said, "you can talk to me or you can talk to Dyson. And don't tell me you're not afraid of him, either. If you weren't you wouldn't have your friends standing guard at the door, waiting for him to show up. He will show up, too. He's on his way. That's what the phone call was about.

"Something else, just so we're both on the same page. See Tim

Foley over there by the jukebox? He's in contact with Ms. Bosland. Ms. Bosland is in contact with her brother Mitch in the Cities. It was Mitch and his cohorts who hired Dyson in the first place. Twenty thousand dollars to put El in the ground. Imagine.

"I, on the other hand, am still interested in protecting you and your friend, although the two of you are making it so damn hard. Will you please help me?"

From the jukebox came the opening *ba-ba, ba-ba* to the old Partridge Family song, followed by David Cassidy singing "I Think I Love You," with nearly everyone in the bar joining in. Cyndy smiled weakly and waved and announced, "Enough, enough now," as she had the first time I witnessed the ritual. For a quarter hour afterward, she was overwhelmed by drink orders. When she found an empty moment, she returned to my place at the bar.

"I'll talk to you, but not now and not here," she said. "Where are you staying?"

"Cabin nine at the motel near the Blueberry Hill Golf Course. Room A. There is no one else staying there, so we'll have the place to ourselves."

"I'll meet you after closing." She pointed at my smartphone; Nina still smiling brightly from the screen. "I'm glad your friend is okay."

Cyndy moved away to serve her customers. I finished my meal and the beer. I thought about ordering a second, yet changed my mind. After all, I had an ambush to prepare.

SIXTEEN

I parked the Jeep Cherokee about twenty feet back from the entrance to room A. The dome light flicked on when I opened the driver's-side door. I used a switch to turn it off and stepped away from the SUV. It was so quiet. Whatever night sounds might have been audible in summer had been dampened by ice and snow. There were no leaves for the wind to rustle, no crickets chirping in the tall grass, no traffic moving on the county road. The only noise that I could hear was the noise I made myself as I trudged across the deserted lot to the cabin, unlocked the door, and flicked on all the lights. I made sure the blinds were tightly drawn across the windows and turned on the TV. I found ESPN and increased the volume until I could easily hear it in the adjoining room behind closed doors. I retreated to room B, locking both doors behind me. I arranged a chair in front of the windows so that I could easily and comfortably see anything entering the parking lot. I unzipped my coat and stuffed its pockets with my gloves and hat. I removed the nine-millimeter SIG Sauer from its holster and set it on the table next to the chair. From the other room I heard an announcer report that the Minnesota Wild had coughed up a three-to-nothing lead to the

Colorado Avalanche, yet managed to win four-to-three in over-time to keep their playoff hopes alive.

I forgot they were playing, I told myself.

And you call yourself a fan, my inner voice said.

The first car appeared at twelve thirty by my watch. Person-ally, I would have waited until the bars closed to avoid the possibility of late-night revelers happening upon the scene, but that's just me.

The driver turned off the vehicle's headlights as it swung into the parking lot. There was a light mounted on a pole near the manager's office, so I didn't have any trouble following the car as it made a beeline toward the only other lights within miles—those shining through the shaded windows of cabin 9, room A.

The vehicle was parked next to the Jeep Cherokee, the en-gine extinguished. Two men emerged. They had left the car's dome light on, so I could see their faces when they opened the doors—Cyndy M's friends tall and small. They were carrying handguns, holding them low. They made their way to the en-trance of room A and stood on either side of it, their backs to the wall of the cabin. Tall knocked on the storm door with the flat of his hand

"McKenzie," he shouted. "Open up."

I, of course, did not respond.

He pounded some more.

"Open up."

"Maybe he can't hear us," small said.

"Whaddaya mean, he can't hear us?"

"The TV is awfully loud."

Tall transferred his gun to his left hand and opened the storm door with his right, propping it open with his knee, and banged on the inside wooden door with this fist.

"McKenzie," he called.

Both he and small seemed mystified when I didn't answer.

Small's voice was so low I could barely hear him when he said, "Try the door handle."

Really, my inner voice said. *Now you whisper?*

Tall reached for the handle and turned it slowly until the latch gave. He cautiously pushed the door open and called out in a low voice, "McKenzie?"

Oh, for God's sake.

I lost sight of them when they entered the room. I could still hear their voices, although I couldn't tell who was speaking.

"McKenzie?"

"Check the bathroom."

"He's not there."

"Where do these doors lead?"

I heard hands rattling the handle of the adjoining door.

"Locked."

The TV was turned off.

"Maybe he's hiding under the bed."

"Don't be ridiculous."

In the silence that followed, I was sure they were both checking under the bed, guns pointed as if they expected me to leap out.

"Where did he go?"

"His car is still here."

"Maybe Dyson got 'im."

"Do you think?"

I opened the outside door to room B and prepared myself to confront the boys when I saw another car enter the lot. The driver of this one didn't turn off its lights. I stepped back inside the room, closing the door gently behind me. I watched out the window as the car drove toward cabin 9. It parked side by side with the other two vehicles. Minnesotans are nothing if not orderly.

"Who's that?" a voice asked from the adjoining room.

"Turn off the lights."

"It's too late. Let 'im think we don't know he's coming."

"Is it McKenzie?"

"I don't know."

"Maybe it's Dyson."

"It's Foley."

"What?"

"Tim Foley. What the hell is he doing here?"

"Wait until he comes inside."

I watched as Foley emerged from the car. He made no pretense of stealth. Instead, he slammed the car door shut and walked purposefully toward the cabin. He, too, was carrying a handgun, carrying it low against his thigh like a gunfighter in those B-westerns filmed in the forties and fifties, the ones where the good guy always waits for the bad guy to draw first. Like the others, he knocked on the door—along with neat, Minnesotans are unfailingly polite.

"Come in," someone said.

Foley opened the door and stepped inside. He disappeared from sight, but I heard their voices.

"Freeze."

"Don't move."

"Don't shoot."

"Drop the gun."

"Put your hands up."

"Drop the gun first."

"What are you doing here?"

"Kick it towards me. Harder."

"Start talking."

"Where's McKenzie?"

"As if you didn't know."

"He ain't here?"

"Does it look like he's here?"

"I was told he'd be here."

"Who told you?"

"Ms. Bosland."

"Are you sleeping with Ms. Bosland?"

"What? No."

"That is so wrong, man."

It was starting to sound to me like a Three Stooges routine, and as entertaining as I found it, I slipped silently outside the door of room B and made my way to the Jeep Cherokee. I climbed inside, started the engine, and put it into gear. I drove forward slowly, inching ahead until the front bumper of the vehicle was flush against the storm door leading to room A. I turned off the SUV, climbed out, and moved back to room B. The boys were still talking inside; they hadn't heard a thing. I pulled the motel's telephone information card out of my pocket and dialed the front office. A prerecorded message told me to input the desired cabin and room number. Instantly, the landline inside room A began ringing.

"Who is that?"

"I don't know."

"Answer it."

"You answer it."

"Let's get out of here."

"What about me?"

"Fuck you."

"Oh, no."

"What?"

"The door. I can't open . . ."

"Is that a car?"

"It's McKenzie's Jeep."

"It's parked against the door."

"We're trapped."

"Are you saying we can't get out?"

"Look for yourself."

"There's got to be another exit."

Someone tried the adjoining door again.

"It's locked."

"I could have told you that."

"Shoot the lock."

"Are you crazy?"

"That only works on TV."

"How do you know?"

"I saw it on *MythBusters*."

"We can go though the windows."

"Somebody might be out there."

"Somebody is most definitely out there."

"What do you suggest?"

I shouted as loudly as I could. "Answer the fucking phone."

Silence followed.

Someone said, "Did you hear that?"

"I think it came from outside."

The ringing stopped, and I heard a voice through the telephone's receiver.

"Hello?"

"Finally," I said. "What a bunch of morons you are."

"McKenzie, is that you?"

"Listen to me carefully. Are you listening?"

"Yes, sir."

"I want you to—by the way, which one are you?"

"I'm Michael. I'm—"

"You know what? I don't care. This is what I want you to do. Call Cyndy M. Tell her to come here. I'll give her thirty minutes. If you don't do what I ask, or if she doesn't show up, I'm going to call the sheriff's department and you'll have to explain why you broke into my room carrying dangerous weapons. Most likely, you'll be charged with assault in the second degree. Your public defender—I'm guessing you don't have money enough to hire a real attorney—he'll probably make a deal, allowing you and your friends to plead guilty to third degree assault, which means you'll be sentenced to five years in prison and out in three and a quarter. However, if you do exactly what I say, and Cyndy does answer my questions, I'll let you go. Make your call. Do it now. In the meantime, put Foley on the phone."

A moment later, I repeated my demands, only in Foley's case I said I wanted to see Ms. Bosland.

Afterward, I bundled up and went outside to wait—partly because I was afraid the boys might try something desperate, but mostly because I just didn't want to hear them talking, anymore.

Ms. Bosland was the first to arrive. She parked next to Foley's vehicle, but did not turn off the engine. Instead, she just sat there watching, waiting. I stood in the shadow of cabin 8 watching and waiting as well, my arms folded over my chest in an effort to stay warm. I had slipped the SIG Sauer into my coat pocket where I could get at it in a hurry, yet at the same time, I sincerely hoped I wouldn't need it. So far the only crime committed by the Deer River crowd that I was aware of was having the wrong friends. God knows I was guilty of the same offense.

The woman had a cell phone clamped to her ear as she twisted in her seat, looking this way and that, probably for me. Finally Ms. Bosland left her car while still speaking on the cell. The boys had kept the drapes closed, no doubt for fear I would shoot them through the window. She moved to the Jeep Cherokee. She looked around it, inside it, even under it. In the quiet of the parking lot I could hear her speaking.

"I don't see him anywhere. Are you sure he's here . . . Well, I don't see him . . . Maybe he left . . . No, you're right. He wouldn't leave his ride . . . I'll look."

Ms. Bosland opened the driver's-side door of the Jeep Cherokee and peered inside.

"No," she said. "The keys aren't here."

I walked out of the shadow of cabin 8 and sidled up to her. She didn't see me coming.

"Hey," I said.

Ms. Bosland was startled enough to scream and drop the cell

phone in the same instant. She spun around and fell back against my SUV, her arms spread wide, as if she expected to be hit by a meteor. I scooped up her phone and spoke into it.

"She'll call you back," I said.

I handed her the phone. Ms. Bosland took it reluctantly.

"The party won't begin until the other guest arrives," I said. "Do you want to sit in your car and keep warm while we wait?"

She nodded.

"Beautiful night, isn't it?" I said. "I mean if it wasn't so damn cold."

"Always winter, but never Christmas," Ms. Bosland said.

"C. S. Lewis," I said. "Very good."

"I started out teaching English."

"And look at you now."

We moved to her car. She went to the driver's side and I went to the passenger side. She opened the door first and started to get in. The dome light flicked on. I opened the passenger door and called her name. She stopped to look hard at the handgun I held up for her to see.

"Please, Ms. Bosland," I said. "Don't do anything rash."

Her response was to climb onto the seat and set both hands on top of the steering wheel. I slipped the gun back into my pocket and sat on the seat next to her.

"Where's your friend?" I asked.

"Camila? She doesn't want to be involved anymore."

"Smart woman."

"Why are you doing this?"

"I could ask you the same question. You're a high school principal, for God's sake. Although not for long, if I don't get some cooperation."

Probably the threat wasn't necessary, but I was cold and tired and still miffed that someone took a shot at my girlfriend. You could say I was in a mood. On the other hand, the expression on her face suggested that Ms. Bosland had never actually considered the possibility that she could lose her career, and I really, really wanted her to.

"I'm not the person you think I am," she said. "I'm not Becky Sharp. I'm not the Marquise de Merteuil or the Wife of Bath. I'm certainly not Fagin."

"You're a woman who loves her brother. Who would do anything to protect her brother."

"You understand."

"I've seen plenty of misplaced loyalty lately."

"I won't betray Mitch."

"Who asked you to?"

I leaned back in the car seat and cocked my head so I could see through the rearview mirror.

"Who are you waiting for?" Ms. Bosland asked.

"Cyndy Desler."

"I don't want to speak in front of her."

"Then talk now."

"Talk about what?"

Show her the gun again, my inner voice said.

Instead, I said, "When you spoke to your brother earlier this evening, telling him that I was in Deer River, did he mention that he and his partners had hired a man named Nick Dyson to kill Ella Elbers for twenty thousand dollars?"

Ms. Bosland paused a long time before she said, "He would never do that."

"Hire a man to kill El, or pay that much to get it done?"

She hesitated again.

"Is that why you're here?" Ms. Bosland asked.

"I intend to disrupt his plans, if that's what you mean."

She nodded her head almost imperceptibly, as if she thought it was a good idea but was afraid to show it.

"The last time I was here, you said you wanted to protect El, too," I said.

She nodded her head ever so slightly again.

"Here's your chance."

"I had no idea what Mitch was involved in," Ms. Bosland said. "Honestly. I thought he and Craig ran some kind of secondhand store. When I asked him to check up on the kids after they moved to the Cities, it was because I was genuinely concerned about their welfare. It didn't occur to me that he would . . . take advantage of them."

"Coerce them into a life of crime, you mean?"

She didn't answer.

"When did you learn differently?" I asked.

"When Tim Foley returned to Deer River just before the holidays. He had stories to tell about the crew—that's what they called themselves, a crew. How they would invade a store; El would behave suspiciously, and she's so pretty to begin with that all the store employees would be concentrating on her while the others robbed them blind. How they would do a snatch and grab—that's another phrase he used. Steal something and dash out the door to a waiting car. Most stores have a don't-chase policy, and those that will chase—Foley told how if something happened, if someone was hurt, they could be in more trouble than the criminal."

"Did Foley refuse to participate in the operation? Is that why he came home?"

"I'd like him better if that were true. No. He came back because he was a poor thief. Inept. He kept getting caught. Half the time the stores would release him without pressing charges. A couple times they prosecuted. On both occasions he had to pay a fine. After the second arrest, the others decided he was more liability than help . . ."

Considering that shoplifters are caught on average once in every forty-eight attempts, yeah, you could see how the others might be annoyed, my inner voice said.

"I enlisted Foley to assist me the day you came to Deer River looking for El, the day you came to the high school, solely because he already understood the circumstances," Ms. Bosland said. "I reasoned there was less likelihood for gossip that might impact my . . . I'm a good teacher, McKenzie. I'm a good principal. There is absolutely nothing between Foley and me. It's important that you know that. There are some things that even I won't stoop to."

"You'll stoop low enough to help your brother, though."

"No, no, McKenzie, I won't help. What he's doing—I'm so angry that he's using my former students the way he is."

"Just not angry enough to do anything about it."

"He's my brother."

"What did you think when El disappeared?"

"Just that—that she disappeared. Mitchell said that El and the others had a falling-out. I had the impression that they didn't part on the best of terms, because Mitch said to keep an eye out in case she came home. I didn't think anything bad happened to her because he said she might come home. Did something bad happen to her?"

"Yes, something bad happened to her." Another vehicle pulled into the motel parking lot; I saw its headlights in the sideview mirror. I turned in my seat and watched as it approached the line of cars, parking at the end. "Now there's hell to pay."

Ms. Bosland watched, both hands still resting on top of the steering wheel, while I slipped the SIG out of my pocket and thumbed off the safety.

"Turn off the engine," I told her.

She did. I held out my hand.

"Keys," I said.

She removed the keys from the ignition and dropped them into my palm. I stuffed them into my pocket.

"Don't go anywhere," I said.

I stepped out of the warm car. Winter slapped me in the face, but by then I was used to it. I had intended to go to Cyndy. She came out of her car in a hurry, though, and marched on me. She must have seen the nine-millimeter handgun resting against my thigh, yet chose to ignore it. As soon as she was within spitting distance of me, she halted, her legs spread apart, her fists pressed against her hips, and shouted, "What do you think you're doing?"

"What do you think you're doing?" I asked. "Sending those punks to mess with me."

"They're not punks. They're my friends."

"Look at it from my point of view."

"All they were going to do was tell you to go home."

"I guess it was the guns that confused me."

"What guns?"

I heard a muffled voice coming from room A.

"After what he did to Tim the last time, we thought we might need them," it said.

"He didn't do anything to me," Tim said. "I slipped on the ice."

"Why are you trying so hard to be rid of me?" I asked.

"This is Deer River business," Cyndy said. "It has nothing to do with you."

"Dyson—"

"Dyson, whoever he is—he'll never find El. He'll never find anyone."

My peripheral vision picked up Ms. Bosland as she left her vehicle. I pivoted, my back to the Jeep Cherokee, so I could watch both women at the same time while staying out of sight of the boys should they decide to open the drapes.

"What do you think of that, Ms. Bosland, since it was your brother who sent Dyson in the first place?" I asked.

"I told you, there are some things even I won't stoop to."

"Is that why you and M joined forces?"

"I don't know what you mean."

"If I may use a somewhat antiquated phrase—the two of you are in cahoots. You pretend to be at odds, yet you've been together in this all along."

The quick glance the two women shared confirmed my suspicions, yet I justified my accusation anyway.

"When Foley arrived, M's thugs—"

"They're not thugs," Cyndy said.

"Friends, then. Jeezus. M's friends asked Foley why he was here and he answered that Ms. Bosland sent him. How would you know I was staying in cabin 9, room A—unless M told you? Something else—M, you knew about Dyson coming to Deer River before I mentioned his name." I gestured at Ms. Bosland. "Which means Mitch must have told her and she told you."

"No," Ms. Bosland said. "Honestly, McKenzie. I never heard the name until just now."

"Then how . . ."

No, no, no, my inner voice chanted. *You have to be frickin' kidding me.*

Cyndy must have seen something in my face.

"What?" she said.

What a nitwit you are.

"McKenzie, what?"

"El's friends, her fellow shoplifters," I said. "Where are you hiding them?"

Ms. Bosland's head snapped toward Cyndy as if she were surprised by the possibility.

"I don't know what you're talking about," Cyndy said.

"Don't lie to me, M. I'm in a very bad mood and I just might call the sheriff's department and have you arrested for conspiracy to commit assault, not to mention aiding and abetting a fugitive. While you're in jail, your little girl can go live with the man who stole your middle name."

Cyndy didn't reply, yet I could see her thinking about it.

"I'll make it easy," I said. "You don't need to tell me exactly where they are. Just tell me that they're here."

"In Marcel," Cyndy said.

"They are?" Ms. Bosland asked.

"They've been hiding here since a week ago last Wednesday."

The day El left your condominium, my inner voice reminded me.

"I thought it best to keep it from you," Cyndy added.

"Because of Mitch," Ms. Bosland said.

"El said to protect them from your brother. I didn't know why exactly until I heard about Dyson."

Shipman was right. She's been right all along. Nuts.

"Where is El hiding?" I asked.

"I don't know," Cyndy said.

"Stop it."

"I don't know where she is. I told her not to tell me."

"Don't ask, can't tell. I get it. That's all right. I think I know where to look." I raised my voice. "You in the cabin."

A voice replied, "Yes."

"Open the window. Throw your guns out."

"No."

"Then I'm not leaving."

"You're leaving?"

"Throw the goddamn guns out the goddamn window."

A few moments passed without anything happening. Cyndy spoke up.

"Do what he says, c'mon," she said.

A moment later, the drapes were pushed aside, the inside window was opened, and the storm window was raised. A moment later, two handguns were dropped outside.

"One more," I said.

I heard muffled voices raised in anger followed by a loud thud. A second later, a third handgun joined the pile.

The three young men watched me through the storm door as I went to the Jeep Cherokee; Tim Foley was massaging his forehead. I started the vehicle and put it in reverse. The two women stepped aside as I backed away from the cabin. I stopped and powered down the window.

"Both of you," I said. "You believe you're virtuous because you've drawn a line in the sand that you refuse to cross. The trouble is the line often disappears. The sand shifts; wind and rain and time work at it, and pretty soon you need to draw another line, and another, and another until you're so far from where you started that you can't even imagine how you got there. Your family, your friends, your students—they're criminals. I understand that you want to protect them because they are your family, friends, students. But they're criminals, and there comes a time when you need to step away, step back across the line, or become criminals yourself. I don't expect you to understand what I'm talking about."

I left them alone in the parking lot without even a glance in the rearview mirror. I was tempted to drive home, yet I was afraid that it was still snowing in the Cities, so I spent the night in Grand Rapids. I figured I had pushed my luck far enough for one day.

SEVENTEEN

The front door of the duplex had been painted and the concrete steps scrubbed. I couldn't see any blood at all, yet being there gave me a queasy feeling just the same.

Nina had not been home when I returned to the Cities. I called her at the club. In a chipper tone she told me she was perfectly wonderful—which I quickly agreed with—and she had saved a couple of voice mails on our landline that I should listen to before I do anything else.

The first was from Bobby. His recorded voice told me that the assistant Ramsey County medical examiner had finally worked up a profile. The blood on the hilt of the knife that Shipman took off Peter Troop *did not* match Oliver Braun's. "So we can't say for sure that it was the murder weapon. Or that Troop did it. Call me."

And tell him what? my inner voice asked. *That you were wrong and Shipman was right? Let's hold off on that for a bit. Wait until you're sure.*

Shelby Dunston recorded the next voice mail, and it came in three parts. The first part was angry. "I knew you had commitment issues, but I'd never thought you'd try to get Nina killed." The second was all exasperation. "When are you going to grow up?" And the third—the third part I still don't entirely understand. "I wish . . ."

Wish what, sweetie?

"I wish . . ."

The unfinished sentence kept repeating in my head as I shaved, showered, and dressed. It was still there when I took the elevator to the underground garage and walked toward my Jeep Cherokee. The burn phone rang; its song echoed off the concrete walls.

"Now what?" I asked.

"I was talking to my sister, my sister in Deer River," Mitch said.

"What about her?" I asked.

"She didn't see you last night."

"She wasn't supposed to see me," I said. "I saw her, though, and the bartender and McKenzie, in a motel parking lot."

"You were there?"

He seemed impressed.

"Interesting conversation," I said. "Told me everything I needed to know."

"What? What did it tell you?"

"Where to look for El. Let's hope I get there before McKenzie."

"But where is she?"

"Hiding in plain sight."

"Huh?"

I turned off the phone. The sonuvabitch was starting to bore me.

Ten minutes later, I was standing outside the duplex. I opened the front door and stepped into the foyer. I leaned toward the artificial flowers in the vase attached to Leon Janke's doorjamb and took a deep breath of their pleasant aroma.

Hard to believe they're not real.

I stuffed my hat and gloves into my pockets, unzipped my coat, and pulled it back so I'd have access to the nine-millimeter

SIG Sauer holstered on my hip. I knocked on the door. Nothing happened. It was late on a Saturday morning, I reminded myself. Maybe Janke was on one of his five-mile walks, if, in fact, he did take walks. The flowers reminded me that it was difficult to know what a lie was these days.

I knocked again. I heard Janke's voice.

"Comin', I'm comin'."

A shadow passed over the spy hole, and a moment later Janke yanked opened the door. He smiled, but the smile quickly went away when he saw that my right hand was resting on the butt of my gun.

"Now, son, I'd say it was good t' see ya, but standin' like you are, that just ain't sociable," he said.

"I apologize. I've had a rough couple of days since we last spoke."

"Not on account of me."

"That's true."

I removed my hand from the gun butt.

Janke smiled and gestured with his head. "Well, now, come on in," he said.

I was surprised to see how neat the duplex was, probably because I had been such a poor housekeeper when I was living alone that I expected everyone else to be as well. The furniture was old. Some of it dated back a half century or more, yet it was all well kept—like its owner.

"Can I offer you a beverage, McKenzie?" the old man asked. "You strike me as a bourbon man."

"I've been known to drink my share, but before you start pouring the good stuff, I need to ask something."

"What's that?"

"Will El be joining us?"

Janke stared at me for a few beats and then smiled as if he had come to a decision.

"She don't live here no more," he said.

"Mr. Janke, I mean no disrespect—"

"So you say."

"El left my apartment on a Wednesday because she thought she was in danger. That very same day, she moved her friends out of this duplex and sent them Up North—to Marcel, to be precise. I was there last night, in case you think I'm guessing. El did it to protect them because she knew what was about to happen. She couldn't have done that, sir, without your knowledge. Or help. Not with that narrow, spiraling staircase. Please. I also believe El stayed here after she sent the others home, that she stayed with you. I believe you took care of her because she didn't have anywhere else to go. You told me you couldn't help but look out for El, for the others, because they grew up where you grew up. So, I ask again—will Ella be joining us for drinks?"

"You talk a lot, McKenzie, but you don't listen real good. She isn't here. I sent her away."

"*Sent* her away? When?"

"After that fella was killed on my front stoop. I've seen things and done 'em, too, McKenzie. When I got off that damn peninsula, I promised I wouldn't hurt no one ever again and I wouldn't stand by while others are bein' hurt no matter how much they might deserve it. I broke that promise a bit when I didn't tell on that little girl, didn't tell the police. Maybe I shoulda. I argue to myself that I didn't actually see it done, so I'd just be guessin', even though, well, my huntin' rifle is missin'. I didn't know that till later though, till a day or so after the police came and went. It shoulda been in a case in the closet; I hadn't used it in years and years. I figured the police, they'd get it right soon enough. You did. Now, you want that drink or don'tcha?"

"You think that El shot Karl Olson—with your rifle?"

"Seen 'im comin' and used it to protect herself. 'Course, like I said, I didn't see it done, and what I think—that ain't evidence, is it?"

"I'd like that drink very much."

"Take off your coat. Stay awhile."

I removed my coat and followed Mr. Janke into the kitchen.

He opened a cupboard door, revealing a colorful assortment of alcohol. The labels on some of the bottles—Grand Marnier, crème de cacao, sherry—gave me the impression that he cooked with it.

"The older I get, the more I like to eat good," he said.

Janke poured two inches of Maker's Mark into each of two squat glasses and handed me one. He raised the other in a toast.

"Absent friends," he said.

"Absent friends."

Janke downed all of his drink while I drank only half of mine. He looked at my glass, raised his eyes to mine, and grinned.

"I didn't know it was a contest," I said.

"Life is a contest, son."

He poured another inch of bourbon into my glass and two into his.

"What're ya gonna do about Ella?" Janke asked.

"I don't know yet."

"The men she—that she might have shot, they threw her off the back of a truck, you know."

"Yes, I know. Unfortunately, it's a little more involved than that."

Janke raised his glass.

"Cheers to those who wish us well, all the rest can go to hell," he said.

"Hear, hear."

This time I emptied my glass while Janke drank only half of his. He grinned some more.

"We're even," he said.

He topped off his glass and refilled mine. I might have protested, except the idea of getting ridiculously drunk was starting to appeal to me.

"Did you know what El and her friends were into?" I asked.

"Not really. I knew it was somethin', though. When they first arrived, money was tight—they were late with the rent a couple of times, complained about how hard it was for a youngster to get work in this economy. Then that Mitch character started hangin' around, and suddenly it all sorta got straightened out, the money thing I mean. I figured the kids musta found decent jobs, but the hours they kept, no one gits t' work those kinda hours."

"You never thought to ask?"

"I ain't their mommy and daddy."

Janke raised his glass again.

"May we get what we want, but never what we deserve," he said.

"From your lips to God's ear."

We heard someone pounding on Janke's front door.

The intensity stopped us both, glasses hovering in midair.

"Now, who'd that be?" Janke asked.

He made for the door. I set down my drink and grabbed his elbow.

"If you don't mind my saying so, you are way too trusting," I said.

"Can't live without trust, son. Can't even drive down the street without trust."

"Nonetheless . . ."

I halted Janke's march to the door and stepped in front of him. The knocking was too loud, too demanding. It sounded angry to me. My internal alarm systems demanded caution. Like Mr. Janke, I had also seen and done things . . .

"Just a sec," I said.

I made my voice sound low and conciliatory. It should have calmed our visitor. Instead, the knocking resumed with even greater vigor.

A copy of the *Minneapolis Star Tribune* was resting on Janke's coffee table. He watched from a safe distance as I picked it up with my left hand and moved to the right of the doorjamb. The pounding continued. I waved the newspaper in front of the spy hole, so anyone watching on the other side would see its shadow.

The door exploded.

The paper was torn from my hand.

Wooden shards and buckshot pierced my palm and wrist.

I heard somebody shout, probably Mr. Janke, but it was like listening to a voice from underwater.

A huge hole appeared in the center of the door.

I saw someone peeking through it. I recognized the young man by his hat—Waldo, from the coffeehouse where I met Emily Hoover, the real estate agent.

I drew my SIG Sauer with my right hand and stepped in front of the door. I used my left to steady the shot. Blood seeped from many holes, but I wasn't feeling the pain yet.

Waldo seemed surprised to see me.

He tried to bring the sawed-off shotgun back up.

I fired five times.

The bullets tore through what was left of the door into his body.

They threw him back against the wall on the far side of the foyer. He died at the foot of the stairs.

I stood there for what seemed like a long time, my gun aimed at the door. My vision had narrowed. All I could see was the hole and the body of the young man beyond. Mr. Janke was at my side; I didn't see him so much as I felt him. His voice was like a rumble in my stomach.

"FUBAR," he said. "That's all I can say, son. FUBAR."

It took a while to gather my thoughts. By then the place was swarming with Minneapolis police, crime scene investigators, and emergency personnel. Mr. Janke was standing next to the door, speaking both carefully and calmly to a couple of uniforms. He pointed at the hole.

"Ain't that somethin'?" he said.

I sat on the sofa. My left arm rested on one of Mr. Janke's towels on my thigh. Most of the wounds had stopped bleeding, yet the pain was intense. An EMT was carefully removing splinters and a few pieces of buckshot from my hand and wrist with a tweezers, occasionally adding to the pain. I tried not to let it show. He told me I should go to an emergency room when he finished for a tetanus shot. I grunted something in reply, I don't remember what. The EMT pulled a tiny lead ball out of my skin and held it up for me to see.

"Will you look at that?" he said.

Everyone seemed to be having a better time than I was.

It finally occurred to me to call Detective Shipman. While the EMT worked on my left hand, I used my right to operate the cell. She answered on the third ring.

"Please, McKenzie," Shipman said. "Don't ruin my day off. I get so few of them."

"I'm sorry, Jeannie."

I told her where I was and what had happened.

"You were right," I said. "You were right and I was wrong. I will bet you a thousand dollars that El is hunting Emily Hoover at this very minute."

"Who's Emily Hoover?"

I explained.

"I'd be really upset that you withheld that little tidbit of information, McKenzie, except that I should have figured it out for myself. I didn't even notice the FOR SALE signs. You just might be a better investigator after all."

"You're a better cop. Jeanne, the kid I shot—he wasn't at the coffeehouse to threaten Hoover. He was there to protect her. From El. And now he's gone. You need to find her."

If Shipman said something in reply, I didn't hear it because Detective John Luby snatched the cell out of my hand. He shook it at me as if it were a Bible and he was damning me for all time. In his other hand he was holding a clear-plastic evidence bag. The bag contained my SIG Sauer.

"You did it this time, McKenzie," he said. "I am going to put you away."

The duplex became very quiet.

"I'm not messing around," Luby said. "You think I'm messing around? I am going to fuck you up."

Yeah, my inner voice said. *Like you haven't heard that before.*

I leaned back against the sofa and closed my eyes. Everyone resumed what they were doing, including the EMT, who kept working on my hand and wrist as if it were all just another day in the life . . .

Headquarters for the police department was located in Minneapolis City Hall, sometimes called the Pink Palace because of its Gothic architecture and the color of its granite facade—or maybe I was the only one who called it that. Truth be told, I was a little groggy after three hours in an interrogation room waiting for something to happen. Not to mention the aching pain in my hand and wrist. I hadn't actually been arrested, so whether or not I had the right to call an attorney was open to debate. In any case, I politely refused to answer any of Luby's questions—the man clearly wanted to put me in the jackpot, and I sure as hell wasn't going to help him. Instead, I waited patiently for the crime scene techs to confirm what Mr. Janke insistently and consistently kept repeating—"McKenzie saved my life."

"You think you're a hero?' Luby told me. "You aren't a fucking hero."

It was the only thing he said that I agreed with.

Finally Luby walked into the interrogation room, leaving the door open behind him, which I took as a good sign. He returned my smartphone.

"There's a hostage situation in St. Paul," he said. "She's asking for you."

———

I forced Luby to drive me to my condominium first. He agreed only because it was about a mile from City Hall and more or less on the way. The address was in the Macalester-Groveland area of St. Paul, not far from St. Catherine University. By the time we reached it, the block had been cordoned off and the houses all around it had been evacuated. Luby's badge got us inside the police lines.

Bobby Dunston stood behind a patrol car with a sergeant and several officers, including Shipman.

"You took your time getting here," he said.

"The DQ had a sale on Dilly Bars." I pointed at a house with a blue and white Kenwood Real Estate sign in the front yard. "Is that it?"

"That's it."

"Why did she ask for me?"

"I don't know. She says she won't speak to anyone else. Mc-Kenzie, you don't need to do this."

"El doesn't want to kill anyone."

"Hell she doesn't," Shipman said. "Emily Hoover was conducting an open house. Elbers was threatening her with a semiautomatic when I arrived. She threw a couple of shots at me. It's been a stand-off ever since."

"Are you armed?" Bobby asked.

"No." I jabbed a thumb toward Luby. "My gun was confiscated."

Bobby drew his Glock and offered it to me. I shook my head at it.

"I'll be all right," I said.

"Famous last words. Take it."

"I'm not shooting anybody else, today, Bobby. I've had my fill."

"Okay. Now, listen to me. Elbers is sitting down. We haven't got a clear shot. You need to get her up out of the chair. Get her into the center of the room."

I turned my head just enough to confirm that members of

the Specials Weapons and Tactics Team were deployed all around the house.

"Let's hope it doesn't come to that," I said.

"We have only a couple hours of daylight left."

"I understand."

I gave Bobby my smartphone. The gesture seemed to confuse him.

"You'll thank me later," I said.

I turned toward the house. Shipman put a sturdy hand against my chest, stopping me before I could take a single step. She held up a Kevlar vest.

"Put it on," she said. "I won't take no for an answer."

"I won't need it."

"This is all on you, McKenzie. If you had told me that Hoover was supplying the locations for the garage sales when you found out six days ago, none of this would be happening. But you just had to prove that you were smarter than everyone else." Shipman threw the Kevlar at me. It bounced off my chest; I caught it before it hit the ground. "Now put on the goddamned vest."

I removed my heavy coat and donned the body armor.

"What happened to your hand?" Bobby asked.

I paused to study the bandages, but only for a moment before putting my coat back on and zipping it to my throat.

"It's been one of those days," I said.

The house seemed almost rustic, with a steeply pitched roof, tall narrow windows, a ground floor built of red bricks, and a top floor of white timber. It reminded me of a country home in England, and maybe that's where the style of architecture originated. It was built at the turn of the century—the twentieth—on top of a small hill. I had to climb a half dozen concrete steps to get to a cobblestone sidewalk at the top of the hill and another half dozen to reach the entrance. The storm door was closed, yet the inside door was wide open. I could see elegant paintings on the wall and a wooden staircase leading to the second floor through the frosted glass. I rang the bell; it chimed like an ancient clock.

"McKenzie?" El called. "Is that you?"

"Yes."

"Are you alone?"

"Yes."

"Come in. Hurry. Please, close the door behind you."

I did what I was told and stepped inside the living room. It was a little small for my taste. A large, stuffed rust-colored chair with arms and a high back stood in the corner. Emily Hoover was sitting in the chair. She was no longer handsome despite the stylish clothes she wore. She reminded me of photos I've seen of women peering through the barbed-wire fence of a concentration camp; there was no hope in her eyes.

El was hiding behind the chair. She came out when she saw it was me and I was indeed alone. She was holding a nine-millimeter Beretta. I recognized it immediately.

"That's mine," I said.

I held out my hand as if I expected her to return it. Life would have been so much easier if she had.

"I'm afraid I need to hang on to it a little longer," she said. "Tell me, Fifteen. How do you think this is going to end?"

"You keep thinking of me as Fifteen. You don't know how much I appreciate that. Look, McKenzie, I know that I'm in trouble, if that's what you mean."

"Trouble?"

The word seemed so inadequate.

El stepped toward me.

"Is . . ." For a moment she was the little girl who appeared at my condominium on a cold Monday evening. "Is Nina—is she . . ."

"She's fine."

"Thank God."

"You missed. Ruined her good coat, though. She's pretty upset about that."

"She must hate me."

"Actually, Fifteen—Nina might be the only person left who's still on your side."

"You, though. Are you still on my side?"

I showed her the flat of my hand and gave it a shake.

"I'm wavering," I said. "Holding a hostage at gunpoint—that's not helping your cause any."

"I didn't mean for this to happen. That police officer came out of nowhere."

"What were you going to do if she hadn't?"

"I just wanted to make her say."

Hoover remained in the chair, staring straight ahead. If she was listening to our conversation, she didn't show it.

"Say what?" I asked.

"What she did. Everything is her fault, you need to know that."

"What's everything?"

"I don't know where to begin."

"Why did you shoot Nina?"

"I didn't mean to. It was an accident. I didn't even see her until they started shooting at me and I shot back."

"They?"

"Mitch and Craig. I walked up to them and they just started shooting."

Perhaps they were afraid, my inner voice said

"Why were you even there?" I asked aloud.

"Mitch and Craig were supposed to be my friends. I wanted to ask why they were helping this bitch hire someone to kill me—some guy named Dyson."

"But . . ." Emily Hoover's voice was so low, that we barely heard it. "But . . . he's Dyson."

"What? What are you saying?" El turned her full attention on me. "Dyson?"

I gestured with my hands as if I had just sawed my assistant in half.

"Ta-da," I said.

"You're Nick Dyson?"

"In a manner of speaking."

El stepped deeper into the living room. She brought the gun up with one hand and sighted on my chest. At the same time, two red dots appeared on the blue shirt she was wearing. They moved slightly and then became steady on her heart. I stepped around El until I was between her and the window. I knew the dots were now centered on my back. I recited a silent prayer. I was sure the Kevlar would stop a nine-millimeter slug even at close quarters. Yet a round from a high-powered rifle . . . ?

"Put the gun down, Fifteen," I said. "Do it now."

She lowered the gun until the muzzle was pointing at the floor. I drifted back to my original position to allow the spotters to see that El was no longer an imminent threat. The dots did not reappear. The young woman returned to the chair and stared down at Hoover.

"I don't understand," she said.

"I was in disguise," I said.

El thought about it for a few beats and came to the conclusion I wanted her to reach.

"You were looking out for me," she said. "After everything I did, you were still looking out for me."

"I said I would. Remember?"

"That doesn't change anything. It doesn't change what this bitch tried to do."

El brought the gun up again, this time with both hands, and pointed it at Hoover's head. The older woman closed both eyes and angled her chin away, waiting for the bullet.

"Fifteen." My voice was too loud. I deliberately lowered it

when I spoke again. "Fifteen, did you really bring me here so I can watch you shoot your partner?"

Both women looked at me like I had just recited the entire Gettysburg Address by heart. El lowered the gun again.

"How did you know?" she asked.

"That you and Emily together were the Boss?" I stepped closer to the woman in the chair. "The clues were all there. Take the time we spoke in the coffeehouse. You said that Mitch and Craig were blackmailing you, that they had video of you buying stolen property. Yet they never heard of you, they had no such video, they didn't know who was supplying the locations for the garage sales, and they didn't communicate with you over the phone like you said. It was all done by e-mail. Your e-mail was the key, by the way."

I stepped back so I could watch both El and Hoover at the same time. I spoke to El.

"They never knew where you were, yet you always seemed to know where they were. For example, you knew Karl Olson was going to Mr. Janke's duplex—"

"I saved your life, McKenzie," El said. "He was going to kill you."

"It sure felt like he was going to kill me. Anyway, you also knew that Peter Troop was going to Oliver Braun's funeral."

"Troop was going to kill you, too. You and the lady detective. I saved both of you."

"Not necessarily," I said. "Troop was surrendering when he was shot."

"How was I supposed to know that? It looked to me like he was attacking you. I was trying to help."

"You know what? That's a good defense. Go with that at your trial. It just might work out."

"But it's true."

"Where was I? Yeah, yeah, yeah—you knew Olson would be at the duplex and Troop would be at the funeral. You knew all about Dyson and that Mitch and Craig were going to meet him at Como Park. You knew that Dyson was driving to Deer River—you did call Cyndy M to warn her, right? It was like you were reading their minds. Or their e-mails." I pointed at Hoover. "That's how the Boss communicated with her partners; how they contacted her. Through e-mails. It's also how you knew Raymond Hangarter"—that was Waldo's real name—"wouldn't be here to protect Emily. Mitch must have guessed from what I told him that I was headed for Mr. Janke's duplex to look for you, and he sent Emily an e-mail telling her so. You read the e-mail that Emily then sent Hangarter telling him to—do what? What did you tell him, Emily? To kill El? Kill me? Kill everyone? Hangarter's dead, by the way."

From the way she hung her head, I guessed that Hoover was genuinely distressed by the news. El didn't seem to care one way or the other.

"Except you're not a hacker," I said. "Fifteen, you don't have those skills. The only way you could have managed it is if you had the username and password. How could you have those unless the two of you shared the account to begin with?

"My only question—who came up with the idea in the first place? To be the Boss. Hmm? Emily, you hired El to house-sit some of the properties you were selling, give them that young and beautiful sheen. That's how you two met, isn't it? So, did you approach her, or was it the other way around?"

"I have nothing to say," Hoover told me.

"Really? Do you want those to be your last words—I have nothing to say?"

"It was my idea," El said. "Staying in those wonderful homes, meeting the people who went through them . . . I knew what I wanted and how to get it. Mitch and Craig had recruited us from Deer River to do their stealing for them, and we went along because we were broke and because—Mitch explained how everyone was doing it and how the stores figured it into the cost of doing business and . . . It seemed like as good a way to get by as any until things improved. Only you're never going to get

rich being just a worker bee. The only way to do it is to become—"

"The queen bee," Hoover said.

"Management," El said. "Only I couldn't have pulled it off
by myself. Look at me. Mitch and Craig, Kispert—they weren't
going to listen to me. So I invented the Boss."

"*We* invented the Boss. You would have been lost without
me."

"I never pretended otherwise, Emily. But shoplifting and selling what we stole—that's one thing. Blackmailing our customers?"

"You're just a kid. I'm old. I'm facing retirement. I don't want
to sell houses for the rest of my life. So we make the extra money
and then we quit. Why did you turn it into such a big deal?"

"People get hurt."

"What do you think stealing their stuff does?"

"That just hurts businesses and insurance companies."

"Is that what you tell yourself? You're a thief, Ella. Admit
it."

"What are you? Whoring around with John Kispert so he'll
do your blackmailing."

"I'm not a whore. I didn't even speak to him directly. It was
just business."

"You tried to have me killed."

"You deserved it."

"Fuck you."

Hoover made an attempt to come out of the chair. El brought
the Beretta up with both hands and sighted on her head. At the
same time, she backed away from the chair into the center of
the room. Red dots appeared on her shirt, three of them this
time.

"Fifteen," I said.

She pivoted so that the gun was pointed at me and turned
back to Hoover. I moved in front of the window, once again putting myself between her and the snipers.

Bobby is going to kill you, my inner voice said.

Two of the dots disappeared; the third remained steady on El's chest.

"Fifteen," I said. "Please. Lower the gun. Please."

"It's all her fault," she said. "Emily's the one who crossed the line, not me."

"Lower the gun."

She did.

The dot remained.

"Please," I said.

The dot disappeared.

"Thank you."

El looked at me. Her eyes were wet with tears.

"Don't be mad at me," she said. "You're my only friend in the Cities. You and Nina. That's why I asked for you. Please, McKenzie, tell me what to do."

In a minute. First . . .

"Tell me what happened," I said. "From the beginning."

El backed against the wall, still holding the gun with both hands, and sighed deeply. Hoover settled back against the chair. It was as if they both were preparing for a long story.

"The Boss thing worked," El said. "Mitch and the others did what we said, held the garage sales at the locations we scouted; security was arranged so nothing bad would happen."

"Raymond Hangarter was my nephew," Hoover said. "Olson and Troop were his friends."

"And then one day I invited Merle Mattson to a sale. She was a Ramsey County commissioner; my boyfriend worked for her."

"Oliver Braun," I said.

"Yes. A month or so later, this . . . this whore—she started blackmailing her. The commissioner blamed me. She complained to Oliver. I knew nothing about it, but Oliver called me a slut and said he never wanted to see me again, and said if I didn't fix it he'd call the cops. I went to Mitch and Craig and told them I wouldn't put up with blackmail. See, I thought it was them and Kispert. I didn't know it was Emily until—until her nephew and his friends tied me up and threw me off the back of my own pickup truck. Do you know why? Do you know why they tried to kill me that way? It was because the Boss wanted to send a message. She wanted everyone to be afraid of her—don't mess with the the Boss—like she was some kind of Bond villain."

"Why didn't you tell the police?" I asked. "Why didn't you tell Commander Dunston?"

"Because, when I woke up in the hospital—McKenzie, I really did lose my memory, I really did forget my name. It was terrifying. But what scared me more, this woman"—she pointed the gun at Hoover—"came into my room and threatened me. She told me to keep my mouth shut about what happened or my friends would get the same treatment.

"McKenzie, I didn't know who she was, I didn't know who my friends were; I didn't remember what happened. What could I tell the police that made sense? They thought I was brain-damaged as it was. I didn't know what to do, so I did nothing. Then my memory returned. It was a day or two later. I went to sleep, and when I woke up, it was all there. Everything. I felt—I felt ashamed. I felt angry. Ashamed and angry that I wasn't the person that I had wanted to be, that I had hoped I was. But I thought if I didn't tell anyone, if no one knew who I was, I could be. I could become Fifteen. She was nice, even if she did hit on you."

We both smiled at the memory.

"Only she . . . Emily—you should have let me go. Instead, you sent Karl Olson. You sent Karl to kill me, goddamn you. That's what made me decide if I wanted to become someone else, first I had to make amends for who I used to be.

"But McKenzie—how do you stop blackmailers without hurting the people they're blackmailing? And what about my friends from Deer River? I called Oliver and told him what happened. I didn't ask for forgiveness. I didn't think I deserved it. I called him because I hoped he might talk to the commissioner and ask her to help me. I knew she was an ex-sheriff, something like that. He said he would. I gave him one of my guns, your guns, for protection. Afterward, I went to the duplex and hustled my friends out of town. I sent them to my friend Cyndy for safekeeping.

"And then they killed Oliver.

"And I knew what I had to do.

"Why, Emily? Why did you kill Oliver?"

Hoover smirked, actually smirked, which I considered amazing given the circumstances.

"Do you expect me to confess?" she asked. "Is that why you brought McKenzie in here, so he could hear my confession? You're so stupid, Ella. Stupid little Barbie doll with a plastic head. It doesn't matter what I say. Don't you get it? You can't use what I say against me. You have guns—"

"Gun," I said. "Singular."

"I'll claim duress. You forced the confession from me. You'll never be able to use it in court."

"Lady, look around. We're not in court."

"That stupid boy. That stupid, stupid boy. He came to my open house in Highland Park with that stupid, stupid gun. He wanted me to confess, too. I told him that anyone could walk in at any time. I told him to wait for me in his car. And he did, too, that stupid, stupid boy. I took a knife out of the kitchen and sat in the car and talked until he relaxed and then I stabbed him. Is that what you wanted to hear, El? How I killed that stupid, stupid boy? Afterward, I shoved him over on the seat and drove his car to the ice arena. I walked the two blocks back to the house, washed off the knife, put it away, and drove home. I slept like a baby, El. Happy?"

El brought the gun up. I had no doubt that finally, she was going to use it.

I stepped in close, grabbed the Beretta by the muzzle, and yanked upward. The gun went off. A single bullet bore into the ceiling above us.

"It's okay, it's okay," I chanted.

I twisted the gun and yanked some more until it came out of El's hand.

"The hostage is safe," I said. "The gunman is disarmed. I'm coming out."

I turned and left the room, left the house.

Shipman was going in while I was coming out. I handed her the Beretta, butt first. She took it without a word.

I continued along the sidewalk and down the concrete steps to the street. Bobby was still standing behind the patrol car, and I walked toward him.

Behind me, the cops were hustling El and Hoover out of the house, their hands cuffed behind their backs. Hoover was resisting. She kept repeating that the police couldn't arrest her, that she was the victim.

Bobby was smiling when I reached him.

"Took you long enough," he said.

I removed the forget-me-not that had been pinned to my jacket and gave it to him.

"You're welcome," I said.

JUST SO YOU KNOW

It was late October with the sun shining bright. I was sitting on the balcony of our condominium, the chair up against the wall as far away from the edge as possible. Nina was leaning against the railing and looking down. Winter had been a long time going—a ball game with the Dodgers in the last week of April had to be rescheduled because of snow, for God's sake. Which was why we were attempting to stretch the following summer as far as we could.

"Shelby called," Nina said. "She wants us to stop on the way and get some ice."

"Okay."

"It'll probably be the last barbecue of the year."

"Could be."

"Shipman will be there. Are you two going to growl at each other all night?"

"Probably."

"These terse replies of yours—I don't feel good about what happened either."

What happened is that everyone went to prison. It took three county prosecutors seven months to figure out where they were going, for how long, and for what crimes, yet no one was spared. Well, almost no one.

The final trial had just ended. The results were in the morning paper. Emily Hoover's attorneys had argued that the statements she made over my cell phone were inadmissible, along with her e-mails and a knife found at the home in Highland Park where she had been conducting an open house the evening Oliver Braun was killed—a kitchen knife, by the way, that the Ramsey County medical examiner proved conclusively to be the murder weapon. Fruit of the poisoned tree, the lawyers called it. The trial judge disagreed. The attorneys appealed. The Minnesota Court of Appeals said, "Nah, nah, nah, nah, nah." Hoover was given a three-hundred-and-six-month jolt in the Minnesota Correctional Facility located in Shakopee.

Meanwhile, each member of the Deer River tribe was convicted of theft crimes and given one year and a day in Lino Lakes. The judge could have stayed the sentences, given the kids probation instead. Apparently he was not in a giving vein that day.

Mitch, Craig, and John Kispert each accepted seven-year sentences in St. Cloud. That was also severe by the standards laid out in the Minnesota Sentencing Guidelines, yet a damn sight better than if they had also been convicted of a boatload of other complaints that were subsequently dropped in exchange for the guilty pleas, including conspiracy to commit murder and blackmail.

That left El, who went to trial for killing both Karl Olson and Peter Troop. Her attorney argued that since her actions saved the life of others, including a decorated member of the St. Paul Police Department, she shouldn't be charged with anything. The argument might have succeeded, too, if El had only done it once. But twice? In the end, she accepted a forty-eight-month sentence for each of two counts of second degree manslaughter, the sentences to be served concurrently, all other charges dropped. That meant she'd be out in thirty-two.

"We can help Fifteen when she's released from prison, can't we?" Nina asked.

"Sure," I said.

Yet El doing time wasn't what bothered me. It was the woman who didn't pay for her crimes.

The day after El and Hoover were arrested, I went to see Ramsey County Commissioner Merle Mattson. I told her that neither El nor Troop killed Oliver Braun—it was Emily Hoover. She accepted the information with a shrug.

"I asked this question before," I told her. "Maybe now you'll answer it. When the police interviewed you after Oliver was killed, why didn't you tell them that the two of you were having an affair?"

"I don't like that word—affair," Mattson said. "It suggests something deceitful. It suggests cheating. I'm not married, McKenzie. Certainly Oliver wasn't. There was nothing dishonest about our relationship."

"Why keep it a secret?"

"Have you ever been in love?"

I flashed on the face of Shelby Dunston, which was inexplicable, and then Nina's, and finally Jillian DeMarais, of all people.

"Frequently," I said.

"I haven't."

The look in her eye, the catch in her voice, the use of contraction—trying to make you believe she was actually in love with the kid? my inner voice asked.

"Partly, we kept it a secret because of my job," Mattson said. "I didn't know how my constituents would take it. Or the party. Yet mostly we kept the relationship to ourselves because I just didn't want to face questions from my family, my friends. Their smirks. I didn't want the headache. It was better this way for him, too. Young men don't respond well to teasing, and given the disparity in our ages, he would have been teased.

"Besides, I knew it wouldn't last. Ms. Elbers, young women

like her—stiff competition, Mr. McKenzie. It was only a matter of time before Oliver outgrew me. Until then . . . I wanted to keep it pure. I wanted to keep it simple. I wanted to remember our love in the years to come as being pure and simple.

"You know what, though? Call the police. I don't care anymore. Call the media. Shout it from the rooftops. I might think differently about it tomorrow. Today—today, I'm proud to have been in love with Oliver. I'm thankful that he loved me."

"Bullshit."

The word jolted her. It was meant to.

"If you really meant what you're saying, Commissioner, you would have told the cops the truth the moment you learned Oliver had been killed. You would have told them that you were being blackmailed and why. You would have told them that Oliver had taken a gun and gone to see Emily Hoover in order to protect you. But you didn't love him enough to even acknowledge his sacrifice."

"McKenzie—"

"You're a public servant. You were a sheriff's deputy. Yet you did nothing to put his killer away. Tell me again how much you cared."

"Don't talk to me like that. I have a reputation for being an honest woman, an honest politician. I didn't want voters to remember me for this. I didn't even know the handbags were stolen. How could I? I thought I was getting a deal."

I had nothing more to say. Neither had anyone else. Because of the way the trials played out, Commissioner Mattson's name was never mentioned. It annoyed me that she never paid for her sins. But then, I didn't pay for mine either.

"I'm thinking of getting involved in politics," I said.

Nina thought that was hysterical.

"No, I mean it," I said. "Start small. Find someone to support in the race for Ramsey County commissioner."

"You don't live in Ramsey County anymore."

"A minor detail."

"I think it would have been better if we hadn't been involved in any of this."

"Then Emily Hoover might have gotten away with murder. The Deer River tribe would still be out there shoplifting, Mitch and Craig still selling what they stole. Kispert would be running his burglary ring and helping Hoover blackmail their customers. El—she might be dead instead of safe and sound in a cozy women's prison. I'm sorry they went to prison, El and the kids, but sweetie, they all crossed the line."

"Is that what it comes down to? Which side of the line you're on?"

"Almost always."

"But we crossed the line, too, didn't we?" Nina said, meaning *you crossed the line.* "We all kept secrets. We all did good things for bad reasons and bad things for good reasons. We all screwed up."

"Yes."

She paused for a moment and then asked, "Are you ready to go?"

"Yes."

Yet we didn't leave. Instead, I kept sitting in the chair and Nina kept leaning on the railing and looking out at the city sprawling beneath her.

"There were no good guys in any of this, were there?" she said.

"Just us."

"Us? What makes you think we're the good guys?"

"We're the ones going to a barbecue with our friends on a Saturday afternoon."